A DEMON'S FASCINATION

THE DEMONS OF YIDDERA BOOK ONE

LOUELLA RANES

PUBLISHED BY LOUELLA RANES

CONTENTS

This book is dedicated to my mom, Carol, who has had to listen

to my stories since I was old enough to talk.

I love you Mom!

YEAR 825

THE BLUE-HAIRED MAN SAT down on a large rock and looked at the destruction before him. The once beautiful and well-kept gardens were now dead wastelands. The trees looked like they had started rotting years ago and were standing by sheer habit. The land was no longer covered in sweet-smelling grass; instead, it was as parched as if it had not seen rain in several hundred years.

It was not just the garden before him that looked this way. It was the whole world. In her anger and despair, she had touched the ground and caused this destruction and desolation in a matter of moments. It would take Y'ddra centuries to recover on her own. And even then, she could never recover all that was lost. The Tarikan and the LuZivot had lost over half of their population, and the Yidderians were down to just a few thousand. The

SeiOrhii had survived but barely, and only because they were next to impossible to kill.

The man lowered his head into his hands and cried for all that had happened. If Yiddera was to survive, he had to find a way to fix things, to fix what he had helped break. He knew that if things were to heal quickly, he would need to make things right with her, but he wasn't sure how. She was not talking to him, which was hard to do as he could not be kept out of anyone's mind once he knew it. They were bonded, and yet, somehow, she had locked him out.

He sat there in miserable contemplation until he heard someone sit beside him. He looked up and saw that the Yidderian Prophetess sat beside him. She sat there quietly, and she, too, gazed out at the barren wasteland, smelling the scent of decay that wafted through the air.

"How. No, why did this happen?" She finally asked of the silent man.

"It is my fault, and I don't know how to fix it." He replied in a broken whisper.

"Dream? Nightmare? Which are you today?" She asked him.

"Neither, just Tayin."

"Well then, just Tayin, show me how this happened, and together, we will find a way to fix it. We must work together to stop this for both of our kind." She placed her hand on his, and instead of pulling away, he allowed the touch.

"From the beginning?"

"That is always the best place to start."

Tayin took a deep breath and showed the Prophetess an illusion that was so real she felt like she was back in time. Before her, the world turned colorful and alive once again. She could smell the fresh air and the sweet scent of flowers and feel a cool breeze brush across her cheek. The Prophetess could hear the rushing of the waves as they lapped on the shores of Kruger despite knowing she was sitting on a rock on Kahlali. She gasped in surprise as a spaceship landed almost at her feet.

PROLOGUE
STILL ON BOARD THE SPACE SHIP

The small redheaded girl sat at a table in the community room of their transport ship, her head down over an open sketchbook. She studiously drew yet another picture of her blue people. The room was full of other teenagers laughing and having a good time between their classes, and though the young girl had many friends, over the last few weeks, she had begun to play less and draw more.

"What are you drawing this time, Alena?" Asked Amalie, her best friend.

The girl looked up, smiled at Amalie, and indicated she should take a seat next to her. She looked around for John, who always seemed to follow Amalie but did not see him.

"He is in the library," Amalie replied to Alena's unspoken question. "So, what are you drawing?"

"I am drawing my dreams again. But I am beginning to think they are not just dreams." She paused momentarily and drew a few more lines on her picture. "I think that they are visions of the future."

Amalie laughed and pushed against her friend's shoulder with her own, causing Alena to mess up the picture. Alena stared at the line of blue that she had just drawn across the page in dismay and then turned to scold her friend when she had another of her waking dreams. Her face went blank, and her eyes rolled into the back of her head.

"Alena." Amalie shook her friend, "Alena, are you okay? What's wrong?"

It took only a minute or two before the vision disappeared, and Alena finally responded to Amalie. "I am okay, but I do not think we are going to make it to Seager if what I just saw is correct. We will be hit by an asteroid that breaks away from a nearby belt and get pushed into an Einstein-Rosen bridge that will take us far away from our intended destination. We will eventually land our ship on a planet inhabited by the blue people of my artwork."

Amalie sat back in her chair and looked at her friend in concern. "Alena, I love you; you know that I do. You are my best friend, but you are starting to sound crazy to me, and."

"But Amalie, I have to tell the captain or someone who can try and avoid what I have seen." She interrupted and leaned in closer to her friend. "How can you call me crazy when you know that some of my dreams have already come true?"

"And to the others." Amalie continued through the interruption. "They already call you the "Prophetess," mockingly. Do not tell anyone what you have told me, or you will be spending the rest of the trip in the psych ward."

Alena jumped out of her chair and ran from the room up to the bridge to see if the captain would speak with her. She was denied entrance and told to go back to school. As she was pushed gently back out of the doorway, she yelled out to the captain. "Watch out for the asteroids; they will push us off course." The door was then shut firmly in her face.

Amalie stood against the wall with her arms crossed in front of her. "I told you not to tell anyone. Now you are going to get in trouble for disrupting the crew." She straightened off the wall and walked with Alena back to the community room. The two girls sat again at the table they had vacated earlier, and Amalie picked up the drawing.

"You are quite good, Alena, but why do you always draw your people with blue hair and spots? Why not just draw them the way people actually look."

Alena grabbed the drawing from Amalie's hand and looked at her friend in consternation. "I draw them as I see them. They are not people like us. They are the people that inhabit the planet we will be landing on."

"Our planet is currently not inhabited. That is why it was chosen for us to colonize." Amalie replied.

"Whatever, Amalie. Do not believe me, but I tell you that what I have been dreaming is real. Not only will we not make it to the planet, but we will find the one we do land on beautiful and dangerous because of the native people. These people." Alena pointed at her drawing. She gathered her art supplies and stood up. "Amalie, you will play an important part in our future, and I, well, I am not sure why or how, but you will be important in saving us from them." Alena walked out of the room, heading down the hall to her living quarters, humming a strange tune in harmony with the voice in her head.

Later that week, the captain walked into the classroom and looked around until he found Alena. He asked the teacher to excuse her and then told Alena to follow him. She left her books on her desk and followed the captain out of the room and into his office. She knew what he wanted. It was known that they had detected an asteroid belt on their sensors just that morning.

"How did you know we would encounter this problem, young lady?" He asked.

"My name is Alena, and I had a dream that we did. It is now too late to avoid it. We will be run off course and be taken light years away from our intended destination." She leaned forward and made eye contact with the captain. "When you start hearing the song, finding another planet will be too late. The song will guide you to one that is dangerous to us. Do not believe its message; do not follow it. Turn away now. Go back to Earth, go anywhere, just do not continue on this current course." Alena implored the captain.

The captain laughed and slapped the table. "Miss Alena, who told you there was an asteroid belt, and who put you up to this weird little joke?"

Alena stood up, placed her hands on the table, and leaned toward the man sitting opposite her. "I am not playing tricks.

One thing I have told you has already come true: believe in the rest of what I say. Start looking for a way around the belt, and you will see that there is only one, but that is where we will be hit by a stray asteroid. That asteroid will knock us into a wormhole that will carry us lightyears away from where we are now, and we will not be able to find our way back." She stood up and walked toward the door.

"Send for me when you start hearing the song, although, by then, it will be too late to correct our course." She walked out of the captain's office without waiting for dismissal. She knew that at only 17 years old, the adults would not believe her until there was further proof of her ability to foretell the future. Still, knowing they could have avoided this upcoming situation if they had just listened to her a week ago was frustrating.

That night, she heard the song again and frowned at its beauty. Somehow, it seemed to beckon her to its source, promising everything she could possibly want, yet it also repelled her. She could hear danger within its tune. It was like a beautiful flower that beckoned its prey to it with a sweet scent, but once the bug got too close, it would gather it up and eat it.

Alena felt deep inside that they were being led into a trap, and they would soon be gathered up and eaten just like the bug. She fell asleep listening to the tune that could not be blocked out of her mind. It invaded her dreams and filled them with visions of a lovely, vibrant planet full of everything they would need to live happily. The air was clean, the water was fresh, and the soil was fertile. But, amongst the beauty of her dream was a feeling of danger. She could see the blue people looking at her, and fear filled her whole body. She felt Amalie take her hand in hers, and the dream version of Amalie told her that everything would work out eventually. Then Alena watched her friend walk over to the blue people and stand with them. Alena woke up in a cold sweat. She was going to lose her best friend to the planet they would land on.

Over the next few weeks, everything she had told the captain had come to pass. They had indeed been thrown off course, 127 Earth years off course, and had no way to return to their original destination, Seager. Seager, named after an ancient female astrophysicist who studied exoplanets and black holes, was their intended landing spot. While she did not discover their world, it was named after her in honor of her many accomplishments. Now, they would never step foot on the planet chosen for their colonization.

It was one year later that the captain began to hear the music. Once he did, he finally started listening to Alena more carefully. During that year, she had predicted many little things that had kept her friends safe, helped with a project they were doing, and even once predicted a malfunction on the ship. This malfunction was instantly looked into and then was found and fixed. Soon, everyone began to think of her as the "Prophetess," not just her friends, and no longer was it said mockingly. She was embarrassed by this title, and if it wasn't for Amalie making fun of her, she did not think she could handle the looks of fear and reverence people began to give her. However, Amalie still saw her as a friend and nothing more.

Every day that passed, and the closer they got to the source of the music, Alena's visions became more frequent. Many were still simple things that came true quickly, such as when she told the captain to skirt around a planet, putting off a deadly amount of radiation. She told him this two months before they saw the globe on their scanners. While other visions were about the planet they would land on, there was no way, yet, to know if these would come true.

After the captain began to hear the music, it took them another eight years to make it to the planet Alena told them was called Yiddera. She announced that a sentient being made up the planet, her name was Y'ddra, and this was the Goddess giving her the visions and singing for them to find their way to her.

They had searched for a long time and could find no other habitable planet within range. So now, nine years after they were pushed off course, they had to land as they were out of enough fuel to make it anywhere else. So, their trip, initially scheduled to take 24 years, had taken 30 long years instead.

The ship floated in orbit around the magnificent planet while the crew used the ship's scanners to search for life signs and what resources were available. They found that there were not any of the needed resources available to build up a technological civilization. Still, resources were abundant if they were to become an agrarian society. With the help of the replication units and 3D printers on their ship, they could live quite well for a century or so. During that time, they would learn how to thrive on the planet without the help of technology.

Despite Alena's insistence that it held an intelligent species similar to theirs, the scans did not find any. There were no signs of the sentient being she stated made up the planet other than the singing that everyone could now hear, and there was absolutely no proof that other beings similar to those she drew existed on the planet. The captain believed that Alena was right, but without evidence and their lack of fuel, he decided to land on Yiddera anyway.

And if Alena was correct and there were beings that posed a threat to their existence, they would also be prepared for that. There was nothing that people who were not as technologically advanced as they were could do to hurt them. It would be easy enough to subdue the native inhabitants or wipe them out entirely. This world was their home now, and the people about to land on it would fight to claim it as their own.

YEAR 1

SEVERAL YOUNG MEN AND one young lady sat on the bluff, watching the commotion below them. They sat and observed without anyone knowing they were there. One of the young men was casting an illusion in front of them, so if one of those working below happened to look up, all they would see was an interesting pile of rocks. They sat in silence for about an hour before whispering amongst themselves.

"They are so similar to us." Daija, the young lady, said to her brother Kest.

"They are more similar to the LuZivot than to us." He replied as he stretched out on his stomach and crawled a bit closer to the edge.

"You are messing with the illusion." Grumbled Tam, the illusion caster.

Kest scooted back from the rocky ledge and scowled at Tam as the other three men laughed at both of them.

Tayin nudged his twin, nearly pushing him over. "If you can't keep an illusion active while Kest scoots around, I would be surprised. But then maybe you are losing your touch, old man." He laughed and nudged his brother, who was 13 minutes older than him.

"Hush, you guys are getting loud. What if they hear us?" Daija whispered.

Raighn yawned and stood up, stretching his stiff muscles. "We have nothing to fear if they hear us. I am in need of sustenance; we all are. Maybe we should have one or two of them hear us." An arc of blue lightning flashed across the sky as he stretched.

"Mind the lightning, Raighn. We were told to watch and watch only. There is to be no interaction until we are sure it is safe for us to engage them. We do not want a repeat of the Kahru." Adym, ever the responsible one, said.

Raighn quickly stopped the lightning and sat silently with the others. All of them remembered the terrifying years of the Kahru. Many of them had lost their parents during that war, and all of them had a loved one or a relative injured or worse by the deadly bear-like creatures. So, no, they definitely did not want a repeat of the Kahru.

They all sat quietly and watched as the giant ship was unloaded, and many more of the beings they were watching came out of it. Several looked like they had just awakened from a very long sleep. Children excitedly ran around the adults and were often scolded for getting in the way. Several females finally gathered the excited little ones up and took them for a walk along the brilliant yellow-sand beach.

The sun was past its zenith when the watchers stood up and left the area. They held hands, and Adym whisked them back to Raighn's house. They settled down on one of the many cushions strewn around the central courtyard. A beautiful stone fountain splashed water down soothingly as a gentle breeze drifted across the group. Wine was brought out for them to enjoy, along with refreshments of cheese and nuts.

"I do not think Y'ddra would have brought us another species like the Kahru. I think they are safe for us to enjoy." Kest began.

"Our father did say that Y'ddra told him they were safe," Daija added as she shifted her legs more comfortably on the pale purple cushion she occupied.

Tam handed his brother Tayin the wine bottle and munched a cheese slice before talking. "Well, there is only one sure way to find out if they are safe and have what we need. One of us has to try."

"And who do you suggest goes?" Tayin inquired after taking a drink from the bottle he was handed.

"I volunteer." Stated Adym. "When one is alone, I can take them somewhere and see if they have the fear we need. If they are dangerous, I can disappear; if they are not, well, then we know. It is easier for me to leave more quickly than it is for any of you."

They all agreed, and Adym quickly asked the Elders if this plan was okay. Being a telepathic race, the Allurans could easily talk with others on a different continent. The reply came back to them that, yes, the plan was okay to implement, but they should wait until tomorrow night when they would all be well rested in case things didn't go as hoped.

Daija decided to leave and headed down the hall until she came to the green door that would take her home; stepping through it, she was teleported to Zeljani. Meanwhile, the men decided to go to the village down the road from Raighn's house and see what was happening that evening. They would all stay in Alendrot tonight so they would be refreshed and on the same schedule as each other. Though only Adym would be in danger, they all wanted to be available if he needed help. So tomorrow, they would watch and wait. Tomorrow, they would find out if they were the ones who needed to be afraid or if the new arrivals would be their prey. Tomorrow was uncertain, but the moon glowed softly through the warm air and promised adventure, so tonight, they would play.

Alena looked up at the bluff that overlooked the landing site and studied it momentarily. Nothing seemed amiss, but she could have sworn that she had seen something move up there. Alena watched the area for a bit longer. Finally, she decided it must have been some animal crawling around the rock formation at the bluff's edge. She sat the box she was carrying down next to several other packets from the ship when she realized what was bothering her about the ridge. Alena did not remember that rock formation being there yesterday.

She sat on the box she had just placed, watched the bluff, and, after several minutes, decided that she must have been mistaken when it suddenly disappeared. She blinked several times and saw that it hadn't disappeared; it had moved. Now, it was further back from the edge, where she remembered it being yesterday.

Alena knew that others inhabited this planet, but no one had seen any of those they shared this world with. She wondered if the reason they had not been seen yet was due to some type of power or magic that kept them invisible. This would explain what she just saw. Alena did not believe in magic, but until she started seeing the future, she had never believed that was possible, either. She hoped the native inhabitants stayed invisible and relatively harmless but doubted this outcome, as many of her visions had shown blue-haired people, who looked similar to themselves, harming her friends. She knew from her dreams that the people who were already here were dangerous to the Yidderians.

Alena smiled at the name. The Goddess Y'ddra was the sentient being that brought life to this beautiful planet and had named the world Yiddera. Embracing their new home the leaders had voted to call themselves Yidderians, as they were no longer Earthlings. There was no going back to Earth. After the ship had gone through the wormhole they had no way of knowing where they were in relation to Earth. Even if they did, they no longer had enough fuel to get them back.

She stood up and looked up at the bluff once more. The rocks were back to exactly where they were supposed to be. Alena went to the ship and grabbed another box. Unloading the necessities from the vessel would take days. And it would take even longer to fabricate the items they would need to build a civilization. Still, several boats were already fabricated so the people could spread out and live on one of the five continents across Yiddera. The necessities would be split amongst the colonists depending on which continent they would be going to and what was needed based on climate and available resources.

The leaders had drawn names randomly to assign people to the different continents. Alena had requested that she go to the continent with the highest mountain peaks. She had always loved the snow or at least the simulation of snow, and from the aerial pictures, the place was beautiful. Alena had seen the perfect spot for a settlement. It was high up in the mountains, and though close to the mysterious Myst, it would perfectly suit her plans for the monastery. Even closer to the blue barrier was a beautiful lake with waterfalls of every color of the rainbow. She could not wait to see such an incredible sight in person.

The leaders had granted her request; after all, she was the Prophetess. Because of her gift of foresight, she was appointed the leader of their newly founded religion that surrounded their newly found Goddess. She frowned at the name but knew it was why she was getting her wish. The people going with her had already named the continent Alenar after her. Though uncomfortable in her new role, she was determined to embrace it. Being the world's religious leader gave her the power she would need to keep the world safe when the blue-haired beings finally appeared.

She was headed back to the ship for another container when Amalie, also on 'moving' duty, joined her. The two women picked up several more boxes, piled them on a cart, and pushed the heavy bundle off the ship and over to where they would be unloaded. The work went much faster and was more enjoyable when shared with a friend.

"I put your name in to join me on Alenar, and it was approved." Alena told Amalie excitedly.

"I know, but I declined it. Alena, I am going to Continent C with John. I have already told you that." Amalie lifted a box off the cart and handed it to someone to catalog and see that it was placed in the correct area.

"But why? You are my best friend, and I would like you to live near me. We will never get to see each other if you don't come and live on Alenar."

"I am going with John. You know he is my partner, and besides, I don't like the cold."

"Well, if you change your mind, there will always be a place for you wherever I am." Alena stopped working and allowed her eyes to follow a tall man with light brown hair and a wistful smile played across her lips.

"He is to old for you, Alena. For Goddess's sake, he was born on Earth." Amalie said in exasperation.

"He was three when he boarded the ship, which makes him only 33. That is not to old for me." Alena stood and watched the man. Luke, she thought she had heard someone call him, took the heavy boxes marked for the construction area from the unloading zone to their designated spot. Then, she turned back to her friend.

"I don't see it lasting with you and John. You will soon get bored of him. You already get lost in your work, and soon, it will consume you because it is the only thing that interests you. After that, John will be forgotten, and he deserves better."

"Thanks for not holding back 'Prophetess'," Amalie said, her voice dripping with sarcasm. "And you think that because my work fascinates me, I cannot have a life with John and an interest in what I do?"

Alena shrugged her shoulders. "It is not that you cannot have both. I just don't think you can have both with John. You need someone to draw you outside of yourself and your work." She again smiled and watched Luke once more. He caught her looking at him and smiled back at her.

"Ugh. I do not understand how you can say that. John is perfect for me."

"Whatever. You only say that because John caters to you and lets you do whatever you want to." Alena lowered her voice as the one who caught her eye walked by again. "I requested that he be sent to Alenar, and they have approved my request."

"Who, John?" Amalie asked in question.

"No, him." She pointed at the man she had been staring at all day.

"We undeniably have different ideas of who would make a good partner." Amalie frowned at Alena. "Let's not argue about who we partner with. I will miss you, but as soon as I get settled in my new place, I will come visit."

Alena held out her hand, and Amalie took it. "Deal." She said over their handshake. "I leave for Alenar in five months and you for Continent C soon after that. So, let's make the most of our time together here."

Alena and Amalie returned to work and over the next few months, helped turn the landing spot into a thriving town. It was paradise, or it would have been if not for the frightful happenings that began soon after their arrival.

Night fell, and Adym found a man standing sentry at the far end of the camp. He was half asleep and leaning against a rock. Adym entered the man's mind and found it easy to infiltrate. This man's mind was similar to his own but much more straightforward. He found the man's fear and smiled that it was such an easy fear to prey upon. This man was afraid of heights. Adym emitted the istotymir, the fear-inducing essence that the SeiOrhii produced to heighten their prey's terror and eventual pain.

The man shuddered and looked around him. Not seeing anyone, he went back to leaning on the rock. Adym, the immortal with the gifts of telekinesis and teleportation, took the man to the edge of the bluff he and the others had sat upon yesterday. He then moved the man so that he was floating in thin air, high above the ground. The man screamed in terror, not knowing what was going on. Adym laughed at the man and lifted him higher. The man shook with fear and started crying. Adym could feel his eyes begin to glow, and his gift becoming stronger the more frightened the man became.

Adym laughed again in delight. He now knew that this would not be a repeat of the Kahru. These new beings were just what they had hoped they would be. Adym smiled broadly, and since he was done with the 'test,' he dropped the man, watching him fall a hundred feet to the ground, and breathed in the heart of his fear. The precious concentration of fear released at the moment of death brought increased strength, power, and excitement to the SeiOrhii, and Adym felt it spread deliciously throughout his body. He looked at the man lying dead on the ground below for a few moments and then let the rest of the SeiOrhii know that these beings were precisely what they needed and wanted. This prey would suit them very nicely. The humans were easy to scare and produced a very acceptable amount of fear for them to feed on. The SeiOrhii would grow strong on this new prey.

For several days, the five young men took turns seeking out fear and found Adym was right; these new beings were what they needed. The Council of Elders decided that if they were such a good source of nourishment for the SeiOrhii, then something should be done to keep them from leaving Yiddera. After much deliberation, they devised a plan to get themselves on the ship to see what they could do to keep it from being capable of going back into space.

Kest gathered the animals and cleared out the area. He watched as the people scattered into the trees and found that the collective fear was intoxicating. Something about the fear of this prey held a sweetness to it. It was akin to a sweet wine. Tam, Tayin, and Adym waited until all the humans outside were gone so they could enter the ship unnoticed. Adym could have just teleported them inside, but they had decided that keeping the humans guessing about what was causing their fears to rise was fun. Eventually, they would start showing themselves, but the unknown kept their prey in a perpetual state of unease.

They were about to have Tam cloak them in shadows when they heard "to hell with this" and saw Raighn standing on the bluff they had once watched the humans from. He cast down thunderbolts of blue lightning, and the ship sparked and smoked. The lights in the vessel went out, and the soft noises it had made went quiet. Another round of blue lightning hit the ship, and people from inside came running out, exclaiming that the ship's internal system had gone dead. People poured out of the surrounding trees and gathered around the spacecraft, looking at the damage the freak lightning storm had caused. Many stated that the animals had known and that they had protected them from being hit by lightning.

Kest scowled, and his friends joked about him being the protector and laughed at him for "keeping our dinner from being burned." Adym took them to the bluff, gathered Raighn up, and left for home. Though they did not follow the plan laid out for them, and Adym reprimanded Raighn for this, the job had been accomplished quite successfully. They had ensured they had a continuous food source for years, perhaps centuries, to come.

YEAR 2

PROPHETESS ALENA SAT IN her little bedroom just off to the side of the chapel sanctuary. She sipped her tea and studied the plans for the new abbey they would be breaking grounds for later this morning. Last night, she had a vision that required her to make a few changes to the design. Alena quickly sketched in the underground room and made changes to the room that would go above it. Satisfied that she had drawn it as she saw in her vision, she reviewed the rest of the plans. She looked at the wall that would be built up around the monastery and decided that another foot higher might keep them safer, so she made a notation for this and a brief sentence stating why the change at this late date. She glanced out her window and saw that the sun was already starting to make an appearance. She smiled. It was going to be a warm late spring day.

She had planned for the ground to be prepared in the late spring as it would ensure the dirt was more easily dug (this wouldn't have been an issue if most of their equipment had not been destroyed). She could have waited another month, but the summers here on Alenar were not very long, and the winters could be harsh. She was still staring out the window when she heard her assistant enter her room. Turning, she saw a look of consternation on the poor woman's face. Sighing, Alena beckoned for the woman to sit.

"Another has disappeared, my lady," Sophie stated.

Alena thrummed her fingers on the desk and frowned. "We must remind the people that they are not to go out alone."

"But the one who disappeared didn't. He headed out to cut wood with two other men as usual. They swear they were all together when Benjamin disappeared. He just vanished. I don't understand what could be causing all these disappearances and strange deaths."

"I have told you and everyone else that this planet was inhabited by others and that they would be dangerous to us. I warned everyone while we were still on the ship before we ever laid eyes on this planet." Alena sighed again and, standing up, went over to the window. "Of course, we had no choice but to land." She thought back to the day that she had told the captain that they wouldn't make it to their intended destination. He had just laughed at her. And really, Alena could understand why. She was only 17 and was known for being odd. It wasn't until several predictions later that the captain began to listen to her.

Alena remembered when she started hearing someone singing a sweet song of welcome. But in the melody, she could also hear the deception. Something warned her that this would be a dangerous place to land. The captain and several others heard the song a year later and followed it. The song called to them and elicited images of beauty, prosperity, and peace. Alena begged them to find a new planet, knowing as she begged it was useless to even try. They needed to land on the next habitable planet they came to, and this one was welcoming them.

They were on that planet now. A world that was inhabited by a being named Y'ddra, who the people decided was a goddess. A year before they landed, she let everyone know that the planet was named Yiddera and that it was inhabited by the blue people she had been drawing since she was a child. Alena had warned them that these people were not friendly and wanted to cause them harm, but no one would listen to her. Why would the Goddess wish to harm them when she was so sweetly welcoming them to her? Their long-range scanners were not picking up any humanoid creatures on the planet, so surely that meant that

Yiddera was not inhabited by an intelligent species. In this one thing, they ignored her warnings, but then, with the lack of fuel, what choice did they have?

Alena sighed and stopped thinking of the past. "Someday, the strange Myst will be locked and hold the others in. Only then will we have peace."

"But Prophetess, when will that be?" Sophie asked, her eyes wide.

Turning back around to look at the woman, Alena answered, "That is not how the visions work. I do not know when; I only know that we will have a temporary peace someday." She did not tell Sophie that the peace would not last long nor that she knew who would lock the gates to bring that peace. She picked up the blueprints from her desk and handed them to Sophie. "Will you please take these to Smith? He will need to review the changes I made before we start. Oh, and tell him I will be at the designated starting point in one hour." She waved Sophie out of the room and turned back to her window.

The window she looked out of faced a densely packed growth of dark evergreen trees. Just walking a few feet into them could cause a person to become lost. Anyone who went into the dark forest tied a rope to the post just outside her door so they could find their way back. The tree cutters were barely making a dent in the forest despite the many trees they had taken down in preparation for building the great Monastery fortress.

She watched a bird land on the tree branch closest to her. This planet was beautiful, and the flora and fauna were incredible, but there was an evil here. An evil that hunted her people. She was not sure why, as none of the people they found dead were eaten. The few people who survived an encounter with the unseen just reported extreme fear. They said it was as if they were being drained of energy through their fear.

Alena remembered the drawing she had made as a child. She often drew people with blue hair, strange blue markings on their bodies, and glowing eyes. Alena knew these were the beings hunting her people, but she had never actually seen them. As far as she knew, no one had ever seen them, except maybe those that had died by their hand. She only knew of one living person who may have already seen these beings, but Alena did not think she had yet. Amalie, her closest friend, was the one destined to free them from the terror they were living in. But the cost for Amalie would be high. Alena wasn't sure how, but she knew that Amalie would live in hell in order to free her people from the unseen.

She had never told Amalie about her part in all of this, only that she was very important to the happiness of the Yidderians. Amalie had laughed at the idea that she would be essential to anything. She said she was just a botanist and an herbalist, not a hero. She had countered by saying it was Alena who was the important one. Amalie often teased Alena for being "The Prophetess." Alena smiled at her memories and then frowned in sadness at the fact that Amalie had chosen to follow John to Kahlali instead of coming up here to the mountains with her. But then she suspected she had chosen Kahlali because its climate was more temperate there than on Alenar and less about being with John, even though Amalie said otherwise.

Alena grabbed her shawl, headed out of her room, and down the path that led to the other side of the grounds. She had chosen this spot for her home as it was well protected by the mountains and the forest on two sides and a steep cliff on the third. The fourth side was a wide ridge that was used as a road to another vast clearing that was already starting to become a lovely little village. Storefronts were going up, and homes were being built there.

The monastery grounds were big enough for the building she was planning that would house the artifacts brought from Earth, a sanctuary, dormitory, kitchens, meeting hall, classrooms, and a ballroom. The rest of the area would eventually contain a place for healers to come and learn, animal husbandry, farming grounds, and whatever else was needed to make the monastery self-sufficient. The pond in the middle of the acreage had already proven to be a good fishing spot when it wasn't frozen. All in all, this was the perfect place for her paradise. She had always loved the cold, and this continent had plenty of that.

She walked to the edge of where the abbey would be built and looked down at the valley far below. There was an extremely narrow path that worked its way up the mountainside. She wondered if it would be possible to carve it out a bit more to make it a safe passage from the fertile grounds below to where she stood. Alena made a mental note to check with Luke to see if any of the equipment they had salvaged from the ship could do that type of work.

When they first landed here on Yiddera, they had plenty of equipment for anything they would need to build. And if they were short on something, they could have had it made, but the strange blue lightning had struck the ship and fried all the electronics, making new fabrications impossible. The humans were surprised as they did not think it was possible to destroy the ship with something as trivial as lightning. The spacecraft that should have been able to keep them supplied with ample necessities for centuries had become a useless piece of metal in just moments.

"Your pardon, my lady. I do not mean to interrupt your thoughts, but we are ready to start, and the workers would like a few words from you to commemorate this occasion."

Alena turned and smiled at Luke. "No pardons are necessary. I was, in fact, just thinking of you and was about to come looking for you." She took his hand and pointed down to the small path far below. "Do you think we can make that walkway safe for use?"

Surprised at the Prophetess holding his hand, Luke did not hear what she had said. "I'm sorry, but can you repeat that, my lady."

Laughing, Alena squeezed his hand and then repeated her question.

"Yes, my Prophetess, we have just the tool for that, and it has enough power left that I think we can get the job done easily, but it would mean doing more of the stonework on the abbey by hand which would mean a bit more time will be added to our plans."

"See it done as soon as possible, please." Still holding his hand, she led him back to where the others waited to begin their work. She stood on a small platform that someone had made for her and then addressed the people in front of her.

"My friends, thank you all for coming here today. This day marks the start of a new life for all of us. Here in the monastery, we will strive to honor Y'ddra, the Goddess that brought us to this beautiful planet. We will do this by teaching others about her but also by enjoying what she provides for us." Alena looked out at all the smiling faces around her.

"We will also bring those interested in the arts to us so that this place will teach others their crafts and enhance the beauty around us. I want healers to know this as a place of learning and come and increase their knowledge and teach one another. I want this to not only be a place of worship but also a home to all who wish to study and improve themselves."

Alena swayed and stepped backward off the pedestal and would have fallen if Luke had not been standing next to her. She saw a flash of a young girl cross her eyes. The girl had white blonde hair with blue streaks in it. Her eyes glowed a brilliant cornflower blue, and she stood holding a round stone the color of Allura, the blue moon that only made its appearance in the sky twice a year. She stood in the middle of the finished monastery and looked straight at Alena, and then she disappeared. Alena took a couple of deep breaths and then allowed Luke to help her back up onto the impromptu stage.

"Sorry, my friends. I am alright now." She straightened up and continued. "This day marks the gathering of those who plan to make this world their home. Thank you all for coming out today to start this huge undertaking. It will take many years, but it will be a monument of our strength, fortitude, and desire to overcome all obstacles in order to claim this world as ours." She bowed her head to those before her and stepped down. She could hear the team leaders gather their volunteers and begin the work.

"Walk with me?" She asked Luke as she started to walk around the perimeter of the soon-to-be-built edifice.

"Yes, Prophetess." He fell quickly into step next to her, matching his long strides to her much shorter ones.

"Call me Alena." She looked up at him shyly, "If you would like."

He smiled down at her and took her hand in his, "I would like that very much."

She smiled back at him and then proceeded to tell him of her vision. "I think it means that at some point, we start having children who will have the coloring of Allura. The feeling I got from the vision was that they would need sanctuary and would find it here, at the monastery. The young lady in the vision was holding something, a rock or gem of some sort. It seemed important to her."

"I am not sure how or why you have the visions, but they have always come true. Some sooner than others. You told us back on the ship that this planet was here, and sure enough, it was exactly where you told the captain it would be. So, if you say we will have blue daughters, then we will expect this and make a special place in the monastery for them." He stopped and looked out at the workers bustling around.

"I must get back to helping the others. Would you like to come over and discuss updating the plans for these new dwellers over dinner tonight?" He asked with much hesitation and no small amount of hope in his voice.

"I would like that very much."

YEAR 3

AMALIE GATHERED UP HER sketchbook and her basket and headed out of the house John was still building for them when she turned back around and grabbed up her 7-month-old son, Ethyn John the Third. She settled him on her hip and readjusted her belongings before swooping up the bag that held Ethyn's. Amalie headed out the door once again and down the path that would lead into town. She hurried along the road that ran down the center of the still-growing village and stopped in front of the bakery. Opening the door, she smiled to see Micksie behind the counter.

"Let me help you with Ethyn." Micksie, whose name was actually Mickayla but was called Micksie because of her love of cooking, came around and scooped up the wiggling baby and gave him a big hug.

"Thank you." Amalie put Ethyn's bag down on a nearby table and sat down in one of the seats. "Is there any way that you can watch him for a few hours? I know it is short notice, but John had to help Thomas deliver a calf from one of the nosorokuh. The calf is stuck, and they are trying to save it and the mother." She set her sketch pad on the table. "I had planned to go out and study the plants in the field next to the wall of Myst. I am looking for a new plant that might be used as a pain reliever or anesthetic to help with the injuries that are so common these days."

"Of course, I will watch this sweet little thing," Micksie said in baby talk as she snuggled the boy.

"I hope he saves the calves. We need to build up the herd. And their milk is so much sweeter and creamier than the milk we used to get from the cows before they all died. It is a shame they couldn't survive on this planet, but thankfully, the nosorokuh is a much better substitute." She kissed Ethyn's cheek and handed him a spatula that she had in her apron pocket. "Take all the time you need. I could love this little one forever if you cared to give him to me."

She laughed as she said this, but Amalie knew it was probably true. Micksie would be a much better mother than she was. Micksie would also make John a much better partner than she herself did. She had to admit she was not the most attentive mother. Her mind was on her studies far more often than it was on her son or on John. Both deserved better. Both deserved someone like Micksie, who was born to be a wife and mother. But she was comfortable with John, and they had been friends since childhood and a couple for several years now.

"Thank you. I will be back before sunset." Amalie kissed her son on his cheek, grabbed her sketchbook and basket off the table, and scurried out the door. She raced back toward her house and into the forest of trees. Amalie followed the small creek that ran straight into the Myst. It was called the Myst because it was a mystery as to what it was made of and what might be on the other side of it. She could not enter the Myst; no one could. For all that it looked soft, and as if you could walk right through it, it was impenetrable. She ran her hand over the Myst and, as always, was surprised at its dewy warmth. She pulled her hand back before the tingle of fear that always followed the warmth could run up her arm.

She sat down in a patch of bright green two-leafed plants next to a bush that had tiny white flowers. She took out her sketchbook and started to draw the parts of the bush in detail. She picked the leaves and drew both sides, writing their dimensions next to the drawings. She did the same thing to the flowers, the stems, and the roots. She then picked a few choice samples and put them in one of the bottles that she carried in her basket so that she could study their properties once she was at home in her lab.

Amalie was tightening the lid on the jar when she heard a noise behind her. She turned around and saw a man sitting in the grass a few feet from her. Amalie was unsure what to do, so she just stared at him as he was staring at her. She saw that his hair was cut short, and he wore a closely shaved beard and mustache that was a medium shade of blue, very similar in color to the moon of Allura. His eyes were the same color, though the irises were an oval shape and the pupils a bit of a darker blue shade. She let her eyes wander down and saw that he had strange blue spots across his shoulders and collarbone. As she looked at him, she felt something enter her mind.

Gasping in shock at the intrusive feeling, she looked back up at his eyes. She felt something probing her thoughts and wondered if it was the man sitting in front of her. She heard a heavily accented male voice say 'yes' in her mind. Her eyes widened, and she scooted backward from him. This was not her thought. This was very obviously the man speaking to her from within her own mind.

"Who are you?" She asked, "What are you?"

"Tam." He spoke in her mind again before flooding her thoughts with images that answered her second question. She saw him watching her from inside the Myst and then walk out of it and sit next to her."

"Oh." She toyed with the flowering bush she sat beside, unsure what to say next. She could still feel him in her mind and found it was not as uncomfortable as it felt a few moments ago.

The two sat there watching each other for several more moments before the man stood up and held his hand out to her. Hesitantly, she took it and stood up with him. His hand was warm, and she found she liked the feel of it despite the slight tingle of fear that it elicited within her. She let him lead her a few yards further down the creek and stopped when he pointed at a scraggly little plant that looked as if it would scratch you when you touched it. She then saw a picture in her mind of him crushing it up and wiping the juice on the wound of an animal. She could tell that the animal felt relief from the pain.

"Will this work on people?" She asked. Amalie felt the man's hand release hers and then run down her back, sending shivers of both pleasure and fear up her spine.

The man cocked his head and then smiled. "Yes." He spoke out loud this time, and his deep voice matched that of the one she had heard in her mind.

"Thank you." She knelt down and looked closely at the plant. She opened her sketchbook, and before she started to draw, she looked up and saw that the man was gone. Shaking her head over the encounter, she started her process of sketching all the parts of the plant, and then she picked several specimens and placed them in an empty jar. Once done, Amalie realized she had been there for far longer than she had planned, so she hurried back down the path and out of the forest. She swung by the house and put her basket and sketchpad on the counter before heading once more into town. About halfway to the bakery, she met up with John carrying a sleeping Ethyn in one arm and a basket of baked goods in the other.

"I am so sorry I am late." She said as she took the basket from him.

A laugh escaped John. Ethyn stirred, and John instantly stopped laughing and lowered his voice. "You are always late. What did you find today?"

"I am not always late, only mostly always." She laughed quietly. "I found a plant that I think will help with pain and another I am not sure what to expect from it."

"Why do you think the one will help with pain? Have you tested it yet?" He asked, switching the sleeping child to his other arm as he opened the door to let them in.

Amalie felt a strong desire to keep her encounter with the strange man to herself. Hell, she wasn't even sure if the meeting had actually happened or if it was a hallucination caused by the first plant. Until she knew for sure, she would keep it to herself.

"I scratched my hand as I picked the plant, and it released a liquid that made the pain from the small injury go away." She lied, but she felt it was a harmless lie. "Would you like me to bathe Ethyn and put him to bed?"

"No, you go on to your lab. I know you are dying to do some research on the new plant species. I will get Ethyn down. I enjoy the nighttime rituals with him." John kissed Amalie on the cheek and watched as she left the house. He saw her cross the yard and enter the capacious greenhouse that she had insisted on building before anything else was built.

Amalie entered her workshop and sat down at the big table. She pulled out her specimen bottles and placed them carefully on the table. Amalie opened the one with the white flowers first and set a petal on a glass slide. She looked at it under her microscope and then did the same to the leaves, stems, and roots. She then crushed each one gently and looked at them under the microscope once more. She mixed the liquid that came out with different solvents and watched their reactions. Amalie took careful notes and found that she could not make any judgments from her findings yet on what the plant might be used for, if anything.

Amalie stretched her back and tried to get more comfortable in her chair when she realized she had been there for many more hours than she had anticipated being. She sighed and thought this was often her problem. She got so caught up in her work that she forgot about everything else. Amalie saw a sandwich sitting on the edge of the table next to a cup of tea that at one time must have been hot but now was quite cold. John must have brought it to her. She smiled as she bit into the sandwich. It was her favorite: goat cheese with tomatoes and pickles on Micksie's freshly baked sourdough bread. She sipped the cold tea and smiled as, once again, it was her favorite flavor, bergamot with just a hint of orange. Someday, she vowed that she would learn to notice him when he entered the room. He deserved to be at least acknowledged even while she was deep in her work.

She finished the sandwich and went back to writing her findings in her journal and jotting down pertinent facts in the sketchbook by the pictures she had drawn earlier. Amalie heard a soft noise at the back of the building and, looking up, was once again surprised to see the blue-haired man sitting there in the corner watching her.

"Hello." She said softly.

He smiled but did not say anything. He just continued to watch her. After a while, this made her feel uncomfortable.

"If you are going to be here, at least say something; otherwise, I am going back to the house and to bed. I am tired." She stood up and made to leave.

"Don't go." He said slowly, as if struggling to find the right words in a language he did not know.

"Alright." She sat back down. "Why are you watching me?"

"I find you," He paused, "Interesting."

"Me? Well, I am not very interesting unless you like people who get lost in plants." She laughed a bit nervously. Amalie was beginning to suspect this man was one of the original inhabitants of this planet that Alena had told her about. He had the coloring and the markings that the Prophetess had always drawn on her people. Prophetess, she smiled inwardly at this term. Alena had said that the people who inhabited this planet before they arrived were dangerous to the Yidderians. If the mysterious troubles they had been having since their arrival on Yiddera were any indication, then she was right. They were not pleasant, which made Amalie wonder if she was the next on this man's list to be killed or terrified in some manner.

"No. You are not. I find you interesting in a different way." He said to her unspoken thoughts.

"You can read my mind?" She asked, setting down her pencil. Amalie realized she found this man more fascinating, at the moment, than her research. A first for her, but then she was also exhausted, and this might be part of the reason why.

"I am telepathic, so in a way, yes." He replied. He stood up and walked over to her. Taking a lock of her light brown hair in his hand, he brought it to his nose and sniffed it.

"You smell of appleberries."

"Oh." She whispered and then pulled her hair from his hand. "How do you know my language?"

He lightly touched her cheek and smiled as she closed her eyes and unconsciously leaned into his touch. "The more I am in your mind, the easier it is to understand your thoughts and your words." He replaced his hand with his lips. He kissed her cheek and breathed in her scent once more.

His closeness and her body's reaction to this man were making her nervous. Amalie did not understand how she could be attracted to this stranger, but she couldn't keep her body from leaning into him and welcoming his touch. She stood up and headed to the door, leaving him standing by the chair she had just vacated.

"Please do not come back here." She closed the door behind her.

Amalie raced into the house and quickly locked the door behind her. She calmed herself down before heading into the bedroom and changing into her nightgown. Amalie crawled into bed next to John and tried to sleep but found herself unable to. After a few minutes of tossing and turning, she quietly got up and went into the living room to read.

She lit a candle and, tucking her feet up under a blanket, started to read one of her botany journals. She did not hear John until he sat down on the couch next to her.

"What is wrong, my love?" He asked as he put an arm around her and pulled her onto his lap.

"I just met one of the beings that live in the Myst. At least, I think I did." She began. "I am not sure, as I was doing research on one of the new plants, and maybe it causes hallucinations. I don't know, but he seemed so very real."

"Did he hurt you? Are you okay?" John ran his hands over her, looking for any injury.

"No, he just talked to me, in my mind. He said he was telepathic, and John, the man looked like the drawings that Alena made when she was young. You know of the people with blue hair and spots." She snuggled up against John. "I don't know; it has been a long day. Maybe I made up the whole thing."

"If you didn't, then you must be careful. I don't want you to go missing as so many others have or go insane with fear." He kissed the top of her head and, picking her up, carried her back to bed. "I could not live without you. I know it is asking a lot, but maybe for a while, could you try not to go anywhere by yourself. Stay with one of your friends, one of the other botanists, or myself if you choose to go out into the forest."

"I think that is a smart idea. Goodnight, John."

"Good night, my love." He tucked her into bed and rubbed her back until he felt her drift off to sleep. Tomorrow, he would talk to the other town leaders about what Amalie had told him.

If there was someone out there causing the evil, then they must be on their guard and come up with a plan to keep everyone as safe as they could.

After John and the other town leaders talked, it was decided that a curfew should be enforced. For safety, no one was allowed out after dark, and if it was necessary to be, then a second person must accompany you. It was also decided that no one should go into the forest without a companion. There were a few grumbles about this, but overall, the villagers accepted it as a temporary measure, though they did wonder how this new rule was supposed to keep the nightmares away.

Amalie knew this was mainly for her safety, and so she put up with the new restriction without argument. She would often ask John to go with her into the forest to gather new specimens, and if he were not available, she would ask Micksie. It was on one of the days she was out in the forest that Amalie came across a flower that looked like a wild orchid, but it was bright green in color. After drawing it as meticulously as she drew everything, she sniffed the flower. It smelled faintly of coffee.

"Micksie, will you come and smell this flower for me?" She asked as she held out the seemingly delicate bloom to be smelled.

Micksie walked over to where Amalie sat and smelled the flower. "Ooh, it smells like coffee." She smiled and took another whiff.

"I wonder if it tastes like coffee, too?" Amalie replied. She sat the flower down and felt as if a headache was starting in the back of her head. She closed her eyes and realized no; it was more like when the strange man had been in her mind. She then heard a male laugh as it told her that the flower made an excellent drink and, if left to dry, tasted like what she called vanilla. Amalie opened her eyes in surprise at the intrusion of his thoughts into her mind.

"Amalie, are you okay?" Micksie asked with concern in her voice.

"I am fine. I thought I was getting a little headache, but I feel okay now." She replied.

"Are you sure? I can run and get John for you if you would like. He may have something that could help you." Her voice was excited and sounded a little breathless.

Amalie realized, at that moment, that Micksie was in love with John. The way she said his name and the way her face went soft spoke volumes. She wondered why she had never noticed this before.

"I am fine. I do not need John to help me with a little headache. Besides, even if I did need his help, I do not know what pasture he is working in today." Amalie made a few notations in her book before setting it down.

"He is in the south field down by the edge of town where the two roads meet. He will be there all day today and for the rest of the week." Micksie replied, picking up the green flower and inhaling its enticing scent once again.

Amalie was reminded that John had told both her and Micksie that very information just this morning. She was ashamed that she had not given it much thought. The voice in her head spoke again.

"As far as I can tell, you often don't give him much thought." The voice paused, and she could almost feel him smile. "But you have given me a lot of thought lately." His voice was warm and inviting.

Amalie frowned at her body's reaction to the stranger. She started to pack up her belongings and the new plant specimens to distract herself from him. She then asked Micksie to help her gather more of the green orchids, and after filling up her basket, the two women walked back into town. As she walked, Amalie thought about what the voice in her head said. It was true; she had thought of the stranger more than she wanted to admit. But then, it was most likely because he was the reason for the extra precautions the town was taking. She pushed thoughts of him out of her head and entered the bakery with Micksie.

She went to the back room behind the counter and picked up Ethyn, who was happily playing with his toys. She gave him a big snuggle and kissed his sticky cheek. He squealed in delight and gave his momma a hug back. Amalie sat her basket on the floor and sat down with Ethyn to play for a while when she heard John's voice from the front of the store. She quietly listened as he spoke a few words to Micksie. She was not surprised by the love she heard in Micksie's voice but was surprised by the care she heard for Micksie in John's voice.

Amalie thought about that for a while and thought yet again the two would make a great couple, but that was not meant to be. She and John were together. Amalie grew up knowing that John would be her partner. He was easy to be with, and while he was not her sole focus in life, she did love him. Amalie scooped up Ethyn and her basket and went out to meet the others. She tiptoed up for John to kiss her cheek and then thanked Micksie for going with her into the forest before leaving the shop and heading home with her little family.

While she followed the rules that were put in place to keep everyone safe, not all the townsfolk were content to. An increase in night terrors occurred, and people reported seeing terrible things that were not there. Those few that had gone out alone either didn't come back or came back in such a state that she was called upon to bring a tonic that would help them to sleep or calm them down. She was thankful she had found the plant that helped ease the pain, as it was called for quite often. Amalie did not like to remember that the only reason she knew it helped with pain was because the very being who was causing the said pain was the one who had told her it would help.

After another month of being good and following the safety guidelines, Amalie absentmindedly went out into the forest alone. She did not mean to, but as she was out walking to her greenhouse lab, she saw a child enter the woods by themselves. Amalie ran out to stop the little one when she realized that she had not thought about bringing someone with her. What if the child she saw was just an illusion? She walked further into the forest, searching for the child but trying to be cautious in case it was a trick. Many of the other villagers had reported seeing things that weren't real.

Ahead of her, she saw the child run close to the Myst barrier, and she hurried to catch up and pull the child away. Amalie tried to grab the hand of the young boy but couldn't. He stood in front of her just out of reach, and she scolded him for going into the woods by himself and reached for his hand once more. Again, the child evaded her touch, then turned and ran straight into the Myst.

Amalie had never seen anyone enter the Myst before and was surprised that this child could go through the impenetrable vapor. Without thinking about it, she ran in after him, dropping her basket as she passed through. She found that the barrier was slightly damp, warm, and smelled of rain. She stopped just inside and saw that the landscape was the same as it was on her side of the Myst. She had expected it to be different somehow. Amalie saw the child she had been trying to catch vanish into nothingness and knew that she had made a mistake and followed an illusion.

Tayin walked through the garden and down the path that led to the border of the Myst closest to the Yidderian village. He smiled as he passed the many fragrant flowers and touched a pale pink bloom on one of the fruit-bearing trees that lined the walkway. He loved the beauty of his home. Unlike Tam, he was very concerned with keeping it orderly and beautiful. Tam was not worried as he knew that the Tarikan would keep everything in order, but Tayin liked to be involved in its planning.

He continued walking until he found his brother. Tam was standing just inside the Myst and staring at the woman studying the flowers on the other side. He watched her for a moment alongside his twin, not understanding Tam's fascination with her. Sure, she was pretty, but she was Yidderian, not Alluran. She was one of those that Y'ddra had brought here for them to feed on. Tam's fascination with this Yidderian woman was not because of this.

"I don't know why she fascinates me, but she does. I want to touch her, taste her, and talk to her." Tam replied to Tayin's unspoken thoughts. He continued to watch the young woman.

"You will cause her fear, so it would be pointless to try. She will never see you as she sees that man she lives with."

"I have visited with her," Tam said.

"Really? And how did that go?" Tayin was surprised as he had not known that Tam had talked with this woman before. They shared their thoughts more closely than any other Alluran did, with the exception of the Tarikan. Twins were very rare among the Alluran people. Not only did they share their mind in a way similar to the Tarikan, but they also shared the gift that would have been given to one of them if they had not been born twins.

Tam, with his gift of deceptive illusions, was powerful in his own right, but Tayin, the younger of the two, had the talent to create dreams and nightmares, day or night. Most with his gift could influence dreams but could not actually make them, and they could only influence one person at a time. He was considered to be the SeiOrhii with the most powerful gift since he could create thoughts and images and then project them into every mind at one time, day or night. He could also keep them in the dreamworld forever if he chose to.

Tayin was a gentle and caring man who knew that his gift could be dangerous. In fact, it was to the Yidderians he fed on, but to his people, it was used for education. He would ease bad dreams when he felt one in progress and would provide extraordinary dreams to them on their birthday. He would often give the children dreams about their history so that learning was more effortless.

In addition to being a dream master, he was the history keeper for the Allurans, which came with the responsibility to keep the history of their world, and he took this very seriously. As a historian, Tayin would remind the Elders and other Allurans of past events that would help with the decision-making of current ones. As the history keeper, he could hear everyone's thoughts. No one could hide their thoughts from him even when they tried to. He was once again surprised that Tam had been able to.

"She told me never to revisit her." Tam turned to Tayin. "But I am going to. I am going to bring her into the Myst."

"And if she doesn't want to come?"

"It doesn't matter. I want her." He stubbornly replied.

Tayin shrugged his shoulders. "I still don't understand this desire you have for a Yidderian female, but whatever. Do as you wish, but be prepared for her to try and get away. Be prepared for her fear and refusal to accommodate your wishes."

Tayin headed up the path that led back to their home. "When will she be coming? I will have the Tarikan prepare her a room." He said over his shoulder.

"No need. She will be sharing mine." Tam said, smiling as his brother laughed. He turned back to the woman and watched. Tam couldn't help but talk to her when she asked the other woman she was with to smell the green flower. He saw her face scrunch up in worry about hearing him in her mind and then watched as she gathered up her basket and walked with the other woman back to their village. He wasn't sure how he would get her to enter the Myst, but Tam knew that he would find a way.

Over the next months, both he and Tayin fed indiscriminately on the villagers and enjoyed the fear that caused them to place strict rules for their people to follow to help keep them from danger. Nothing these Yidderians did could actually keep them safe, but the two men allowed them to think it did. Tayin and Tam only had one disagreement in the time that followed. Tayin found Tam feeding on a group of young Yidderians and stopped his brother from continuing. Tayin disagreed with feeding on the young of any species. He felt that they deserved a peaceful childhood. Tam, like many of the SeiOrhii, didn't care. Food was food, whatever age they may be. After a terse argument, Tam gave in to Tayin and went in search of an adult to feed upon.

Since humans came to their planet, the SeiOrhii had been allowed to indulge whenever and however much they wanted to. The fear of these people strengthened their gifts and helped nourish their bodies. The SeiOrhii, the immortal race of the Alluran people, needed the fear and pain of others to survive. They did not know what it was about the fear of others that kept them healthy, but it did. Without this fear, they felt weak. Each time they fed, their eyes glowed brighter, their gifts became more potent, and they felt more powerful. It was a heady sensation.

After over a month of watching, Tam knew how to get the woman he wanted into the Myst. She could be lured out of her house by the sight of a child going into danger. He could not use a real child as he had promised Tayin that he would not hurt the young, but he could create an illusion of one heading into the Myst, and she would follow. He waited until she was alone one day and out in her garden.

Tam saw her head to her greenhouse, basket, and sketchbook in hand, and he created a child that looked like one he had seen running around the village. As he knew she would, the woman headed after the child and right into the Myst.

Amalie tried to go back through the Myst gate and found it once again impossible to pass through. She tried and tried until she felt a hand on her shoulder pull her away.

"It is not passable unless an Alluran guides you through."

Amalie looked up into the incredibly blue eyes of the man she had met a couple of months ago. She shrugged away from his touch and backed away from him. Her body meeting the now solid barrier.

"Alluran?" She asked absently.

"That is what our people are called collectively." He answered as he walked toward her and placed his hands on her shoulders, then leaned down and kissed the tip of her nose.

"Please don't." She said, her voice quivering with fear and, she hated to admit it, excitement over what might happen next. Something about this being drew her to him in an unsettling way. He backed up and stared at her before taking her hand and leading her along the beautifully kept path that led away from the Myst gates. Amalie looked back at the Myst and saw that she could see straight through it, sort of like a window. Yet she knew that on the other side, you could not see into the Myst. Amalie turned her eyes away and looked at where they were going. At this point, she had no hope of escape, so why torture herself by looking back?

The path through the woods opened onto a well-manicured lawn with flowers of every color and size speckled throughout it in magnificently kept beds. Trees such as she had never seen lined the perimeter of the garden. She could hear water off in the distance and wondered if it was the river on the other side of the Myst gates that she heard. She continued walking, her hand held tightly by the strangers until they came to a small, intimate alcove next to another section of the Myst barrier. Amalie saw that the water she heard was coming from a stream that fed a pool lined with bright red gems. Next to this pool was one of crystal-clear rocks. It was a bit larger, and part of it disappeared under the Myst. The area was beautiful, and she ached to draw and study every new thing she saw.

The man let go of her hand and sat down on the soft grass. She sat across from him and was pleasantly surprised by the cool mint smell that was elicited by the slightly crushed ground cover.

"Why am I here?" She asked.

"Because I want you to be." He replied.

She looked at him and saw that, to him, this was a sufficient answer. Amalie picked a blade of the thick grass and brought it to her nose. The mint smell intensified, and she wondered if it would be good to ease nausea. Would she need to make it into a tea, or could it just be eaten? A laugh brought her out of her thoughts.

"Either would be fine, but it has a bitter flavor and so should be mixed with honey." He told her.

"Oh." She hesitated, "Thank you for the information." She sat the plant back down on the ground, unsure of what to say next.

"Your name is Amalie?" He asked, putting the emphasis on the wrong syllable.

She corrected his pronunciation, and when he said it right, she nodded her head and smiled at him.

"And yours?" She asked.

"I told you the first time we met." Was his reply.

Amalie scrunched up her face and thought back to that day. She remembered how she felt when he touched her but could not quite remember what they had talked about. She focused more on the moment and finally remembered.

"Tam?"

"Yes." He leaned over and kissed her lips.

Amalie once again pulled away from him. This time, he followed her with his body and pushed her down in the grass, lying gently on top of her.

"Please let me up." She said to him. Her body was tingling in every spot that he touched her. She had never felt this level of excitement or desire for anyone before. The shivers that rolled through her body made her uncomfortable. This man was not John; he was one of the monsters.

"No, I like it here." He replied and kissed her once again.

She pushed against him and could not get him to move.

"I don't care if you like it there. Get off me." She pushed him, and he complied and rolled over. Amalie sat up, shaking with want of him. "I have a partner and a son," Amalie told him more to remind herself than anything else.

"So." He said as he, too, sat up. "You are not his Korsyon."

"Korsyon?"

Tam looked into her mind and found the word he was looking for in her language. "You are not bonded with him for eternity. You do not carry his heart next to yours."

"Bonded? Oh, you mean married. No, we are not yet. But I do love him and mean to be faithful to him."

Again, she felt him intrude into her mind. It felt a bit like a headache about to come on, but not quite as unpleasant.

"He does not set you aflame. You," He searched her thoughts before continuing. "You love him but are not in love with him. He makes you feel comfortable. I want to make you uncomfortable. You will notice me when I come into the room, no matter what you are doing."

Amalie was unsure how to respond. It was true that she loved John but was not in love with him. They had been friends their whole lives, and becoming a couple seemed the obvious next step. It seemed the natural thing to do. Maybe he did not set her aflame, as Tam said, but he was gentle and reliable, and he was her best friend. She did not need more than that. John was a wonderful father and took up the slack when she got lost in her work. That was what she wanted in a partner.

"No, it isn't. You want excitement and someone to distract you from your work." He stated, rolling over onto his side and looking down at her as he ran a hand over her belly.

She sighed and knew that what he said was once again accurate, but she didn't want to hear it. "Please stay out of my mind."

"I cannot. You think very loudly."

Amalie stood up and walked to the red waters, and then sat back down. Taking off her shoes, she dipped her toes into the relaxing pool. It was warmer than she thought it would be. She sat with her back to Tam and felt the instant he moved toward her. She could feel his presence before he wrapped himself around her and slipped his feet into the water as well. Amalie sat up straight and tried to keep from leaning against his bare chest but, after several minutes, could not maintain the uncomfortable posture and so relaxed against him. She could feel him smile.

"How long are you going to keep me here." She asked, kicking the water with her feet.

"Until I am bored of you." He ran his hand down her arm and pulled her closer to him.

She turned her head to look at him and, finding she couldn't see his face from this angle, turned back to look at the waters.

"Then please get bored fast. I have much to do back home."

Tam laughed at the terseness in her voice. She obviously did not like his honest answer. But she was Yidderian, and he was not. He could not keep her forever; she would not live that long. He untangled himself from her and, taking her hand, helped her up.

"Come, I want to show you my home." Tam started running and was delighted when she willingly ran with him.

It had been six very long months since John had found Amalie's basket at the edge of the Myst gates and six very long months since he had gone to the council to get help in searching for her. They had spent almost two weeks searching the woods and the lakes before the party had given up. Her body was not found, and no signs, other than her basket, had been found either. Everyone but John was convinced that she had been killed by the mysterious beings as so many others had been before her.

John still had not given up. He searched for her every chance he got but with no luck. He stood against a tree looking at the crystal lake that faded into the Myst and knew, somehow, that she was inside the barrier. John pushed away from the tree and touched the warm vapors, deciding as he did so that he needed to see Prophetess Alena. She had always said that Amalie was important. Maybe Alena knew when Amalie would return to him. Perhaps she could tell him how and why Amalie was so important and if it had anything to do with her disappearance. The Prophetess was sure to know how he could get her back.

John entered his house and smiled to see Micksie in the kitchen making dinner. She had moved into his spare room two months after Amalie had disappeared so that she could take care of Ethyn while John was out searching for Amalie at all hours of the night. She would take Ethyn with her to her family's bakery every day and then bring him back home so that he would be there when John returned. It was nice to come home to a home-cooked meal and to have someone to talk to.

"Micksie, I am going to Alenar to see the Prophetess. I will leave early next week to make it to the shore on time to catch the monthly boat. Would you like to come with Ethyn and me?" He asked, popping a freshly baked roll in his mouth. He smiled at the explosion of warm, gooey cheese in the middle of it. Micksie was a fantastic cook.

"I would love to." She smiled and handed him another of the bite-size rolls.

After dinner, John bathed Ethyn and put him to bed, and then sat in the living room with Micksie. She was wrapped up in a blanket on the armchair by the window. The snow falling softly outside made a perfect backdrop for her. She was a pretty woman with dark chestnut-colored hair and soft brown eyes. John stared at her for several minutes before sitting on the couch and putting his feet up on the coffee table.

"John, put your feet down. They don't go on the table." She sat her book on one of the end tables. "Would you like me to pull up the ottoman for you?"

"No, don't get up." He took off his shoes and stretched out on the couch so that he could look at her.

"Do I have something on my face?" She asked.

"No, I was just noticing how pretty you are and thinking about how glad I am that you are here. But I was also thinking about how selfish I am being to you. You should have a family of your own to care for, and here I am keeping you from finding someone to start one with."

Micksie pulled the blanket tighter around herself and smiled shyly. "I am very content to take care of you and Ethyn. Right now, you are all the family that I need." She knew that he still loved Amalie, but as time passed, she hoped John would come to love her more. Micksie was as convinced as everyone else that Amalie was dead, and soon, she knew that John would see the truth in this. Until then, she would be his friend and dream of the day that he would want more than that from her.

"Thank you for being willing to come with me. It will be nice to have a friend on the long journey." He folded his arms up under his head. "We will need to start packing tomorrow and gathering supplies for the trip."

"I will make sure everything is ready by Monday so that we can get a nice early start Tuesday morning." She stood up and walked over to the hallway that led to her room. "If you need anything tonight, you know where I will be." Micksie disappeared from his sight.

John continued to look out at the snow falling for a while longer before deciding to head to his room. He had often been alone while living with Amalie. She was always working late into the night and rising early in the morning. He rarely saw her, and she was always busy with work. He had never truly felt lonely with her, but now, living with Micksie, he saw how lonely he had been even when Amalie was there. As much as he still loved her and wanted to find her, he wondered what it would be like to live with Micksie. Not as they did now, but as a couple. John knew that she cared for him and that she would welcome something more than friends, but he wasn't ready to take that step yet. If he did, it would mean there was no going back. It would mean that he was giving up on finding his best friend and his first love.

He got up from the couch and headed down the same hall that Micksie had. He paused at her door and looked into the room. She always left her door slightly open so that she could hear Ethyn in the night. He looked at her as she pulled off her robe and smiled at the beauty of her shapely body. She was nicely rounded in all the right places. He watched as she pulled on a nightgown and then crawled into bed. He laughed softly as he heard her say, "Goodnight, John." She had known he was there the whole time.

"Goodnight, sweet Micksie." He replied back and then entered his own room.

The trip had been arduous. The boat had hit an unexpected storm, and many of the passengers had been sick, but finally, they made it to Alenar. John and Micksie, with Ethyn in tow, were in one of the few remaining shuttles. They were comfortable little ships that held 20 people and flew in the air. Only three of them had survived the destructive lightning that had killed most of the electronics they had brought with them from Earth. The Prophetess was given one, and the other two were used by those who requested them from the elected leaders on Kruger.

The flight was a quick one from the docks to the thriving little village outside of the Monastery walls. John and Micksie disembarked and found a room available at the inn next to a tea shop. They unpacked and then went to refresh themselves with tea and a light repast at the shop next door. Once done, they started the long walk to the Monastery. They reached the walls and were allowed to enter. They were then directed to the little chapel where the Prophetess Alena was still living. They were told that if she was not there to ask around for Luke, he would know where to find her.

Fortune was with them, and they found Alena sitting at a table outside of her house. She smiled when she saw them and got up to give John a big hug. She then hugged Micksie and took the young Ethyn from her arms. Alena sat back down and handed the squirming child a cookie from the tray on the table.

"It is so good to see you both." She said. "Sit, have some refreshments and some of the last of the snowfruit juice. The fruit grows on trees and has a white rind, but the flesh is a shocking red color. It tastes similar to pineapple." She poured each of them a glass of the iced drink.

They chatted for a while until Alena could tell that John was getting frustrated by the idle conversation. This was very unlike him as he was usually very convivial. Alena handed the child back to Micksie and then cleared the table.

"Micksie, why don't you take young Ethyn to the kennels? They are over by the entrance to the Monastery grounds. You passed them on the way in from the village. There are a couple of new litters of mini rex. Let Ethyn pick out a male and a female to take back to Kahlali with you." She turned to John, "They are amazing at keeping pests and rodents out of the gardens and work well in herding smaller animals." She walked with Micksie to the gate and pointed her down the path with a reminder not to go near the construction site of the Abbey as it could be dangerous.

Alena sat back down at the table and looked at John. "She is gone, isn't she?"

"Yes, for the past six months. I have searched but cannot find her. I feel that she is trapped in the Myst with those monsters." He shook his head in frustration. "I don't know where else to look or how to get into the Myst to find her. I am here to beg you to help me."

Amalie looked at him sadly, "I cannot. She is where she is meant to be, John. There is nothing you can do but move on."

"I cannot until I know that she is alive or dead. This not knowing is driving me crazy."

"She is alive, and you will see her again, but John, she is no longer yours. I don't think she ever really was. She will emerge from the Myst one day, and I do not know how, but when she returns, peace will happen for our people. No longer will we be tortured by those that live inside." She paused and then decided to tell him the truth.

"Amalie will no longer be the happy person she was. My vision shows that she will live out the remainder of her life in agony." She took a sip of her fruity drink. "John, move on with your life. She would not want you to waste it mourning her or searching for her."

"I know, but how can I move on and be happy knowing that she is out there somewhere and in pain?"

"I never said she was in pain. She is content. That is all I can tell you as that is all that I know from the visions that I have seen that concern her." Alena paused for a moment and looked at John as he spoke once more.

"I am thankful that I have had Micksie by my side through this. She has been good for Ethyn. She has helped him not miss his mother."

"She has helped you as well, I think. You should settle down with her and give Ethyn some brothers and sisters. You do know that she has been in love with you for a very long time."

"I realize that now but didn't before. I have been seeing her more as the amazing woman she is and not just as the friend she was. I think that I have been so wrapped up in the idea of Amalie all my life that I never even thought to notice someone else. Micksie makes me feel noticed and cared for. She is helping me heal from losing Amalie. I am not yet ready to move on, but Micksie makes me want to." John paused and then got up to leave. "I don't know if I will ever stop loving Amalie, though."

"I know. And that will be part of her tragedy." Alena stood up and followed John down the path toward the Kennels. There, they found Ethyn playing with two rex pups. One was a female who was brown and had a lavender stripe down its back and a lavender front paw. The other was a male with a purple and black brindle pattern. They were beautiful. John picked out another male and female but of the regular size and then thanked Alena for her advice. He put the young Rex in a basket, and with Micksie carrying Ethyn, they headed back to the hotel.

They stayed for another week and were taken on a tour of the monastery grounds. They looked at the area mapped out for a maze and another for an herb garden. They were in awe over the size of the vegetable garden and the nearby flower beds. The nosorokuh were huge creatures, built like the Earth rhinoceros but covered in thick wool, and often broke through the pasture fences. John helped reinforce the fence around the nosorokuh pasture and offered advice on the building of the barn and veterinary clinic. He added a few things to the drawing that he had found helpful in his own pastures.

Micksie traded recipes with the local bakers and bought several starter plants of different herbs that they did not have in Kahlali and promised to send some of hers back to those she traded with. All in all, the trip was healing and productive. Together, the family headed back to Kahlali with a new outlook. Micksie was happy because she knew that John was feeling more at peace with the loss of Amalie, and that might mean he was ready to see her as a woman and not just a friend. John was happy because of his newfound peace and because of the woman who was helping him to heal.

Amalie had been in the Myst for almost seven months, and though she missed her son, Amalie found she was happier where she was now than she had been outside of the Myst gates. Tam had been right when he had told her she would never be able to ignore him, even when she was busy working. All he had to do was walk into a room, and she knew he was there. Amalie had tried hard to ignore him, but she couldn't.

She found him intriguing, intelligent, and oh-so-very sexy; his touch set her on fire. This made her feel guilty. Amalie had truly loved John, still loved him, but she had never felt for him the way she felt for Tam. Though insistent, Tam had never forced her into his bed; she had chosen to be there. She shared bliss-filled nights and unforgettable days with him.

Tam took her into the forest and showed her many new plants to draw and study. He let her know what they were used for or gave her hints and let her figure it out for herself. The plant that she had studied but wasn't sure what it could possibly be used for, she now used daily. It was used to prevent pregnancy, and all you had to do was chew the leaf. She found that you could also take it in tea, though this diluted its potency, so you had to drink at least two cups for it to work.

Tam was what Alena had told her she needed in a partner. He was one to help her with her interests but did not let her lose herself in them. Tam did not like being ignored, and as she could not forget him even while entranced in her work, he never was. All he had to do was walk into a room, and her body knew he was there.

He helped her learn not just about the many plants that grew within the Myst but also about the people that lived within its borders. She saw that the Allurans were a fantastic race of people. They truly cared for each other and made sure each and every one of them had everything they needed for a happy life. They were meticulous in caring for Yiddera and Y'ddra, the sentient being that inhabited the planet. Amalie was told it was this being that spoke to Alena and to Brecher, one of the SeiOrhii Elders.

Tam was a SeiOrhii, one of the immortals. In the short time she had been here, she had learned that he and the others like him fed on the fear, and sometimes pain, of other species. She discovered that Y'ddra lured other beings to this planet by singing to them so that the SeiOrhii might feed. Amalie was told that this kept them strong and their gifts powerful. This fear that they reaped from others kept them immortal.

Tam had never been shy about this and offered no apologies for it. Amalie heard the screams of his victims and tried to close her mind to their cries of terror. His friends would 'hunt' with him and then sit around the table talking about the many and varied human fears. Never once did they think that maybe she did not want to hear about their exploits. Amalie usually left when their talk turned to how they tortured and fed on her neighbors, friends, and fellow Yidderians.

Despite knowing what Tam was and what he did, she found herself falling in love with him. Amalie had tried not to love him and, for the first three months, was successful, but somewhere along the way, she became used to this way of life and learned to overlook the aspects of it that she did not like. She began to see Tam as not someone to fear but to love.

Amalie walked along the border of the Myst and thought of her life with Tam. It was one that she never wanted to give up. She had never been happier, or if she was honest, angrier than when she was with Tam. They got into fierce arguments and yelled at each other. They also laughed and teased and loved. The only thing keeping her from being perfectly happy was knowing that

John would probably still be out searching for her. She knew he would have trouble moving on until he knew whether or not she was dead or alive. And if he suspected she was still alive, John would not stop searching until he found her. Amalie also knew that her son was now living without a mother. He deserved to be raised in a loving family with two parents. Tam had taken this away from her son, which was something they argued about often.

As she walked the barrier, her hand trailing in its softness, she came upon the spot where she had disappeared and saw that John was sitting there in the bright green grass talking to the Myst. She sat down opposite him, knowing that he could not see or hear her. She cried silently to herself as he spoke.

"You missed Ethyn's first birthday. It was hard without you, but we managed to make it festive for him. Micksie baked him a cake, and he smashed it with his little fist, trying to grab a piece. I made him a wooden boat, and we sailed it in the pond. He is getting so big." John smiled in memory.

"We went to visit Alena. They are doing good work on the monastery and making good progress on its construction. I was given two pairs of rexes to start breeding here in Kahlali." He paused, and his voice started again, this time with a little hitch in it, "She told me you were content in there and that someday I would see you again. She said that you would no longer be mine at that time. Amalie, I know that you can't hear me, but I want you to know that I am sorry that I was not there to protect you. I am sorry that you are not here to see Ethyn grow into the fine little man that he is. I will try to bring him to this spot on his birthday so that if by some chance you are also here, you can see him or not, as I am not sure you can see through the Myst." He stood up and paced in front of the barrier between them.

"Micksie moved in with me. We are happy, Amalie. Ethyn needed a mother, and, well, she is a good woman. She makes me feel needed and wanted. She smiles when I enter a room and puts down whatever she is working on to give me a hug. Amalie, you were my first love, but I hope you will be happy for me and for us. I won't let Ethyn forget you, I promise. None of us will forget you." He stood there staring at the Myst for a few more moments and then walked away.

Amalie sat there for a while longer, crying silently. She cried for the life she was no longer a part of, and her heart ached over the release she felt at John's words. Amalie felt, for the first time in months, that it was okay that she had moved on. John was going to be okay, and Ethyn would be well taken care of. If she could not be there to care for her son, at least John and Micksie were. They would spoil him, and he would never lack for love.

In a couple of months, on Ethyn's birthday, she would come back to this very spot and see her little one. By then, he would be two and maybe not so little. She stood up and headed back home, pondering how quickly this strange place had come to feel like home. She smiled in anticipation of seeing Ethyn soon; she would not feel quite so separated from him if she got to see him on his birthday.

Alena enjoyed having John and his family there with her for the week. She had been impressed with his knowledge of the new animals that they had found on this planet. She had known that the nosorokuh produced heavenly-tasting milk but had not known that they could also be eaten. She also appreciated his advice on how to better construct their grazing areas and kennels for the strange-looking rex.

She watched the interactions between Micksie and John and knew that they were already forming a happy family. For all that John was upset at the loss of Amalie, his childhood friend, and first love, she saw that he was more relaxed around Micksie. The two worked well together. It made her smile to see Micksie doting on John. She had often thought that Amalie ignored him too much and that he deserved someone who actually saw him.

Alena was sad when they left and worried that John would continue his search for Amalie. She hoped that he would let Amalie go but knew that was not going to happen anytime soon. Maybe she had given him what he needed to move on, at least, even if he never fully got over her. As she was watching the couple and little Ethyn leave, she felt Luke's hands on her shoulders.

She leaned into him and appreciated his companionship. They had been together about a year now but had not yet moved in with one another. Her place was too small, and he shared a house with several other single men. She hoped that it would not take much longer to get the first floor finished and roofed so that Luke and herself could finally be together every night.

"You have received bad news?" He asked as he walked with her back to the little chapel.

"Yes and no." Was her reply. She laughed at the look of consternation on Luke's face. She knew he hated her mixed answers.

"Sorry. Yes, the news was bad in that my friend Amalie has gone missing. She was taken into the Myst. It was not unexpected news, though. I have always known that she would disappear into the Myst; I just wasn't sure when."

"I am sorry for the loss of your friend. I did not know her, but I feel I have always known her from your stories. So why was the news not bad?" He asked.

Alena opened the door to the chapel and invited Luke in. The two sat in one of the pews that took up the main room.

"Her disappearance is the countdown to our freedom from fear. She is the one who sets the chain of events in motion that leads to an era of peace and prosperity for our people. Though it saddens me that I will lose my friend, it is what must occur for the good of our people."

"You will lose her, but you have not yet?" He looked confused at her answer once again.

"She will return, and it is in her return that the peace we want begins, and her hell starts. It is in her descent into her own private hell that I will lose her." She sat in silence next to the man she loved and respected. She could not have accomplished all she had so far without his strength and his love.

YEAR 4

"Tam," Amalie laughed as she ran away from his reach. The pair headed out of the house and into the small grove that they considered their own private paradise. It was covered in hanging vines, which made it into a secluded little room. The plants grew so thick that noises were blunted and hard to make out.

He caught up with her and pulled her down into the sweet-scented grass. Brushing the hair out of her eyes, he leaned down and kissed her.

"You are happy today." He said.

"How can I not be? I am with you." She replied with laughter and love in her voice.

"You are not always happy, though." Tam pulled her on top of him and held her closely.

"At times, I miss my son. I would be completely happy if he were here with me. But since he can't be, I will have to be content to wait and see him only on his birthday each year." Amalie whispered, knowing that he did not like to hear of her life before him. As she suspected he would, she could feel his body tense, and she sighed.

"Tam, I love you, and I am here with you. I made that choice a few months ago. I cannot see anything changing my mind about the way I feel for you. I belong here with you, and if, at times, I miss the outside world, that is okay. I am not going to leave you for anything or anyone out there." She kissed him passionately.

The two made love well into the night and only came up for air when they heard Tayin walk by. They knew that he needed something as he was making a lot of noise and giving them plenty of time to redress. He stopped just outside of the little grove, and while Amalie waited for him to say something, Tam sighed and kissed her as he stood up.

"I need to go. Tayin and I have been summoned by the Elders." He lifted the vines and exited their paradise.

Amalie started to ask how he knew as no words had been spoken, but then she stopped herself. She had been here a bit over nine months now and knew that they did not need to use their voice to speak to one another. She was still getting used to this. It was frustrating, as most of the time, this was the way they communicated with each other, and she often felt left out. She laid back down and decided not to let it bother her. Tam would tell her what he was needed for when he came back. She smiled to herself. Until then, she would take a nap, as she did not get much sleep during the night.

"You spend too much time with her," Tayin said in greeting.

"So what? I enjoy her company." Tam replied as he walked along the path that would lead them back home.

"Do you know what they want?' Tam asked after a few minutes of silence.

Tayin opened the green door that would take them to Zeljani. He allowed Tam to enter first as he was the eldest and leader of Kofira. He thought it odd that the humans had renamed their continents, but he guessed it made sense. They needed to call the land masses something, and not knowing the Alluran names made up their own. Kofira was called Kahlali by the Yidderians, and Zeljani was Lijiang. He stopped his random thoughts and answered his twin.

"No, but we will soon find out." He stepped through the door and appeared next to Tam on Zeljani, half the world away from where they had just been. The two walked down the hall and were met by Raighn, who had arrived just before them. The three nodded their heads in a quick hello and entered the meeting room, where Kest and Adym waited for them at the table. The group of men stood behind their chairs until the Elders arrived and were seated before taking their own seats.

Elder Elcrys, the oldest living SeiOrhii, started the meeting. "I have all called you here so that you might hear the disturbing news that Elder Brecher has received from Y'ddra." She then turned her attention to Brecher.

Brecher was the only Alluran who was not telepathic. He had been injured in the war with the Kahru, and though he had survived the injury, he had become mind blind. Brecher could no longer hear the thoughts of other Allurans. It was a lonely existence for one among a telepathic race, but he was compensated by the fact that he was also the only one who could hear and talk to Y'ddra directly.

He cleared his throat and then began speaking. "As you all know, the woman, the humans call the Prophetess, had a vision soon after arriving on this planet that said that they would have peace from the evil that inhabited Yiddera. She also stated that she was unsure when, but she knew that the evil would be locked away."

He gazed at the young men before him and then continued. "Y'ddra has told me that this prophecy will come true soon, but not to worry, as a Yidderian with blue hair will come along in time and set us free." He ran his hand through his shocking electric blue hair and looked once again at the group before him and then at the other Elders. "I do not know what any of this means. I can only assume that we are the evil that the Prophetess talks about, as Y'ddra told me that we would be set free. But how we can be locked away or what that even means, I cannot say."

Kest spoke up. "The gates cannot be locked by someone who is not Alluran. Y'ddra created the gates and their key to keep us safe from enemies, not to keep us locked away. There is no way that this prophecy of hers can come true."

"But it can and will if Elder Brecher understood Y'ddra correctly, which I am sure he did." Adym looked around the room, "What I do not understand is how the gates become unlocked. How is it possible? Yidderians do not have blue hair?"

Raighn answered Adym with sarcasm. "I thought you understood how babies were made, cousin. A Yidderian and an

Alluran could potentially create offspring together. We are compatible in many ways."

Brecher paced the length of the table before stopping behind his chair once more and looking straight at Tam.

"Is it possible?"

Tam shrugged his shoulders, "I guess, but I make sure she chews the opfrodij leaves every night. I do not want children. Unlike my brother, I do not care for the little pests."

Tayin nodded his head in acknowledgment of this remark. He wanted lots of kids someday. Tam did not.

"The one destined to let us out, if we are the evil that is spoken of, is not of concern yet. What is of concern is how to make sure that the prophecy does not come true. This particular Yidderian has predicted events that have, in fact, come true and things that are yet unknown. Let us pretend this one might happen. Do any of you have suggestions on what we can do to keep this one from coming to fruition?" Elder Elcrys asked.

No one spoke for several minutes. The faces surrounding the table looked to be in deep contemplation, from the Elders to the leaders of the houses. The only face that looked as if it might have an answer was Tayin, and he looked as if he did not want to voice his thoughts. Elder Saniel stared at Tayin for a few moments before asking him to share his thoughts.

"I hesitate to share as it is most unlikely." Tayin stalled and then looked at his brother, whose eyebrows were starting to raise as he read his twins' idea.

"No, she will not be the one to lock us in. Just because you do not like her, do not assume that she will cause us harm. She has no idea where the key is kept or what it looks like, and I don't plan on telling her. Besides, she loves me and would not do something that would hurt me." Tam replied to Tayin's unspoken words.

Brecher could feel the tension rising between the two brothers and knew that it must soon be dissipated as Tam had quite the temper, and he did not want an argument to occur between the two. He was always amazed at the differences between them. Tayin was the responsible twin but also the one who was quick to laugh. He was easygoing, studious, and cared for the people he took care of with passion. Tam was quick to anger, loved playing around, and did not really like responsibility, but, as the eldest, he did his duty as needed. He left most of it up to his brother, who was very willing to take it on. Tayin should have been born the eldest, but that was not the case.

"Tayin, Tam, settle down. Tam, see that she does not learn of the key's location and make sure that she stays away from it. I agree with you that it is unlikely that she would do us harm; she seems to care for you. The humans are not capable of harming us as far as we can tell, and she has had plenty of chances if she was going to do anything." Brecher pulled out Elder Elcrys's chair and helped her to stand.

"If any of you have any ideas, let us know. Otherwise, you are dismissed." Brecher started to lead the Elders out of the room, leaving the five men still sitting at the table when Raighn spoke up.

"I have a possible idea," Raighn said lazily as he straightened from his slouch.

"Yes." Elder Elcrys said as she sat back down.

"I destroyed most of their technology, but their ship still exists. Maybe there is something on that vessel that can lock the Myst gates that we do not know about. Would it not be wise to make sure that the possibility no longer exists?"

"What do you have in mind." Asked an intrigued Adym.

"You and I can sink it somewhere that it cannot be retrieved. You can move it as close as you can to the water, and then I can break the land underneath it. I will then cause a huge swell to pull it even further out into the ocean. Once there, Kest, you can get the water livyatans to help you pull it into the black crevasse just a few miles off my shores. The Yidderians cannot rescue it from there. They will not have the means to."

"It will be hard to move, but I think I can do it. That is a sound plan, cousin."

"Always the sound of surprise," Raighn said in irritation. Though he was Adym's cousin, the two were not the best of friends. They often butted heads. Raighn liked to go with the flow, and Adym was just plain uptight in his opinions.

Elder Elcrys stood back up and took Brecher's offered arm. "See to it then, boys. I would like it done as soon as possible, please." With that, she left the young men to talk and plan amongst themselves.

Tayin stood up and followed the Elders toward the door. "I will leave you all to it. I have some thinking of my own to do."

Adym looked at his friend with concern as he heard a touch of melancholy in Tayin's voice, which was not typical of him.

"I am fine, Adym. I will meet up with you later." Tayin smiled and then left the room. He walked down the hall and through the red door that would take him home.

Tayin arrived back home and headed down the path that led toward the Myst gates leading into the Yidderian village. He had always worried about having the girl here, but Tam was not to be deterred. Once he had an idea, he would not let go of it. Amalie was an obsession for his brother and drove all thoughts of responsibility out of his head. She was dangerous.

Tayin had taken on many more of the responsibilities that Tam should be focused on, and usually, this would not bother him, but lately, it was starting to wear. Tam was his twin, his best friend, and now he often felt like a third wheel. He shook his head over his thoughts and the feelings of jealousy that they brought forth. Tayin knew that one day they would find partners and spend more time with them than with each other, but how could his brother's partner be a human female? There was no way that she could bond with Tam. It wasn't possible; her life was too short, and she did not have a compatible heart.

Tayin passed the house that belonged to Amalie's family and turned around to stare at it for a few moments. He saw the man come around the corner and head toward the big greenhouse in the back. Tayin stepped back into the tree line so as not to be seen. He watched as a very young boy came running up behind the man. He was scooped up and thrown into the air, and Tayin heard his high-pitched squeal of delight. He watched the two play for a few minutes before they headed into the building and shut the door behind them.

Tayin smiled to see that the man was a good father. He knew that the child's mother missed him. As much as he disliked Amalie, he would tell her that her son was being well cared for. She deserved this small comfort. Tayin continued walking until he came to the edge of town. He watched the bustle of the small village and was intrigued. The Yidderians were running around laughing and talking about a party that would be held that evening in honor of the holiday. He listened closer and heard that they were discussing what costumes each would be wearing.

He found this peculiar. What holiday were they celebrating, and why did they wear costumes? Tayin decided to go back home and question Amalie about this celebration. He walked the edge of the village until he came back to Amalie's house, where he quietly entered the home and looked around. He came to a bedroom, and not quite entirely under the bed, he saw a small box labeled *Amalie*. Tayin opened it and found it full of drawing supplies, a tiny pale-yellow sweater, and a locket that had a picture of two people in it. The couple looked enough like Amalie that he decided they must be her parents. Without thinking, he grabbed the box and left the house.

Tayin walked into the Myst and searched for Amalie. He found her sitting by the red pool, her feet splashing the water while her mind wandered aimlessly. He sat down next to her and quietly handed her the box he had found. She looked at him in surprise as she opened it. She pulled out the locket, and Tayin saw her eyes glitter with unshed tears as she clasped it around her neck. She then took out the sweater and held it against her.

"Why?" She asked.

"I was in your village and so decided to stop by and look at where you used to live. Not sure why. I guess I was just curious." Tayin moved a little farther away from her as he spoke. He looked at the beauty of the glistening stones shining brightly in the water.

"He is a good father. Your little one is being well taken care of."

Amalie reached out a hand and put it over Tayin's, who instantly moved away once more and out of her reach.

"Thank you, Tayin. This means a lot to me." She gently folded the sweater back up and laid it safely back in the box. "This sweater was made by my mother and worn by me as an infant and then by my son. It makes me feel not so isolated from my past to have these things. Again, thank you." She saw him nod.

"I know that you do not particularly like me, so this gesture of kindness surprises me, though it shouldn't. You are a kind and caring man."

"You are right; I do not, but my dislike is unimportant. I do not think you are good for my brother. Something tells me you are a danger to him, possibly to all of us, yet I am unsure how this can be." He paused as a concerned expression flitted across his face. "If I could avoid his anger, I would let you go back to your family, but he would know that I helped you leave the Myst, and I would hear about it for centuries. You are a minor inconvenience compared to that."

"Glad to hear I am only a minor inconvenience." Tayin could hear the smile in her voice.

The two sat in silence for a while until Tayin asked about the upcoming holiday that was being celebrated in her village.

"Oh, it must be Halloween."

"What is Halloween? He asked.

"It is an old Earth celebration that honors the end of summer and the beginning of harvest and to scare away the demons that come haunting. Halloween, which falls on the second day of the celebration, is one where people wear costumes to ward off the ghosts, goblins, and demons that roam this one night. It is thought that on this night, the veil between their world and ours is thin, and the scary beings can then enter our world and walk amongst us. The costumes are thought to confuse them so that they cannot tell if the person wearing one was a fellow beastie or a tasty snack. At least that is how some people celebrate it."

"Tell me more." Tayin was curious. As a history keeper, he was fascinated with all history, even the history of the Yidderians.

"Well, here on Yiddera, we decided to celebrate it for basically the same reason. On the first day, we have a community picnic to celebrate the end of the summer season. After the cookout, the single women put their names in a box that they decorate so that it can be chosen by one of the single men on the night of the Halloween party. This is a kind of match-making ritual. Last year, a few of the matches actually worked out, while some were quite humorous. It is fun but not serious.

On the second day, we celebrate Halloween and wear costumes to confuse the demons that enter our world from theirs. It is a night in which being scared, at least a little bit, is welcomed.

People come up with scary costumes and decorations for this reason. It is fun.

Midnight is when those who participated in the matchmaking choose their boxes. These couples then do a last dance, and this signals the end of the celebration. The children also celebrate by wearing costumes, but they perform tricks for treats. It can be funny, though some of the things the kids do show talent. It is interesting to see what they come up with." She paused, and a smile graced her pretty face as she thought of last Halloween.

Tayin watched her for a moment and could see why his brother found her fascinating. Her conversation was educated and easy. She was also quite pretty with her soft brown eyes and hair. And her smile made her lips look fuller and pinker. He looked away and asked her about the third day.

"On the third day, we collect our baskets and gather the last of the summer berries and fruits. Families and friends go out together, and the couples from the night before go out alone to see if they are compatible with each other. Then, as the sun sets, we light huge bonfires in honor of the coming winter season." Amalie paused for a few minutes and then continued. "As the years go by, some of the traditions will become more firmly entrenched in time, and others will fade, and different ones will take their place. Here on Yiddera, we need to incorporate customs that fit our lives here and not hang on to the ones we had on Earth. I think Halloween will persist through the centuries, but I am not sure how it will look then, compared to now."

Tayin thought of what she had told him and decided that it sounded like an intriguing party to attend tonight. After all, if the Yidderians liked to be scared on this night, then it sounded to him as if they would welcome him. He could supply the scare for them, and they could provide the fear for him. He stood up and, without a word, left Amalie still splashing her feet in the pool of dreams.

Tayin cobbled together a costume, and then, as the sun began to set, he headed out to join the humans in their celebration. He followed a small group of people heading to the largest building in the village. The sun had set an hour or so prior, which made it easy to follow without being seen. He entered the brightly lit room and found a corner hidden in shadow to watch the Yidderians in their celebrations. A few walked by him, but he could see them shudder in discomfort, so they did not stop to talk. Finally, at midnight, he decided to participate. It was time for him to enjoy the holiday.

Tayin brought them all to a state of semi-sleep in which they could all still participate in the upcoming fun, but he could induce a communal nightmare. He slowly brought forth nightmarish images into the corners and recesses of their mind and watched as they all looked around the room to find the source. He breathed in the fear that permeated the hall. Then, he fully unleashed the istotymir and brought the monsters to the forefront of their thoughts. He grew stronger as they started to scurry around in fear. Tayin noticed that while they were afraid of what was happening, they also got enjoyment out of the situation. Many had a nervous excitement interspersed with their fear, which he found interesting. It did not take away from his pleasure. No, instead, it added an unexpected spice to his feast.

Finding his experiment quite fulfilling, he released them from the nightmares and their waking sleep and listened briefly to the buzz of voices that erupted in question at what had just happened. Tayin left the room and exited the building with new knowledge and understanding of the Yidderians. They enjoyed fear. Not in the way that he did, but still, they did find pleasure and excitement in it, at least to some small degree.

Tayin walked back to the Myst and decided that this holiday was one that he enjoyed, and he hoped that it would stick around for centuries. He would join in the celebrations again. He fell asleep that night thinking of ways to make the Yidderian's Halloween celebration even more thrilling next year.

"What is it with you and Tam?" Adym sat down on one of the many cushions that surrounded the low table in front of the small fountain that sent cooling sprays around the warm courtyard. He helped himself to a glass of wine and some of the fruit that lay before him.

Raighn sat up and pushed the redhead off him, covering both her and the brunette. He couldn't remember their names, but that was not important. Both he and the women had had their fun, and as soon as Adym was gone, he would feed and then send them on their way. He walked over to where Adym sat, pulling a pair of pants on as he went.

"They welcome my attention, so why not have fun with them." He replied lazily, popping a grape into his mouth as he sat on a cushion across from his cousin. "What brings you here this early in the morning?" He filled a glass of the slightly bitter red wine that he liked and took a drink. He then waved over one of the Tarikan and ordered breakfast for both him and Adym.

"We need to get that ship moved. It has been a week since you brought up the idea, and I would like to see it finished. It will put all our minds at ease to not have that eyesore on your shores and wondering if it is the cause of our incarceration." Adym thanked the Tarikan, who brought them their food, and enjoyed a sip of the hot vanilla coffee that Raighn served.

Raighn bit into a buttery roll, swallowed, and then replied to his cousin. "Moving the ship can wait until the sun is more fully up. I did not get much sleep last night."

"I can see that," Adym said sardonically.

"My overly responsible cousin, I will meet you and Kest on the shores of the place the Yidderians have named Anchorage once I have finished eating." He glanced over at the two women starting to wake up and smiled back at Adym. "It may take me another hour or two, but I will be there." He patted the pillows next to him, and the women wrapping blankets around themselves went over to sit by him.

Adym gave Raighn a disgusted look and finished his coffee. "Two hours Raighn. Two hours until I come back and move your new toys to the top of my highest mountain." He stood up and walked out of the courtyard, heading to the yellow door that would take him to Kest.

Raighn scowled at his cousin's retreating back before turning his attention back to his food. He knew that Adym would do as he promised and so set about retrieving the fear he needed from the two women. He entered their minds and found that one of them was afraid of thunder, and the other was afraid of drowning. He held out his hands and walked with them to the beach. Ah, such simple and easy fears to exploit.

Raighn found Adym standing on the bluff that overlooked the giant ship. He saw many humans working on trying to fix the damage that he had caused soon after the Yidderians had arrived. Despite the futility, he was amused at their diligence in trying to fix the unfixable.

"I have been thinking, cousin, that instead of breaking the land, I will try using a windstorm to help you move the ship into the water. I would hate losing any piece of Lioleta that I can possibly save. Kest," Raighn said to the giant rex that came walking up behind him, "We need to get the people out of the ship so that it is lighter in weight."

"Done," Kest said and then ran down the hill, calling other predators to him.

Adym and Raighn watched Kest leading the pack and scattering the Yidderians as they approached. Within a few minutes, the humans were out of the ship that was now being guarded by the animals. Adym placed a hand on Raighn's shoulder, and they appeared instantly at the side of the great vessel.

Raighn waved his hands, and the wind picked up with tornado-like strength. Adym lifted the ship off the ground, and together, the two men pushed it out into the ocean. Once there, Raighn pushed the wind out to sea, and huge waves appeared, causing the giant vessel to go further out into the waters. Its weight caused it to sink with each wave that pushed it. A giant green tentacle latched onto one side of the ship, and then another tentacle and another joined the first and pulled it even further out until it finally disappeared from sight. Adym scrunched up his face in concentration and floated above the ocean, helping the monsters move the ship, as Kest changed from a rex into one of the livyatans and jumped into the water, unfurling his tentacles to help pull the vessel into the trench.

The mission was accomplished, and the humans standing in the tree line and behind their buildings watched in bewilderment as the blue-haired men destroyed their last link to Earth, their last ability to make the things they needed. This planet did not have the resources it needed to duplicate all that they had now lost. They watched as the animal changer turned back into one of the blue-haired men and as one of the others laid a hand on each and then watched as the three beings disappeared from sight.

The couple lay gazing up at the sky, entwined in each other's arms, enjoying the aftermath of their intimacy. Their legs were still in the brightly colored waters of the lake below Rainbow Falls, their heads on the soft grass that surrounded it. The day was peaceful, bright, and unusually warm for this time of year.

Amalie turned over to face her lover and smiled. She marveled at his love for her and hers for him. Their differences should have made them incompatible, but somehow, they made it work. Amalie reached out her hand and ran her fingers through his beautiful blue hair. She smiled again when his eyes of the same shade opened and looked at her.

Tam kissed the tip of Amalie's nose and pulled her under him once more. She stared up at him, excitement building at what was to come, when she saw a shadow cross his face. He became more alert and rolled off her and into a sitting position, watching the trail that opened up to the right of them. Amalie saw a man walk into the opening and stop when he noticed the two of them. She closed her eyes as she felt the energy shift around Tam, and her fears started rising from deep inside her mind. She put her hand out to remind him that she was there, but he looked at her and grinned his wicked grin.

"I am hungry." He stated simply.

Tam released the istotymir, and the level of fear Amalie felt increased tenfold. She was not Alluran, but still, she could feel the man's fear from across the lake. She opened her eyes and saw that shadows without form were making their way over the rocks, from behind the trees, and out of the lake. Amalie had never seen Tam feed on anyone, but she knew that he used his gift of illusion to terrorize those he fed on. She stood up to leave. She did not want to see this part of him. He turned his glowing eyes on her, and she felt frozen in place with her own fears.

"Tam, stop." She asked of him and shuddered when he laughed and entered her mind so that she could experience the feeding with him. He turned back away from her and concentrated his efforts on the man in front of him.

The images started taking shape, and she could see all sorts of weird illusions. The Yidderian was afraid of snakes, and Amalie watched as several serpents slithered over the rocks coming up behind the man. The young man turned to look at the writhing beasts and walked backward up the trail and closer to where she and Tam stood. Amalie realized that Tam was herding the man closer to him and wondered why. He could feed on the man at a distance. Tam did not need him to be close.

The man stumbled over a rock and splashed into the lake, only to find a serpent of considerable size rising out of the waters and hovering over him. Amalie could feel the power and strength that Tam was receiving from the man's fears and the enjoyment of his torture, and she tried to push him from her mind but was unsuccessful.

Tam continued guiding the man toward him. The snakes were everywhere. The man screamed as one made to strike, and he tried desperately to get out of the lake and onto dry land. Amalie knew that had the man reached out, he would have realized the snake was just an illusion and couldn't actually harm him, but his own fear kept him from seeing the haze around the edges of the image.

The man made it out of the water and came face to face with Tam, whom Amalie now understood why he was drawing the man toward him. Tam took on the appearance of the undead and moved closer to the man. While the illusion around Tam was make-believe, he could now touch the man, thus making the twisted fantasy seem very real. His touch made the man's fears peak, and he cried out in horror and fear.

Amalie, through her own fear, whispered, "Please let him live."

Tam ignored her and drew the poisonous serpents ever closer to the man, who was now too weak to stand and was pleading with the monster in front of him to release him from his terrors. Tam leaned over him and gently caressed the man's face with his fingertip. He felt his prey's heart race uncontrollably. He placed a finger on his prey's lips to quiet his cries and licked his own as if getting ready to take a bite of the man. Tam put his face, covered in the mask of the undead and his hair writhing with hissing vipers, closer to his victim and breathed in the essence of fear that the man released at the moment of his death.

Tam dropped his illusions as he savored the sweet morsel of fear that still lingered in the air after his victim's demise. Once he gathered all he could, Tam looked at Amalie, who stood away from him and reigned in the istotymir so that her fear would ease. He looked at her pale skin and frightened eyes and smiled as he walked over to her.

"Come, my love, let us finish what we started before we were so deliciously interrupted." He pulled her close and kissed her with rising passion.

Amalie, still shaking in fear at what she had experienced, was confused at her reactions to this Alluran. She now had a fear of him that she had not had before but also felt her own desire rising for him as he touched her. A thought passed through her mind that maybe he was showing who he truly was to see how she would respond. Tam was still the man she loved, was, in fact, the same person she knew him to be, but now she had seen firsthand his evil and was shocked she could still feel safe in his arms. She wondered if he would grow weary of her someday and feed on her as he did the man who lay dead just a few yards from where they stood.

"No, you will always be safe with me. I will never feed on you." He kissed her again and, taking her hand, led her up to the cave that lay behind the falling water and into the warm red pool of dreams.

The sun rose over the mountains and highlighted the beauty of the forest, the lake, and the building that was slowly showing its magnificence. Alena looked on in pride as the villagers started arriving to begin the day's work. The building's basement had been constructed, and the ceiling had been placed. The first floor was built, the structure for each of the different rooms had been established, and the supporting walls were completed. Today, they would begin on the ceiling, and once it was built, they would then be able to start using it safely. It was to be four stories above the basement with ample open space under the roof for storage and extra rooms as needed. At each corner, Alena intended to put four apartments that could house the mysterious blue girls that she saw in her visions.

Alena wrapped a blanket around her shoulders and walked around the structure. It was going to be beautiful once completed, and she couldn't wait. The final destruction of the ship had slowed the progress more than she had hoped it would, but without the fabricators, her workers had to make most of the parts by hand. This would not be that much of a bother, but they also had to make new tools and supplies from the resources found on this planet, and as the planet survey had found, there were not many resources similar to those that they were used to on Earth.

She was deep in thought about how they would finish the lighting and the plumbing when she felt Luke's arms slide around her waist. She smiled and leaned against him, enjoying this quiet moment together. Alena felt him rest his chin on her head.

"It is coming along well, I think." He said.

She nodded her head in the affirmative and asked him what he thought they could use for plumbing and electricity.

"We have many of the necessary things to finish the plumbing already, and with the many hot springs in the area, water could be used to help heat the building. As for the electricity, we will have to use candles until we can find a way to store the solar energy that we plan to use." Luke took her hand and led her to the edge of the cliff to show the work on the path she had requested was finally finished.

"We will have to start on a fence to keep people from falling off this ledge and to protect those using the newly widened path," Alena remarked. "I will add that to the growing list of tasks."

The pair meandered the paths that had been laid out and pointed out things that were finished or were being started. This massive undertaking was coming along quite nicely. They made their way into the village, sat at the tea shop, and had orange scones with orange and clove tea to break their fast. Once done, Alena asked Luke if he would postpone his work for the morning and walk with her to the nearby lake.

"The falls are quite spectacular in coloring, and I heard that several different edible plants were found surrounding the waters. I would like to pick some so that I can plant them in my garden. I would also like to finally look at the colored pools in person. I am tired of hearing about their beauty secondhand."

Luke agreed to act as her escort, and the two requested a lunch made and found a shop that sold baskets. Gathering these items, they began the trek up the mountain that led to the path that would take them down to the springs.

Alena gasped in awe at the beauty of the falls. The colors sparkled brightly in the early morning sun. The lake below the falls was filled with every color of the rainbow, and the five waterfalls fell in grand cascades down into the beautiful lake. She held tightly to Luke's hand as she climbed down the rocks that led to the cave of hot springs. Upon entering, she was surprised at how warm it was within the cave.

The vast cavern held four hot springs, each of a different color. The first she came to was brilliantly colored reds and pinks. Alena dipped her hand in the water and felt that it was warm, like bath water. She found that the water itself was not colored; it was the crystals inside that gave the pool its brilliance. Alena walked with Luke to the next one; bright oranges and yellows shone like the sun. Luke smiled when they came to this one. It reminded him of both a sunset and a sunrise.

Down the sloping path and in the middle of the cave was the largest of the pools. It held every green color imaginable. They both reached a hand in and found the water a bit warmer than the pink pool was. They continued down to the next hot spring. It had a stone bridge across it, and the falling water fell violently on the half of the pool that overlooked the lake below. The part of the pool that was in the cave was peaceful. The colors started out as pale lavender and turned to purple, so dark that it was almost black on the waterfall side. Alena and Luke looked at each other in wonder as lightning seemed to flash in it periodically. They walked over to the water that ran down the back of the cave.

This water fell over crystals of blue, the blue of the Alluran moon. It disappeared into the floor of the cave. Alena tried to walk closer but was lightly repelled away from it. She was surprised and tried once again. And, once again, she was pushed aside.

"How do you think the water is going through the rock floor?" She asked Luke.

"I don't know, but this whole place sort of creeps me out. Look." He pointed at each of the pools, and above them flashed images somewhat like the lightning seen in the waterfall above the purple pool. The red basin held images of dreams and nightmares. The forms drew you to them with feelings of joy and love and yet also made Alena and Luke back away in fear.

The yellow/orange pool had animals playfully jumping around and chasing one another, while the green pool showed images of the cycle of life, from a seed of a tree sprouting to the tree withering away. It was magical.

"Alena, let's go. I do not feel comfortable here." Luke tugged on her hand and tried to lead her out of the cavern.

"No, I don't want to go just yet. I need to be here." She said, pulling him to the green pool once more. "Join me in the waters?"

Reluctantly, he agreed, and the two undressed and entered the temperate pool. They splashed around and played until Luke began to feel comfortable. Alena turned their innocent play into a more intimate experience. The two made love in the healing waters.

Alena lay her head back against the edge of the pool, her body still wrapped around Luke's, when a vision took her by surprise. She shook, and her body became submerged in the waters, and she could not catch her breath as the vision raged in her mind. She felt Luke's strong arms lift her out of the water and onto the rock floor of the cave. Her mind was still lost in the future. She could not quite make out what the vision was trying to tell her, and she struggled to understand.

"Help me." She unknowingly cried aloud and then felt Luke pick her up and take her out of the darkness. Once the sun hit her face and she was away from the cave, her mind cleared, and she saw the vision clearly, but she still did not understand the words that were repeated over and over again in her mind by the Goddess.

Nature will rise and become our salvation from Nightmare.

Nightmare will become Dream.

And only Dream can save us from Nature's wrath

and keep her from destroying the world.

The words flooded her mind, and she found herself unconsciously repeating them as she heard them. Her mind saw the world turn green and grow darker and darker before becoming light once again.

Finally, the vision stopped. It felt as if it had been waiting for her to have the words and image burned into her mind before it stopped. Alena sat up and rested her head against Luke's shoulder. She took several deep breaths and could feel her head clearing.

"Are you all right? I have never seen a vision hit you that hard." Luke held her against him and caressed her hair.

"I am good. I do not understand what I have seen, but eventually, I will." She raised her head and looked around for her clothes. When she didn't see them, Alena asked Luke to please get them for her as she knew she was not meant to enter the cave again. She watched as he left and wrapped her arms around her knees to ward off the chill of the air around her.

She heard a noise coming from up the path and saw a tall, handsome man coming toward her. He had shoulder-length dark blue hair, and spots of the same color crossed his shoulders and marked his collar bones. He scowled at her and came to a stop in front of her.

Both of them looked at the mouth of the cave when they heard Luke hurrying toward her with her dress and the blanket she had used for warmth.

"Do not hurt him, please." She said, at the same time, the strange man waved his hand toward Luke. She watched as Luke was pushed back into the cave and held there with an invisible hand.

"Why do you come here?" The honeyed voice asked her.

"I wanted to see the Rainbow Falls that so many have told me of, but I have never had time to see," Alena replied.

"Do not come again. These waters do not belong to you or your kind." He held his hand out to her, and Alena, though uncomfortable in her nakedness around this man, took his hand and allowed him to help her stand. She felt waves of fear rush through her at his touch and quickly withdrew her hand from his.

"I will make these waters forbidden to all." She told him.

"You must be the one they call the Prophetess." He stated.

"I am."

"Let it be known that any who come to our sacred falls will be killed. It will not be a comfortable death that they experience, so it would be wise to make your people understand the seriousness of my words."

Alena looked at his eyes and saw that the irises were oval in shape and were the same blue as his hair. She saw his sincerity in them and nodded her head in understanding.

"I will make sure they heed both your words and mine." She stared at him and took a deep breath to help ward off the fear she felt of this man.

"May I ask a question before I leave?"

The strange man looked down at the small woman and, in her mind, answered her unspoken question.

"I do not know the meaning of what you just saw."

"Thank you for your answer. I will figure it out, but I was hoping you might have insight." She stepped back and again was surprised at the answer to the unspoken question in her head.

"He is fine. I will let him go in a few minutes, and you can get dressed." The blue-haired man walked back up the path and stood there watching as the two hurriedly dressed and raced up the trail and back home.

Once back at the little chapel, Luke sat on the bed they shared and waited for Alena to sit next to him.

"Who or what was that?" He asked.

"That was one of the original inhabitants of this planet. He," She paused to find the right words, "He is dangerous. He let me go because of who I am, but no one must ever visit Rainbow Falls again. It would mean death to any who do." She stood up and went to the chest of drawers, took out a dry dress, and changed into it.

"They are telepathic. This is how they find out our deepest fears. Many times, I have wondered if it was our own fears causing those who encounter these beings to go crazy. The ramblings of the few that have been returned to us often speak of terrors." She shook her head. "I need to meditate on what I saw in my vision and on this encounter. Do you mind if I take a few hours of time to myself?"

Luke put his hand on her shoulders and kissed the top of her head. "Take all the time you need. I will be down at the construction site if you need me." He kissed her once more and left her alone.

Alena pulled out her paints and painted the sky as she saw it in her vision. Then, she overlayed it with the words that were still repeated in her head. She needed to figure out how to impress upon the people the importance of staying away from the beautiful waters. The slightly eerie feeling that she and Luke got from the cave itself would help, as she was sure that if they felt it, others had as well.

That evening, she had a meeting with the elected community leaders at the local tea shop. Once they had all arrived and settled themselves, she began. Alena stood up and walked around the table until she came back to her original spot.

"I have met one of those that live in the Myst." She raised her hand to silence those around her as they all began talking at once.

"I was at the place we call Rainbow Falls, and one of them came to me to warn me away from them. It seems that the falls are a sacred spot for these beings, and it would be in our best interest to respect their wishes and leave that place alone."

"Why should we give in to them?" The hotel owner asked.

"We all have seen the results of an encounter with one of the mysterious beings. This particular man warned that if any of us entered the lake or the cave around the falls, they would kill us." Alena looked at each and every face seated at the tables around her. "This man was very serious. He let me go so that I could warn you all of the consequences of disobeying his command." She put her hand on Luke's shoulder and continued with her speech.

"We have felt the fear that the waters hold, and we have seen what the being could do. He held Luke inside the cave by some invisible means that I could not begin to figure out. He answered my questions without me asking them verbally. He talked to me within my mind.

Friends, there is no reason to risk our lives or those of our loved ones by going there. Help me keep people away from the sacred waters of the Allurans." She paused and wondered at the word. She could hear the man's voice inside her head telling her that this was what their race was called. She silently and politely asked him to leave her mind and not enter it again. She felt his hesitation and then his acquiescence as he left her. She felt her face whiten at the encounter, so she closed her eyes and took several deep breaths before she continued.

"I forbid any entry into the falls, the lake, or the cave. It is off limits, and if anyone disobeys and somehow survives the

Allurans wrath, I will see to it that they are severely punished for their disobedience." She took her hand off Luke's shoulder and sat in the chair next to him.

"Prophetess, you have never made a law without consulting the other leaders of the world and us. Why now?"

"It is within my rights to make laws without consulting anyone. I have always felt it best to collaborate with you all, but in this, there will be no discussion. My order will be obeyed. She stood up once again and, nodding to the people sitting with looks of shock on their faces, she left the tea shop.

The next day, she set several older children to deliver her written order to all the shops and homes within the village. She then sent several copies with a few volunteers to take the order to all the towns around the world. She wanted no one to mistake her authority on this. She set guards to watch the three paths that led to the falls so that if someone did try to disobey the new law, they would be caught and brought to her.

Raighn snuck up behind his sister, who was peering out at the budding human village, watching the people laugh and joke with one another as they worked on building yet another house. He grabbed her waist and laughed aloud at her squeal of fright.

"Raighn, you scared me," Nicollete said as she readjusted her hat back into place.

Raighn placed an arm around her waist and watched the villagers with her. "You are too easy to startle, my sweet. What are you doing out here alone and without permission again?"

"I find these creatures fascinating. They are not the usual type that Y'ddra brings for you to feed on. These beings look so similar to us. The talk is in a weird language, but it is somewhat like our own. And like us, they build, and create, and."

"And they will kill you if they find you out here alone." Raighn interrupted.

"I look like them way more than you do, dear brother. I bet I could walk among them, and they would not notice my differences." Nicollete started to walk around the tree she was hiding behind when she felt Raighn pull her back.

"No. That is not a risk I want you to take. What would I do without you if you lost your bet?" Raighn put his hands on her shoulders and turned him to face her. "Promise me you will not come out here alone again."

"I will promise if you promise to walk me into the village tomorrow so that I might see what these people are like up close." She put her chin up in the air like she often did when she was trying to be demanding.

Raighn knew that she would come out alone again if he did not take her, so he made her the promise. He kissed her forehead and turned her back toward the Myst gates.

"Brother, we will be recognized as two of the "evil creatures" if you do not start wearing a shirt when you are amongst them. I will have one made for you."

"I will wear it for you but only while in the village. Nicollete, please be careful. You are not SeiOrhii, as much as I wish you were, and so, therefore, can be hurt by these people."

"Did you know that they are now calling themselves Yidderians? It is funny, isn't it? But then they also think of Y'ddra as a being to be worshiped." She skipped ahead of Raighn, picked a light pink flower, and then brought it back to him.

She placed it in his long midnight blue hair and kissed his cheek. "I will be careful, brother."

Raighn found Nicollete waiting for him the next day by the same tree. She handed him a beautiful lavender silk shirt, which he quickly put on with a grimace. The thing clung to his ridges, and he shrugged and wiggled until the tunic was in a somewhat comfortable placement.

"Why must I wear this thing?" He grumbled.

"I told you yesterday that you would look more like a Yidderian in it and, therefore, will draw less attention than you would otherwise." Nicollete scrunched up her eyes and looked up at Raighn. "Well, not much less. The girls are going to look twice as usual."

Raighn laughed at her and, taking her hand, walked out of the tree line with her and into the growing village. They walked along the road and into the village square. They sat at a table, and Nicollete, who had a better grasp of the Yidderian language, ordered a drink called cider and something called "cheese fries."

The two loved the tart apple and strawberry-flavored drink but found the "cheese fries" odd. They did not eat much of what they were given, which was for the best as they began to get strange looks. The two siblings stood up and continued walking down the village road, trying their best to blend in.

A small group of young women came up and started flirting with Raighn and giving Nicollete jealous looks. She laughed at them and told them not to worry as Raighn was her friend and nothing more. The women relaxed and started talking to them. Raighn was used to women fawning over him and welcomed their advances. He thought of which one he might enjoy later that night and then thought that maybe he would enjoy two of them. Without realizing it, he started to release the istotymir, and the women became nervous.

"Raighn, you are scaring them," Nicollete said silently and then excused them from the group.

"If you are going to walk amongst the people, you must learn not to scare them." She looked at him sideways. "As one of the Yidderian sayings goes, 'You will catch more bees with honey, so be honey and not something they fear.'"

Raighn acknowledged her wisdom and concentrated on not scaring the locals. This worked until a man came up and noticed that his hair was blue in the sunlight. He swung the hammer he was carrying at Raighn and barely missed. The man then grabbed Nicollete and told her to get behind him, and he would protect her from the "evil" being trying to take her. She played along and cowered behind the man, silently laughing at the situation.

"This is not funny, little sister," Raighn spoke to her quietly as he again sidestepped the man who was trying to protect his sister from him. After a while, he got irritated by the man and brought lightning down next to him. The man backed away in fear and tripped over Nicollete's skirt. Raighn stood above him and enhanced the man's fright before flashing another bolt of lightning above him. He breathed in the man's fear and felt his eyes glow brighter as the man cowered before him.

"Grab me, and let's get out of here." He heard Nicollete say in his mind. He thought it a strange request but did as she asked. He ran with her back into the trees and then into the Myst.

"Why did you want me to grab you? You can run perfectly well on your own." He said as he sat her down on her own two feet.

Laughing, Nicollete adjusted her skirt and her hat before answering. "Cause now they think that you kidnapped one of their own, making me seem like one of them and not an Alluran. If I am seen again, I can tell them that you fed on me and then let me go. As long as I keep my hair covered by my hat, they will not see me as an Alluran but as a Yidderian. I will be safe among them."

"You are a brat. You planned for this to happen, didn't you? You used me to prove that you would be safe amongst them." He pulled her hair and then messed up the hatstrings that she was so particular about keeping neat.

"I did; I admit it. I set out to prove that I would not be recognized as different, and I was right." She took off the tussled hat and carried it in her hands. "So, which one of the pretty girls are you going back for?"

Raighn opened the door of his house and gestured for her to enter ahead of him. "I think I will have both the brunette and the redhead. They looked delicious."

Nicollete nodded her head and told him to be careful when entering the village tonight, then kissed his cheek and headed to her living quarters within the citadel. She thought that maybe she would reintroduce herself to her would-be protector. He looked like he might be fun for an evening or two.

YEAR 5

Alena smiled at the crowd surrounding her. This was a moment of great accomplishment. Tonight, they were all standing in the ballroom and celebrating their first Ontscheppen in the monastery. This holiday was a combination of celebrating their landing on Yiddera and the Earth holiday Christmas.

It was bitterly cold outside, and while in the past they had celebrated it around huge bonfires, it was nice to be warm and cozy in the spacious room. Tonight, they would partake in a feast and dancing, and some of those who practiced the various performing arts would be providing the entertainment.

She was sitting at one of the tables that had been set up and was sipping on the sweet snowfruit juice she loved and eating a warm, savory pastry filled with meat and a variety of vegetables. She was happy. Alena felt the kick of her active child and smiled in wonder that soon she and Luke would be parents. She had workers diligently finishing her quarters within the great monastery so that she could have her child born in this magnificent place. But tonight, no one was working. It was a celebration.

The celebration was joyful, and the people who had been working so hard over the past year felt pride in the accomplishment that allowed them to be indoors for the holiday gathering. Alena watched her followers laughing, eating, and, for the first time in months, forgetting their fears.

Amalie sat on a cushion around the beautiful fountain that graced this particular courtyard in Raighn's estate. His house was decorated in blues, greys, and purples and was both voluptuous and comfortable. It was a place that invited you to sit and stay awhile. She was sitting next to Tam, who was absently running his hands through her hair and listening to the four attractive men that they visited with.

The talk was of the mundane. Raighn had just let Adym know that a vast blizzard would be hitting the mountain range that Adym called home and would bury them in several feet of snow. Adym had asked that Raighn move the storm toward the west canyon, and Raighn had replied that he would be out at the beginning of the blizzard to push it in the direction Adym had requested.

Amalie still found awe in these men's abilities. Raighn, without much thought, could change the weather's direction. He could even stop the storm completely if he was so inclined. She listened to them for a while longer before shifting her position so that her head was in Tam's lap and soon drifted off to sleep.

"The children will be learning about the war of the Kahru tomorrow in school. Tam, will you be there to show them what they look like? I do not want to scare them with nightmares." Tayin asked his brother.

"I will help you teach them if I must, but you will need to soften their dreams tomorrow evening," Tam replied.

"Why do we need to show them what they look like? Isn't an explanation of them enough?" Questioned Kest.

"I want them to see what the Kahru are like so that if they ever come back to Yiddera, the children are prepared. I do not want us taken by surprise by the beasts ever again." Tayin said quietly.

"Tam, if you would rather not help Tayin in the lesson, I would be glad to help. That is one of the creatures that I can take the shape of." Kest offered.

"Thank you, Kest, but I would rather an illusion be cast than an actual Kahru to appear. I would not want you to take on the beast's qualities and accidentally attack anyone." Tayin said seriously.

"Unlike the actual Kahru, I do not have poisoned claws. I can take on their shape, but I cannot fully become one." Kest responded to Tayin.

"Let Kest go with you. I never like teaching the brats."

The rumble of Tam's voice brought Amalie out of her light slumber. She had heard the conversation of the Kahru but, not knowing what they were, had not paid much attention. She stayed lying in his lap and enjoyed the way he still absently played with her hair. Amalie smiled inwardly at Tam's reluctance to help Tayin with the children. He did not like kids and did what he could to avoid them. Tayin, on the other hand, did what he could to teach them. Tayin was the kindest person she had ever met, human or Alluran; Tam was probably the most selfish. Both men were fiercely loyal to their friends and loved ones, but they butted heads often on several issues.

Amalie still did not understand why the Allurans thought Tayin was the more dangerous of the two, more dangerous than any of the other SeiOrhii. Yes, he had the gift of dreams and nightmares and could give them to several people at once, but Tayin was a gentle soul and would never abuse this ability. He used it to feed on humans, but even then, he never used it against their children and often gave those whom he fed upon good dreams to ease their fears once he was done with them. Of all the SeiOrhii, Tayin was the one who gave her hope that someday, the humans and the Allurans could live together in some semblance of harmony.

The talk turned to the weather once again. There was flooding on the plains of Geltahn, and Kest was asking Raighn if he could dry the waters out so that the planting season could commence. Amalie drifted back to sleep, lulled by the deep tones of their voices.

"What do you think of Luka?" Alena looked up at the man sitting next to her.

Luke reached over and gently touched the soft, downy, reddish-blond hair of his newborn daughter.

"Isn't that a boy's name?" He asked, taking the little one from Alena and kissing the tiny face. He held her in his arms, rocking her softly so that she would not wake up.

"So what? I like it, and it has a strength to it while still sounding a bit feminine." Alena laid down on her pillow and waited for his answer.

"Welcome to the world, little Luka," Luke said and watched as his daughter opened her eyes and scrunched up her face. She let out a howl, and Luke laughed, handing her to Alena. "Either she doesn't like that name, or she is hungry."

Alena took Luka and fed her. "I think the name is lovely, and if you are okay with it, I would like that to be her name."

"It is a fine name." He adjusted his position so that he was lying on his side next to Alena, their baby feeding in between them. "She is beautiful, just like her momma."

"Did you notice her birthmark?" Alena whispered.

"I did." He answered in a serious tone. "What do you think it means?"

"Probably nothing, but as she was conceived that day at Rainbow Falls and the mark on the base of her neck is blue, I do wonder. Maybe she is the first of the many children who will be born with markings native to this planet." She wiped the bow-shaped mouth of her daughter and tucked the swaddling more firmly around her.

Alena looked out the window and gave a small jump, which woke Luka, who once again started crying. Alena adjusted her nightgown and picked up the child, holding her close and trying to quiet her down.

"Luke, we have visitors." She said quietly as the two men at her window disappeared and then instantly reappeared inside their room.

Luke put a protective arm around Alena, "What do you want?" He asked of the man they had seen once before.

The one they had not yet met answered. "Our Elders were told by Y'ddra that you had given birth to a daughter and that as we will be sharing our world with you, we should welcome her." He walked towards them and placed a hand on Luka's head. "She has the feel of one who has bathed in the springs but is not SeiOrhii."

Alena and Luke felt him enter their minds and leave almost as quickly as he had entered.

"Ah, that makes sense." The man turned to the other one. "Did you know that she was conceived in the green waters?"

"No." was the one-word reply.

"We have a gift." Alena was handed an intricately carved box that glowed with a soft pink light from inside of it.

"What is it?" She asked, handing the box to Luke.

"It is a dream box. I have infused it with crystals from the pool of dreams. Place it by little Luka's bed at night, and she will always have good dreams. Consider this a gift from Y'ddra."

He stepped away from them and, turning his back to them, stared out the window. The man they had previously met turned away and placed a hand on the other. Then, he stopped and turned his head back to them. "Y'ddra is the one that has asked us to present you with this gift, and we will honor her in this, but many of us do not care for peaceful relations with you. Do not consider this gift as an invitation to return to the falls. It is not. I still stand by what I said before. We will kill anyone who goes there. I do not agree with this offering of gifts to those we feed on, but I do as the Elders and Y'ddra require me to." He turned back to his partner, and then, in a blink of an eye, the two disappeared.

Alena and Luke stared at the window wide-eyed and concerned for their safety. If these men could appear and reappear at will, nothing could protect them. The high walls they were building and the security doors at the front of the monastery were all for nothing. They could literally go anywhere they wanted, and nothing the Yidderians did could stop them.

"What do we do?" She asked Luke.

"We do what we have always done. There is nothing else we can do, but I am not sure that we should put this box near Luka at night. We do not know what consequences it will have if we do."

"I would like to keep it in here with us for a while to see what it does if you do not mind, my love." Alena requested.

"For now, I will place it in the hidden room, but when you are back on your feet, we can bring it out for you to experiment with."

Luke straightened up and got out of the bed. He gathered the box and, going over to the hidden door by the window, he went down the stairs and placed the box high up on one of the shelves. He watched the box become brighter, and then the pink light faded back into a dull glow.

Amalie sat on a blanket, sketchbook in hand, studiously drawing the scene in front of her. She worked on the picture of the five men standing a bit off in the distance yet still in front of her. Their laughter brought a smile to her face. She had already drawn two of the five. The first was Adym, tall, dark-haired, and standing with pride and with a bit of responsibility. Even when he was supposed to be having fun, he looked a bit serious. This was quite in contrast with the man standing next to him.

Kest never stood still. It had taken Amalie some effort to portray his picture as full of life as he was. He smiled, laughed, and bounced with every breath he took. He was the shortest of the five men, but only when he was in his Alluran form. He could transform into one of the beasts called the Giant Rex. They stood well over twelve feet tall when on their hind legs.

Amalie put the finishing touches on his spiky electric blue hair and moved on to draw the third man. Raighn looked similar to his cousin Adym with the same midnight blue hair and piercing eyes, except Raighn's were the aquamarine color of the water. But something about Raighn was sexy and drew the eye.

Not that a woman would ignore Adym or any of the five men, but Raighn drew a second and third glance. He moved with sensuality. His voice was felt, not heard; his light-colored eyes looked at a woman as if he knew exactly what she wanted and was willing to give it to her. She let her mind wander as she drew him. Unlike Tam and Tayin, who were solid muscle, Raighn was more elegantly built.

Like all the men gathered in the small circle, he was bare-chested and bare-footed. She was not sure what their aversion to shirts and shoes was, but they rarely wore them. Raighn's chest was turned slightly toward her, and she drew the gleaming symbol he wore on his chest. As she drew it, she began to wonder what he would be like in bed. Amalie knew many of the Alluran women gossiped about him, and though some speculated as she did, many had first-hand knowledge.

She wondered if he was like Tam. Gentle when needed but more often rough. She smiled at the thought and remembered last night with Tam. She still had the marks from their play. As she continued thinking, she heard a faint 'enough' in her head and looked up to see Tam with a scowl on his face. She realized she had been thinking loudly. Embarrassed, she put her head back down and continued her sketch. But before long, she was once again back to thinking about what the difference between Tam and Raighn would be in bed. She bet Raighn was leisurely and took his time, or maybe not. She looked up again as Tam reprimanded her once more.

Raighn winked at Amalie before saying, "Anytime you want firsthand knowledge, just let me know. I will be happy to educate you on our differences."

Amalie blushed and then laughed as Tam hit Raighn, causing him to fall back.

"Sorry, Tam, but if she wants to know, I am willing." He laughed at his friend as he backed away from another punch.

Amalie finished drawing Raighn as well as Tam and Tayin. She added some quick sketches of the background and then put away her drawing. She would add more detail and color later. The men still laughed and joked with each other, but as she was not telepathic, she could not hear them unless they spoke directly to her. Amalie lay back on the blanket and fell asleep in the quiet of the garden.

She woke when Tam picked her up and carried her back to the house. The evening was cool, and the first moon was making an appearance in the early evening sky. The second moon would make an appearance in about an hour or so. She snuggled up against Tam's chest, resting her head on his shoulder and enjoying the feel of his warm skin on her cheek.

"Do not think that I will share you." She heard his voice rumble deep in his chest and knew he spoke aloud for her sake.

"I would never ask you to. My thoughts were random and just thoughts. I have no interest in any of your friends or any other man for that matter. You are the only man I want or need." She put her arms around him and kissed his neck.

"See that it stays that way." He kissed the top of her head and continued into the house and into their room. He placed her on their bed and sat next to her. "Join me in the shower?"

"Gladly." She quickly disrobed and followed him into the shower.

"Shirts are uncomfortable on our spine," Tam said. It took Amalie a few minutes to figure out what he was talking about before she realized he was answering one of the questions she had mused about earlier.

"Oh. Why?"

"The fabric rubs on the ridges, and as you know, they are very sensitive to touch." He sucked in his breath as Amalie ran a hand along the spine of one of the ridges knowing that this excited him.

"Hmm, maybe I do not want you to go about with your back bare. I wouldn't want anyone else to touch you in a place that excites you." She purred and ran her hand down his back again. Tam picked her up, sat her down on his erection, and pushed her against the shower wall. Their lovemaking was quick and rough, just the way they both liked it. She bit his shoulder when she came and then rested her head against his. He held her until she quit shaking before soaping her body once more. While rinsing the suds off, she asked him about the bare feet.

"We like the feel of the ground on our feet. It connects us to Y'ddra." He turned off the water and started towel-drying Amalie.

"You are happy here with me?" He questioned.

"Very." She took the towel from him, dried him off, and then guided him back into the bedroom. "I do not want to be anywhere else." She pulled on a shirt that was way too big for her and rolled up the sleeves. "Come, let's get something to eat and then take another shower."

Tam laughed and let Amalie take him by the hand and into the kitchen.

Tam and Tayin meandered the fragrant garden that surrounded the kitchens of their home. The bold colors of the vegetable plants mixed pleasantly with the more muted colors of the herbs. The smells were a variety of sweet and spicy and mingled in a way that brought a smile to Tayin. In the distance, they could make out the group of Tarikan that were separating the herbs into different baskets so that they could make teas and spice blends after the herbs were sufficiently dried, and across from them worked another group preparing vegetables to be pickled and stored for the coming winter months.

The two brothers continued their leisurely walk and found themselves leaving the gardens and walking down to the river that eventually led to the farthest edge of the Myst. The river was miles long and would take them past the LuZivot village if they walked far enough. Today, they had no destination in mind; they just walked together for enjoyment. They came to a bend in the river and sat on a bench that Tayin had placed there. The tall weeping trees swayed gracefully in the wind and hid the pair from the sight of anyone who might pass by while still affording them a view of the water.

"You have something on your mind. Would you like to talk with me about it?" Tayin inquired of his brother.

"It is nothing, really," Tam replied.

"It is, though. I can see that you are concerned about Amalie. Why?"

"She is always talking about her son. She wants to see him, and I do not want her to." Tam leaned back and spread his arms across the back of the bench.

"There is no harm in letting her go see her son. You know that she will only be gone for a day. Amalie cares very much for you and will come back."

"Will she, though? What if she goes and then finds she wants to stay with her brat? What if she chooses not to come back to me?"

"Then you go get her, but I know she will not leave you. She misses her child as any parent would, and it is only to be expected that she would want to hold him again. Let her go." Tayin suggested.

"No. I don't think I will. Instead," Tam stood up and headed back toward the gardens, "I think I will take care of this little problem. If the brat is no longer here, she cannot leave to see him." Tam smiled at his plan and picked up his pace.

Tayin frowned at his brother and hurried to catch up to him. "You cannot do that. First, I will not allow harm to the child, and second, she would never forgive you if you killed her son."

Tam turned around and, walking backward, replied back to his brother. "But she will never know what I did. Unless you tell her, there is no way that she can place the blame for his death on me. I will console her, and she will eventually get over him, and then I will never have to hear of her wanting to leave me again."

"Tam, she is not leaving you. She only wants to visit him for one day. One day every year is not much for her to ask of you. It is such a small thing. Let her go, and when she comes back, she will be pleased and thankful that you let her visit her child. It is a win-win for you both."

Tam stopped in front of the garden gates and sat on the brick wall. "No. I like my idea better."

Tayin stood before his brother and let his disapproval shine in his eyes. "I will not permit this action. This child is innocent and does not deserve to be punished for your selfishness. For your insecurity over his mother." He ran his hand through his hair and stepped closer to his brother. "By Y'ddra Tam, look into her mind, and you will see that you are her world. She will never leave you. I see it every time I look at her. I cannot shut out her thoughts or anyone else's, as you know, and I tell you the truth. Amalie will come back. She misses the boy, but you are her home, her life, and her love."

Tam looked stubbornly at Tayin and started to argue with him. "It does not matter. I want him gone. I do not want to hear of that brat ever again, and this is the only way to make that happen."

"I will make sure that you dream of the child every night for eternity if you harm him," Tayin argued back.

Tam jumped down from the wall and pushed Tayin away from him. He went through the gate, followed closely by Tayin. Not wanting the Tarikan to overhear the argument, he continued it silently.

"Do what you want, and I will do what I want. Dammit, Tayin, I am the eldest, and you will leave this decision to me. Do not threaten me with ill dreams. This is between Amalie and me, and if I want to end the brat's life, that is my prerogative."

"It is, and it is mine to use my gift as I see fit. I will make sure that you never have a moment's peace. I will not only show you his face in your dreams but also tell Amalie that you did this terrible thing." Tayin calmed his voice. "Tam, please, if you do not let her see the child, then so be it, but do not harm him."

"Fine, I will not kill the boy, but if she leaves the Myst to see him, I will make sure that it is the last time she ever sees him." Tam stormed off into the shade of the veranda.

"Promise me you will not hurt him," Tayin yelled to his brother's retreating back.

"I promise," Tam yelled back, disappearing into the house, leaving Tayin standing outside, only half satisfied with his brother's departing words.

Amalie walked with Tam into the Hall of Memories, a place they kept as a sort of museum, and gritted her teeth at his words.

"No, you cannot leave the Myst," Tam spoke angrily. "Forget about the world and those that live outside of the Myst. They are no longer important to you." He walked a bit ahead of her and then sat on a chair by one of the display cases.

"But they are still important to me. My son will always be important to me, and his third birthday is in less than two months from now. I want to see him, hold him, and give him kisses. I do not want him to grow up thinking that I did not love him." She said back to him, anger evident in her voice.

This was an argument they seemed to have often. She could not understand why he would not let her see Ethyn. Last year, she had been allowed to see him through the barrier of the Myst, but this year, she wanted to see him in person. She had promised that she would return and that she would only be gone for a few hours, but Tam would not listen to her. She had even asked him to come with her, but he would not even consider this.

"Tam, I am going. I will get someone else to take me out of the Myst if you will not. I love you, and I promise that I will come back, but I am going." She turned to look at the items in the display case, her back turned to Tam.

This display case was filled with things that had been collected from a war they had waged with another race of beings that Y'ddra had brought to the planet for them to feed on. Amalie did not know the story as Tam was not one to talk of the past, though he had told her that at one time, they had fought with a bearlike race called the Kahru; after she had asked him about a conversation, she had overheard about them. One of the items in the case was a book that had the word Kahru written on it. She still could not speak the Alluran language, but she could pick up a few of their words. When Tam spoke of the Kahru, he said the name with such emotion that it stuck in her head.

She turned her head toward Tam when she heard him stand up. He came up to her and placed his hands on her shoulders.

"I said no. There will be no more discussion of this." He turned her around. "Hear me well. If you leave the Myst, I will find you and bring you back."

"But you already know where I will be." She interrupted in exasperation and turned back to the display case, her hand closing over one of the objects in an effort to control her anger.

He continued as if she had not interrupted him. "I promise you that I will not tolerate disobedience in this. You are mine, and I will not let you go back to those that you once knew. I mean it, Amalie. I will come for you, and I will fill those you visit with fear and feed on that delicious bit that they will produce with their last breath. Your son included."

"You are a demon!" She cried out in frustrated anger. Amalie, still gripping the object she held tightly in her fist, turned and hit him. The look of shock that appeared on Tam's face mirrored her own as the claw she held penetrated deep into his chest. She felt his blood flow hotly down her hand and only let go as he started to fall.

"Tam. By the Goddess, Tam, how? How?" She cried and put her head on his forehead.

"Run, Amalie, run as fast as you can." Blood squirted out of his mouth as he coughed. Amalie wiped it away and kissed him.

"How? You cannot be hurt. I didn't mean to hurt you. I didn't know that anything could." She sat there and cried, watching his life slowly fade as the blood poured out of the wound caused by the claw in his chest.

"You don't have time. Run, my love, run, and don't look back. He is coming." Tam's voice was fading as his life left his body. He reached up and tucked a strand of hair behind Amalie's ear. "In all ways that matter, you are my Korsyon, and everything I have done was to keep you with me. I never wanted to risk you choosing to stay with anyone but me. You are my heart. Now run." His hand dropped from her face.

Amalie kissed Tam. "I don't want to leave you. I love you. What can I do to fix this?"

"Take the blue stone and run!" He said with all the force he had remaining, and Amalie knew that she had to do as he told her to. Tayin entered her mind, and she jumped up and ran. She turned and headed out of the room, stopping briefly as she saw the key to the Myst locked in a cabinet by the door. Tam had not meant to tell her of the key, but in mentioning the war with Kahru, he had also mentioned the creation of the key, and now he told her to take it with her. She broke the glass, grabbed the key, and took off running as fast as she could. She could feel anger and pain envelop her mind, and nightmare images tripped her up, but still, she ran. Tayin knew what had happened. He knew what she had done.

The violent storm came out of nowhere, and the captain had trouble keeping the ship on course. He signaled for the bell to be rung so that the colonists could prepare for an immediate evacuation should one be called for. He cringed as blue lightning hit the mast and sent it crumbling into the sea. The captain could not find any land nearby to steer the ship toward. Only the great expanse of Myst loomed before him. No one had been able to get through the thick, glittering blue wall before, and if the ship hit it, they would all be lost. It would break them apart and send them all to drown in a watery grave.

The captain made one last effort to steer the ship away from crashing into the Myst and back out into the water, but the storm made it impossible. He was concentrating so hard that he jumped when he felt a hand grasp his shoulder firmly. Turning, the captain found himself face to face with a man, a man with glowing blue eyes and dark hair that waved in the wind. Fear seeped out of him, and he tried to release himself from the stranger's hold. He failed. The man only held him tighter.

He glanced around his ship and saw the passengers either passed out on the deck or huddled around each other, shaking from some unseen nightmare. He saw that a second man, this one with hair the blue of the Alluran moon, was standing casually at the rail. The intruder laughed at the people as they scrambled to escape their fears. The terror induced by the two strangers (how did they get on his ship anyway?) paralyzed the passengers and made it impossible for anyone to abandon the sinking vessel.

The captain heard the man next to him tell him to hold tightly to the helm, and for some unknown reason, he complied. He gasped in surprise as the ship glided smoothly into the Myst barrier. The storm instantly calmed, and the boat was no longer in danger of capsizing. The captain looked toward the shore and saw two more fearsome-looking men. One put his hand in the waters, and instantly, the ship was surrounded by what might be best described as giant shark-like creatures. He could only assume this was to ensure no one would leave the vessel. The other man caused a gentle wind to start back up with a flick of his wrist, bringing the ship to land safely on the shore.

Finally, the man holding onto him let go, and the captain felt the easing of his unnamed fear. He listened as the man told him to lower the ramp and have his people exit the ship. Knowing he had no choice, the captain did as he was told. Once on shore, the three hundred or so people were subjected to their darkest fears. He looked at his people shaking in terror and then at those that caused it. This planet was not the paradise they had hoped it would be, but then the young Prophetess had told them it would not be. The captain looked around and saw that the man who had stood at the railing gathered the children and sent them into what he hoped was just a deep sleep.

Stoically, the captain tried to ignore his fear. It seemed to him that the four young men were gaining strength the more his people trembled and cowered before them. Could it be possible that the four were feeding on them? He was no longer capable of helping his passengers; he could barely remain standing himself when the terror eased somewhat before increasing tenfold. He looked at the man guarding the children, and what the captain saw on his face almost made him feel sorry for the monster. The last thing the captain saw before the nightmares consumed him was the man crying out in grief and anger as he fell to his knees. The captain came to, momentarily, and watched as the nightmare creator was whisked away into nothingness by the one that had guided them through the Myst barrier.

The remaining two monsters stared in shock and bewilderment for several minutes before both of them went running to the Myst gate. The captain saw them place their hands on the now solid barrier. He watched as they tried to push through it. He watched as one of them turned into a giant cat-like creature and tried unsuccessfully to force his way through the Myst. Then he watched the man turn into a marine animal and try to swim out of the Myst enclosed waters. Finally, the captain watched as the other sent great gusts of wind and lightning at the barrier, trying to penetrate it. Both men failed in their attempts to open the Myst barrier.

The captain realized that if the fear-evoking monsters could not leave the Myst, his people could not either. They were trapped here, too, for how long, he was unsure.

Tayin gathered the children, eased them into sleep, and gave them beautiful dreams so that they would not remember the fear around them when they woke. He turned to join his friends in feasting on the exquisite fear of the Yidderians when pain such as he had never experienced before lanced his heart.

Darkness fell over the bright day, and nightmarish phantasms began to surround everyone around him. Seeping out of the minds of those he held captive from their nightmares, the specters were finally allowed to walk in reality. While Tayin had the ability to make people see the same nightmares, he had never had the ability to bring them to life, but in this moment, the images were as substantial as he was.

His body rejected the gift that was being forced upon him while his mind quickly assessed how to use it. Tayin fell to his knees and cried out in agony as his brother's gift became his, and he cried out in pain with the knowledge that there was only one reason this was happening.

He felt Adym's hand on his shoulder as he reached out to Tam and saw the horror that was waiting for him. He thought quickly of Amalie and knew the minute she heard him in her mind. He saw her jump up from Tam's body, grab a small round blue stone from its glass cabinet, and take off running for the Myst gates.

Tayin felt Adym transport him to Tam's side. He looked down at his brother and saw the Kahru claw that impaled his chest. It was too late to save him, but he knew that Adym would try. He raced after Amalie as Adym swiftly tried to take Tam's body to the green pool underneath the rainbow-colored falls in an effort to save him. While his heart ached to be with his brother, he knew that he had to catch Amalie before she took the key out of the Myst.

Tayin was coming for her. No longer the gentle and kind man she had known him to be, he was now the demon that she had accused Tam of being. Amalie was outside, running across the grass as fast as she could while the beautiful day grew dark as violent images appeared all around her. For a brief moment, she wondered at the illusions stepping out from behind the trees, coming for her, and wondered if Tam was going to be alright. But the images were not the same as the ones he produced. These were more real. She could smell the hot breath of the nightmares surrounding her.

Amalie ran. She was almost to the edge of the Myst gate when Tayin entered her mind with force.

"Amalie." He shouted, causing her head to feel as if it exploded, and her nose began to bleed.

The mounting fear caused her eyes to blur and her mind to lose focus. She tripped and dropped the precious stone that she carried. She quickly scooped up the round Alluran blue crystal and crawled toward the gate. It was almost impossible to keep moving with the pain she was feeling, with the fear that poured out of her. She had never felt real fear of Tayin before, but now she understood why they all had told her he was the most powerful and fearful of them all. He was twisting her thoughts and turning them into nightmares that she could not ignore.

Amalie pulled her foot through the Myst as Tayin reached her. Instantly, the Myst gates locked, and she stopped crawling across the grass. She was safe. Tayin could not follow her now. Her head exploded in pain once more, and she realized that she was wrong. Physically, he may not be able to follow her, but he knew her mind and, even through the Myst, could get to her there. The nightmares felt as if they were eating her mind.

"Amalie." Tayin roared in her head as he raced out of the house and across the grass and saw that she had almost made it to her goal. He reached deep into her mind and found her nightmares and brought them to life. Images of Tam's death flooded the area, and all of her other fears surrounded her as she ran. He released the istotymir and enhanced the fear she was feeling already. Tayin watched as she stumbled at the edge of the gate and then watched as she crawled the rest of the way to the other side. He had been about to grab her and keep her from leaving the Myst when she quickly pulled her foot through the barrier, and he lost his chance to keep the key from going with her.

Taking the key out of the Myst had sealed the gates with a soft click heard throughout Yiddera. Tayin knew that no one inside the Myst could leave until the key was returned. He stood at the now solid barrier and stared at the woman looking back at him. He stared for several minutes before noticing that she had dropped part of the key where he was standing. He picked it up and held it firmly in his hand, knowing that if they were to ever be free again, this part of the key would have to be reunited with the piece that Amalie still clutched in hers.

"Why?" Tayin choked out the question from a throat tight with unshed tears, his fierce eyes penetrating into her very soul.

"I," Amalie began through the tears that were pouring down her face.

"Why?" He yelled at her.

"I didn't mean to. I didn't know it would kill him." She folded her knees into her chest and cried as if her heart was breaking. Her body trembled with sorrow and with the feel of Tayin's grief invading her thoughts.

Tayin did not care for her tears. He violently entered her mind and brushed past all of her guilt and sorrow over what she had done until he found the answer he was looking for.

"I would not have let him kill your son. The conversation you heard us having ended with him promising me he wouldn't harm your child." Tayin stated.

"He didn't always do as you asked, nor did he always keep his promises. And the last conversation he had with me belied his with you." She whispered through her tears. "I would never have done it if I knew that it would harm him. I love him. I didn't know it would kill him." Amalie sniffed and wiped a tear from her face. "How? How did it? You are eternal; nothing permanently damages you people." She asked angrily.

"The claw of the Kahru is one of the very few things that causes death to our people." He answered through gritted teeth.

Tayin leaned his head against the Myst and placed both hands on the barrier. He closed his eyes tightly in pain and felt his breath catch as Tam's last breath left him. He breathed out slowly. "Stand up and listen to me well, Amalie." He waited until she did as he requested before continuing.

"You have woken the demon inside of me, and I will unleash him on your world as soon as I am free to walk the whole of Yiddera once again. You will regret what you did every moment of your life. I will haunt you and cause you to relive the moment of his death every time you close your eyes. You will feel my pain and anger every time you see Tam's face in your mind." His blue eyes glittered with unshed tears and an anger that was foreign to him.

He stepped even closer to the now completely solid barrier. "I will be free, and when that day comes, I will unleash my demons on you and yours. I promise that I will kill you, your friends, family, and loved ones in revenge for what you have taken from Tam and me. And if you are gone by the time I am free, I will not rest until every last person that may carry your blood in their veins is gone. I will kill them and drink of their fear. I will relish the last moment of their death, knowing that the strength it provides me will help me hunt down the next one and the next after that."

He backed up from the woman he had started thinking of as a friend despite the nagging feeling that she was dangerous. Now, he looked at her as if she were poison. "There will be no way for you to stop my revenge. There will be no way for you to hide from my wrath, my pain, my demons. You will pay for Tam's death and for locking us in the Myst." He turned and walked away from her and headed to place the one part of the key they still had in their possession back in the room where it belonged.

He then collapsed in grief and cried, knowing he would never see his twin again. Never argue with him, laugh with him, hug him again. The new gift coursed through his body, and Tayin's sadness and anger increased as he felt the gift become stronger within him than it had ever been with Tam. He could feel it mingle with his abilities, and each one enhanced the other. He could now bring his nightmares and dreams into the waking world, making them as real as he and anything else was. The two gifts melded into one potent ability, making him the most dangerous SeiOrhii that had ever been.

Adym arrived at Tayin's side and placed his hand once again on his friend's shoulder. "Tayin, you have to stop." He gently told his grieving friend. "You are causing nightmares and darkness to envelop everyone. You are scaring the children."

Tayin drew in a deep breath and looked at his friend. He could see that Adym was right, and with great difficulty, he reigned in his misery and allowed the nightmares to fade and the sun to shine through the darkness once again.

Adym sat down next to Tayin and placed an arm around him. "Can you handle it?"

Tayin knew that Adym was asking if he was going to kill himself. The few times that twins had been born among their kind the death of one had caused such torment that the other had taken their life. The bond between twins was similar to the Korsyon, and while twins did not share a heart, they did share their minds in ways that other Allurans could not. This emptiness he now felt in his mind was excruciating, but he nodded his head yes to Adym.

"I can. I will." He leaned against his friend. "I will because I have made a promise to Tam and to Amalie. I will live for the rest of eternity in order to bring my promise to life. After that, we will see."

The two men sat in silence together. Each was grieving the loss of a friend and brother and grieving the loss of their freedom.

Amalie sat in the grass and watched Tayin walk away from her. She was shocked at the anger she had felt emanating from him. Her mind reeled over the promise of revenge he had made her.

She knew that he meant every word of it. He did not lie. Her life and her son's life would be in danger if he were released.

Amalie looked at the blue crystal that she held in her hands. She needed to get this key somewhere far away from Tayin and hide it somewhere that he would never find it. Amalie thought of several places but knew that anywhere she might hide it, Tayin would find it in her mind. Amalie knew that she had to give it to someone and have them hide it for her. She thought of John and knew that she could not give it to him. He would never be able to hide it well, and Tayin would break into his mind quickly.

Alena. She would give it to Alena. The Prophetess would be able to hide it, and she would ensure that it would never be found. Amalie would head to Alenar first. She would see her family after she returned from hiding the most precious object in all of Yiddera. The only thing that was keeping her and Ethyn safe, keeping all Yidderians safe, from the demons in the Myst.

She looked at the Myst and felt her heart breaking. Amalie scooted toward the barrier and leaned her cheek against it, feeling its warmth and vitality. She allowed herself to cry over what she had mistakenly done, over her loss of a life that she had never thought she would have and now would never get back. Amalie cried for Tam, knowing she would never see him again. She would never laugh with him or argue with him. Amalie would never again feel his touch on her body. She cried, knowing that it was her own anger and thoughtlessness that had caused the pain of so many people.

And she cried for Tayin. She had changed a decent, loving, and thoughtful man into one filled with hate. She wept for him, knowing that while she would live with this mistake all her life, so would he, and his life was never-ending. One day, her pain would end, but his would continue for all time.

She allowed herself to wallow in pity and grief for a bit longer before she stood up, wiped the blood from her face, and started the long trek to the docks, where she could find a ship that would take her to Alena. She wasn't sure how long she would have to wait for it to arrive. If the schedule was the same as it was two and a half years ago, it would be there in two weeks. She would have to hurry to make it in time. She ran her hand once more over the Myst and then walked away from where her heart had stopped beating.

Nicollete was sitting in the sand that made up the hidden beach by the cave that she had recently found and started using to meet Kian. She played with the miniature rex that he had brought her as a gift. Kian was Yidderian, and she almost gave it away that she wasn't when she was handed the beautiful little pup. She had exclaimed in joy at being given a miniature kiraly and then caught herself. She could see in his mind that he was confused as this new species had just been sent to them from Alenar a few days ago. Nicollete knew that they had yet to learn that the kiraly came in three different sizes. She saw that, as far as they knew, the precious little pups only came in two sizes. They did not yet know of the giant version. She brushed over her mistake by saying the pup must be a miniature as it was so tiny and that the name Kiraly had popped into her head, so she must name it that.

Kian had told her that they were calling the species Rex as they were said to look similar to a dinosaur from Earth that was known by that name. He had never heard of such a creature on Earth, but the resident wildlife zoologist had told him all about the scary things. He then went on to explain that while they did look like the rex, the pups also had the same soft floppy ears and short brindle patterned hair as the hound dogs on Earth did. Kian had told her that he hoped they would make good pets.

She had replied, using what she saw in his mind, that she hoped so too, as the Yidderians born on Earth were missing their pets. She then thanked him for the gift, and now they sat together with their feet in the cool, wet sand, playing with the young animal. They were laughing and having a good time when Nicollete felt more than heard a slight click in her head. Goose bumps covered her arms, and she went pale.

Nicollete opened her mind and found that many voices were discussing the click and what it could mean. She asked Raighn what was going on, and he quickly replied that he wasn't sure, but it seemed that Amalie had locked the Myst gates, and now they were unable to get out.

Nicollete stood up in a panic. If the gates were closed and Raighn could not get out, then she might not be able to make it back home. She started running the opposite way of the village but was stopped by a hand on her arm.

"Nicollete, what is wrong?" Kian asked, his voice full of concern for her, the rex held in the crook of his arm.

She could not tell him what was wrong. He wouldn't understand, and her answer would put her in danger. Nicollete shifted her feet, trying to pull away, but knew she needed to give him some explanation, or he might be inclined to follow her.

"I forgot to do something important. Will you take Kiraly to your house and watch her for me? I need to do this errand, and then we can meet back up later this evening." She said in a rush, hoping he would accept her answer and leave her to go on her way.

He nodded his head yes and then gave her a quick kiss on the cheek. She watched as he turned back down the beach and headed toward the village before pulling up her skirt and racing toward the closest area of Myst that she could. She ran straight at the Myst, hoping she was wrong and that it would let her through, but she was met with a solid barrier that knocked her to her feet. She got up and pounded her fists against the gate but could not get inside. She kept hitting at it and trying until, finally, she allowed herself to accept the truth. The Myst gate was impenetrable. Nicollete leaned against it and, sliding down into a sitting position, cried in disbelief at being locked out of her home.

Nicollete felt the Myst shimmer behind her and knew that Raighn had joined her, his back to hers, on his side of the Myst. She could feel his anger and his sadness with the situation before them. They sat there together in silent misery, each not sure where to begin.

"How?" Nicollete asked, finally breaking the awful silence.

"She killed Tam with a Kahru claw and then took the key outside of the Myst." His voice shook with anger. "That is all I know right now. Tayin is inconsolable. Adym took him to his room of peace to help calm his mind. We are not sure that Tayin is going to come out of this alive."

Nicollete broke out in a new round of tears at the loss of Tam and the possible loss of Tayin. She cried over the loss of her home and the loss of her way of life. She knew that nothing was going to be the same, and Nicollete knew that Raighn was bubbling over with anger at her for once again leaving the Myst to go into the Yidderian village. While it was okay for her to be out of the Myst, usually, she knew that for the first few years that a new species tried to take up inhabitance on Yiddera, no one was to leave the Myst without permission and without being accompanied by a SeiOrhii. This was a safety precaution put in place over two thousand years ago to prevent another occurrence, such as what happened with the Kahru.

"I am sorry, Raighn." She sobbed.

"Why are you outside of the Myst?" Raighn asked, his voice holding barely controlled anger.

"I enjoy learning about the Yidderians, and I have made friends among them. I was always careful to hide my origins. Raighn, I never thought in all the realm of possibilities that there would be a danger of being locked out of the Myst." She turned to look at him through the shimmer.

"That is just it. You never think of the consequences." He took a deep breath, running his hands through his long, dark hair. "I am sorry, little sister. I do not want to start an argument. I frankly don't know what I am going to do without you. Nicollete, I cannot keep you safe any longer. I cannot come and rescue you if it is discovered that you are not human."

"I know." She whispered, tears choking her words.

Raighn turned to her and looked into the face of his youngest sister. They had been close since she was little, and she was still so very young, barely 300 years old. How was she going to survive without her family? How was he going to survive without his closest friend?

"What are you going to do?" He asked her.

Nicollete knew that he considered her his responsibility and knew that she could not leave him with this feeling of guilt at not being with her.

"I am going to live and prosper and make the humans dependent on me. I know things about Yiddera that they do not. But first, I am going to see if any other Allurans got stuck out here with me, and if there are, then I am going to help them make the best of being on this side of the Myst that we can. I am one of the only Allurans that can blend in well due to the darkness of my hair; many of the others will not be that lucky." She smiled sadly.

"I wish things could be different, but they are not, and I have to make this work. I have no choice."

"I will do what I can to get you back. I promise." Raighn said.

"There is nothing that you can do. But I can. I can look for the key. The Yidderians do not know that I can listen to their thoughts. I will listen, and I will find the key and bring it to you when I find it." Nicollete promised.

"It doesn't matter as long as you stay safe," Raighn told her.

She smiled to herself and replied, "Of course, it matters. It may be the only way that I can make it back home." Nicollete put her hand up to the Myst, and Raighn put his hand against hers, causing the Myst to sparkle with their touch.

"Raighn, stay with me for a while. As much as I don't want to admit it, I am afraid of what is to come."

"I will stay as long as you want me to." He replied and leaned his head against the Myst, settling in for as long as she needed him to. The day passed, and the sun was beginning to set. Nicollete knew that she must leave as Kian would soon be coming to look for her. She stood up and stretched and told Raighn to go home.

"I need to leave and start back to the cave that I use for shelter while out here. Kian will be looking for me, and I need to start acting like a Yidderian if I am to now live with them." She wiped her face on the hem of her skirt, trying to erase the tear stains that ran down her face. "Meet me here tomorrow morning?" She asked with hope in her voice.

"I will be here waiting for you when the sun starts to peak over the horizon." He replied and then reluctantly turned away, leaving her to walk alone with the humans.

Adym looked around the room where he sat with Tayin. It was a large room that had walls lightly covered in the same Myst that made up the barriers, but instead of being Alluran blue, it was a pale pink color. In this room, there was an oversized comfortable couch and a long table against one wall that held music stones, each with a different song placed inside it. Each piece was created with a specific job to do, and that was to calm Tayin's mind.

Adym knew that on the opposite side of the room from this table was a door that led to Tayin's living quarters, but today the peace in this room was needed. Adym sat quietly next to his friend and reflected on the memory he had of this room. He was around one hundred rotations of the sun older than Tayin and so remembered the strange activity that went on once Eniko knew she was expecting.

The Tarikan started building a whole new wing onto the already large house. They left the rooms empty and plain, to be designed once the occupant decided what he would want it to look like, but this outer room they spent a great deal of time in. They were very particular in making it acoustically sound. They made sure that the room was asymmetrical and that the floor was covered with soft, lush carpeting.

Adym remembered trying to get into the room once it was finished, but the door had no handle. Instead, the Tarikan had made a small hand plate that they said could open the door once the twin who would use the room was born. It had come as a surprise to Adym and to everyone that Eniko was going to have twins. Twins were rare to the SeiOrhii.

There were a few twins born among the Chosin, those chosen to be a sacrifice to Y'ddra but not among those SeiOrhii that were not Chosin. The two sets of twins that had been born to the immortal race of Allurans had both died tragically. The first was a female who had bonded with a LuZivot. She died when her partner did, and her twin could not live with her twin's death or the gift that got passed to her. The extra ability caused her to become insane, and so she took the poison that weakened a SeiOrhii enough to slow their healing process down and then used her sister's ability to teleport and dropped herself on a sharp rock. She was found days later, and by then, she was dead.

The second set were males born with the ability to shift into the giant rex. During the war of the Kahru, one of the two was killed. The one left, with the extra power to transform passed to him by his brother, figured out how to become a Kahru himself. He fought the Kahru as one of their own and helped the Allurans reach safety but lost his life when two of the enemy tore his animal body in half, making it impossible for him to heal. But then, he had not wanted to heal. He had chosen his suicide to be death by the Kahru.

Tam was born first, and thirteen minutes later, Tayin was born. Once Tayin took his first breath, a wave of pink Myst swept through the house and entered the locked room. Everyone took this to mean that this room was meant for Tayin, and after three rotations of the sun, they were proven correct.

Every Alluran child was taken to the Rainbow Falls once they were three rotations old. It was at this age that they would become attracted to one of the colored pools if they were SeiOrhii. Those not attracted to one of them were pulled toward the multicolored lake below, and this signaled everyone that they were LuZivot, the long-lived, not SeiOrhii, the eternal. Once in the pool of their chosen color, they changed into SeiOrhii or into Chosin.

Tam and Tayin were drawn to the red pool of dreams. Tam became a powerful illusionist, and Tayin became the master of dreams. Tayin also felt the rush of their world's history enter his mind. The young child cried in pain at all the information he received. Unlike other historians, he could not block out the thoughts of others, nor could he block out the entire history of Yiddera. His father, Adorjan, rushed him back home and placed his tiny hand on the plate of the mysterious room.

The room opened immediately, and once inside, the history went into the pink Myst and allowed Tayin to breathe. He touched one of the song stones, and his little body stopped quivering with the overload of information he had received. He was able to relax enough that he could push the thoughts of every Alluran aside.

Adym brought himself out of his reflection. This room, created specifically for Tayin, was a balm to his fractured mind. Adym watched his friend and saw that while concentrating on the sounds that played softly around them, Tayin could reign in his anger and grief over the loss of his brother. He hoped it would be enough to keep his friend from going crazy.

"I will survive. I have already told you that I would not follow the path of suicide that previous twin pairs have taken." Tayin said quietly, his eyes closed, listening to the soothing sounds and sending his thoughts into the Myst of the room. "I cannot say that I will not go crazy, but I will not off myself."

Adym nodded his head and continued sitting by his friend. He had been instructed by the Elders not to leave Tayin alone, and so he would not.

"I need to see Alena now." The woman told the man for the fourth time. She tried to go around the man blocking her path, but he grabbed her arm before she could make it around him.

"You will address her as the Prophetess, and as I said before, she is busy and will not be seeing anyone outside of the regularly scheduled meeting hours. Of which I also told you that the next one will be in two days." The man dragged the woman over to the gate and told her to be on her way.

The woman screamed in frustration and swung at the man, hitting him squarely in the jaw. While he was recovering from the unexpected blow, the woman took off running toward the monastery.

"Hey, get back here." The man yelled as he ran after her.

The woman looked back at the man, quickly gaining on her, and ran smack into another man. He grabbed her to keep her from falling just as the one chasing her finally caught up to her.

"I am sorry, Luke. I couldn't stop her."

Still holding onto the woman, Luke answered, "It is okay. I will take care of this. Go back to your post." He guided the woman over to a nearby bench and sat her down.

"Now, what is so important that you hit someone for doing his job?"

"I must see Alena. I cannot wait." The woman stood up and once again tried to walk to the monastery doors.

"I can get you an appointment with her first thing on Wednesday, but today, she has made it clear that she is not receiving visitors."

"She will see me." The woman said and looked around the man for a way to continue on her mission.

The man smiled and steered her back the way she came. "Wednesday, she will see you on Wednesday. Give me your name so I can place it on her appointment calendar."

Through gritted teeth, the woman answered him. "Amalie, my name is Amalie."

The man stopped and stared at the woman next to him. He did not know what Alena's friend looked like, and he had only ever heard the name Amalie in reference to the friend who went missing in the Myst.

"Come with me." He guided her into the magnificent foyer of the monastery. "My name is Luke, by the way."

Amalie frowned. She didn't care who this man was. She was just glad that, finally, someone was taking her to where she needed to go.

"You are taking me to Alena, aren't you? It is important that I see her right away." Amalie hugged her bag closer to her as she said this.

"Yes, I am. She is in a meeting with the world leaders, but she will want to be interrupted to speak with you." Luke knocked on a set of double doors and whispered to the servant who answered. They waited for a few minutes before Alena appeared.

Alena saw her friend and held her arms out to her. "Amalie."

Amalie rushed into the waiting arms and burst out crying. She cried as if her heart was breaking and continued crying as Luke guided the two women toward their living quarters. He sat them down on the couch, rang for drinks and refreshments to be brought, and then discretely left them to their long-awaited reunion.

Alena held Amalie until the tears slowed.

"You knew, didn't you?" Amalie asked Alena.

"I told you that you were important to our peace, but I didn't know how you would be." She answered evasively.

Amalie looked at her friend, scooted down the couch away from her, and took a deep drink of the cold water that Luke had sat on the table.

"That is not what I meant, and you know it."

Alena looked at her friend sadly. "I knew that you would not be the same once you came back. I know that you will never be happy outside of the Myst." She reached for a glass and brought it to her lips. Before she took a drink, she asked, "Are the gates locked?"

At that question, Amalie once again broke out into violent tears. Her sobs shook Alena. Knowing there was nothing she could say or do at this time, she just let her friend cry. She stood up and opened her front door and saw that Luke was waiting on a bench down the hall should she need anything. Alena asked him to carry Amalie to their bed. He did, and Alena tucked her friend in and sat with her as she cried herself to sleep.

Alena took Luke's hand and sat with him in the living room. She tucked her feet up under a blanket and laid her head back.

"I think sleep will be good for her. She is worn out from her tears."

Luke nodded and started massaging Alena's feet. She sighed in pleasure and began to relax into the ministrations when she heard a loud cry of fear coming from the bedroom. Both she and Luke jumped up to see what was going on.

Alena was the first in the room, and she saw a still-sleeping Amalie sitting up in bed, watching something that no one else could see. She kept repeating, "I didn't mean to" over and over again. The pain in those words hurt Alena to hear. She left Luke to lay Amalie back down and sit with her as she went into the kitchen to make a sleeping draught that was known to give the drinker a dreamless sleep.

She woke Amalie up enough to get a few sips down her and then left the room once again. She paced in front of her window until it drove Luke crazy. He rested his hands on her shoulders and told her to go outside and find Luka.

"Go play with Luka. She might calm you down. I will sit with your friend and come and get you when she wakes up." He steered Alena toward the door and kissed her soundly.

The sun was starting to set when Amalie found Alena sitting in the sweet-smelling light green grass that surrounded a beautiful pond; in front of her played an infant just beginning to crawl. Amalie sat down cross-legged next to her friend.

"She looks like you and a bit like the man, Luke, I think he said his name was, who brought me to you." Amalie tossed a squishy ball to the little girl and smiled briefly at the squeal of delight that she issued.

"Her name is Luka, and I see more of Luke in her than myself," Alena replied as she took a turn throwing the ball to the baby, who tried to catch it and fell over backward from her sitting position. Alena gathered the little one up and gestured for Amalie to follow her.

The two women took the baby to Luke, and after Alena fed her daughter, they left the monastery and headed up a path that led to the little chapel. Alena opened the door, started a fire in the fireplace, and then curled up on the bed so that she and Amalie could talk comfortably.

"I killed him." Amalie started saying, a lump in her throat, making it hard to get the words out. "I didn't mean to, but I killed him." She stared into the distance for a moment with silent tears running down her face. She laughed wryly. "I do not know how

I have any tears left. I have been crying for the almost three weeks it took me to get here. I can't seem to stop."

"Tell me of the nightmares," Alena whispered.

"They are given to me by his brother. As if I needed his help remembering every detail of that day. They were twins, and now I am tortured by Tayin every night. Every time I close my eyes, I see his face looking at me accusingly. I deserve it. I deserve to feel his pain, and I deserve to relive my love's death every night."

"You loved the one you killed?" Alena asked her.

"I loved him more than anything. I feel like I am dying every day that I am not with him." She paused and hung her head in shame. "We were arguing. I wanted to see my son in person on his next birthday, and he didn't want me to leave. He was always afraid that I would choose not to come back to him, but how could I not come back? He was my everything." She took a deep breath and continued.

"I was so angry at him for not listening to me, for not trusting that I would not leave him. I picked up the first object that I could find within my reach and hit him. I was just as shocked as him when it entered his skin, and he started bleeding. Until then, I thought nothing could hurt him. They are eternal."

She turned to her friend, hoping for understanding and maybe forgiveness.

"I have seen them fall from great heights and recover from the injury within a matter of hours. I have never seen anything puncture their skin, not even so much as scratch it. How could I have known that anything I did would bring about his death or any of their deaths? I didn't even know that they could die." She sat silently for a long while.

"He told me to run. I didn't want to. I wanted to stay with him, but he insisted. And I knew why. He told me to take the blue stone, so I grabbed it," She pulled a blue stone out of her bag and held it tightly in her hand, "and I ran. I could feel his brother coming for me. The nightmares became so intense that I almost did not make it out of the Myst, but I knew that if I didn't, I would suffer unimaginable pain. Part of me wanted to let his brother catch me, but the other part knew that I wouldn't have grabbed the key if this was my true wish."

"What key?"

Amalie held out the round Alluran blue stone for Alena to look at. Alena took it and could feel the pulsing of energy within the perfect orb. She noticed it had a crescent moon-shaped hole going through the center of it.

"What is the hole for?" She asked, handing the stone she had once seen in a vision back to Amalie.

"This is the key that locks the Myst gates. It is a two-part key. When both parts are united and they are taken out of the Myst, the gates lock intruders out, but Allurans can enter at will. When the pieces are separated, the gates lock in a way that no one can enter or exit the Myst, be they Alluran or the enemy. In order for the gates to ever be opened again, the two pieces must be brought back together." She tucked the crystal back into her bag. The Allurans are stuck in the Myst." She turned her head away from Alena as tears once again flowed down her face, "and I can no longer get back to them."

Alena was shaken by the sadness in her friend's voice. She now understood why the vision had told her that she would live out the rest of her days in hell. To see your love's death repeatedly playing in your head every night without end would be hell for anyone, and knowing that you are the one that caused that death would feed the guilt day after day. She had known that Amalie was okay within the Myst, but she would never have guessed that Amalie would have fallen in love with the one that took her.

She was deep in thought when something Amalie had said clicked in her mind. "Did you say that the one brother is responsible for giving you nightmares?"

"Yes. He can create the most amazing dreams and the most hellish nightmares. Why do you ask?"

"The day that Luka was born, two men with blue markings came to visit. They said that Y'ddra had told them to come and welcome the Prophetess's baby. One of them gave me an intricately carved box that he said would give Luka pleasant dreams every night if she kept it by her bed."

"He would give a gift such as that. Though he would never hurt a child, I would advise that you do not keep it by her bed. He is no longer the kind and caring man that he used to be." Amalie stood up, added another log to the fire, and then sat in the comfortable armchair by the window. She looked out at the night sky and felt a small sense of peace for the first time since that horrible day. Alena had always had a calming effect on her.

While looking at the two moons that hung high in the night sky, she told Alena of her time in the Myst. Of her love and his friends. How they were a telepathic race of people, how they were immortal, and why they fed on the Yidderians. She talked about their need for the fear of others to stay strong and powerful. She told Alena funny little stories of all that she had learned while living there. She talked for hours. It was nearly dawn when she turned serious once more.

"They are demons, Alena. If the gates are ever opened, they will hunt me and mine down. They will not be as nice to the Yidderians as they currently are."

Alena raised an eyebrow at this. The beings that fed on the Yidderians were anything but considerate now, and she hated to think what they would do once free again.

"So, what are you proposing we do about this?" Alena asked.

"You are the Prophetess and, as such, have the power to make people listen to you. Make them understand that the Myst is evil and that those living within are demons that will torture and feed on them. Make sure that no one anywhere would ever want them to be free. Make no mistake that if free, this world will be a living hell for everyone."

Amalie once again stoked the fire and then sat on the bed and pulled a blanket over her. "Do what you can to keep people away from the Myst. I am not sure what to do exactly, but religion is a powerful tool. Use it to make people believe that the Myst encases hell." She took the crystal key out of her bag again and handed it to Alena.

"Hide this in a place where no one will ever find it. Do not tell me where you take it or where you hide it. He will find it in my head if you do. It must remain "lost" to all. It must be well protected and never found."

Alena took the key and knew precisely where it belonged. Y'ddra had given her the vision of the hidden room just for this item. She placed the key in the pocket of her dress and promised Amalie that it would be well hidden.

Alena stood up and, taking Amalie's arm, led her out of the cozy little room and out of the chapel itself. They entered the cool, crisp morning air and walked the path that led back to the abbey.

"Come, let's have a bite to eat, and then I will show you to the guest room. After a good rest, we can talk some more as I show you the Monastery grounds. I am quite proud of them." Alena asked the first servant that she came to for breakfast to be brought to the guest quarters next to her rooms and then showed Amalie into a beautiful room done in sunny yellows and spring greens. Amalie sat on one of the comfortable armchairs that she knew had been fabricated by the ship before it was destroyed. It had the synthetic feel to it that many of the items brought from Earth or created on the ship had.

After a cup of tea and a muffin, Alena left Amalie to herself. She entered her own quarters and smiled to see Luke asleep on the couch. He had obviously been waiting for her to return. She tucked a quilt over him, kissed his cheek, and went to her own room to think of all that Amalie had told her and what she should do with the information.

Alena had never wanted to create a religion but inadvertently had. Now, she was being asked to take that religion and turn it into something that would create fear in her followers. She had intended it to teach love and respect for the planet, and she had hoped that she could eventually broker peace between the original inhabitants and the Yidderians. With her gift, she had foreseen that this was a possibility, but Alena had also foreseen that it was unlikely.

The Allurans, as Amalie called them, were now locked in an impenetrable barrier by the hands of the one Yidderian they had trusted. She knew that trust was no longer there and the already fearsome people would not be reasonable. Humans were vengeful creatures, and she had no reason to believe that the Allurans were any different except that they had gifts that made their vengeance terrifying.

Yes, she would do as Amalie asked. Alena would start tomorrow by changing her peaceful religion to one that taught that Y'ddra had brought them to this planet to keep the 'demons' locked in the Myst, and should they ever be let free, well, she would have to think about that possibility before coming to a decision on that. Alena, while knowing that Y'ddra had created the original inhabitants to be what they were and knowing that the humans were brought here for the Allurans, would have to teach against the Goddess. No, she would have to change what she knew to be true of Y'ddra and turn her into a Goddess that stood behind the Yidderians and not her own creations. Alena would use fear to turn them from the truth.

Alena sighed. The Allurans used Yidderian's fear to make themselves stronger. To save the people from this, she would be using their fear to keep the Myst gates closed. Fear was a powerful thing, and no matter which way she looked at it, Alena knew that fear was the only thing that would work. This planet was destined to keep her people afraid, and instead of the Allurans, she would be responsible for their fear. Her religion would now promote the hate of others instead of acceptance.

Snuggling further into her pillow, she tried to clear her mind of these troubled thoughts and finally fell into a restless sleep full of dreams and nightmares about the future.

After 27 days of watching over Tayin, Adym needed a break. He left Kest to sit with their friend and went home to enjoy the cool mountain air that was like a balm to his soul. He sat in his favorite room, a room decorated in soft yellows and whites, and looked out the large window at the softly falling snow.

Concern over Tayin had been the priority since the Myst gates closed, but now Adym began to think about what this new situation meant to all of Yiddera and to all of the Allurans. The Rainbow Falls were now unreachable, which meant that the sacrifices to Y'ddra could not happen. If the Chosin were not able to die for her at the required intervals of time, then her colors would eventually fade, and she would not have the energy to support and heal the planet.

Adym knew that they could survive being locked away, though it would be challenging as they did not do well in confinement. They had plenty of Yidderians in the Myst with them, so while food would be sparing, it was still there, but Y'ddra would be without. He stood up and walked to the window and decided that maybe he could still leave the Myst. He was, after all, a teleporter.

"Adym."

He heard Raighn call to him. "Yes."

"If you are going to try to leave the Myst, would you do it from Lioleta instead of trying it on Elynas?"

"Why?" He questioned his cousin.

"Because Nicollete got locked out of the Myst. She is on the Yidderian side, and I would like you to make sure that she is alright." Raighn said with grief in his voice.

Adym instantly appeared in Alendrot and sat down on the sand next to Raighn, looking out of the Myst.

"Are you sure she is out there?"

Raighn picked up a handful of sand and let it slip slowly through his fingers. "Yes. The day the gates closed, I met with her, and she told me to stop worrying over her as she was safe in the village among the Yidderians. Adym, she has no one to ensure her safety, no one to help her if she needs it." He scooped up another handful of sand. "I kept telling her it was not safe to go into the village as someday she is going to be identified as an Alluran, but she would just laugh and tell me she was perfectly safe."

"How is she now that she knows that she cannot get back into the Myst?" Adym asked the solemn Raighn.

"Nicollete says that she is okay, but she is bewildered at her change in circumstances and not fully sure what she should do. I feel so helpless. I am her big brother. I should have been able to protect her, but I never imagined that she would be locked away from her home."

Adym stood up. "Well, if I can make it out of the Myst gates, I will try to bring her back with me, and if I can't, I will help her in any way that I can to keep her safe and comfortable in her long years of isolation."

Adym walked to the Myst and tried leaving, but it rebuffed him, so he disappeared once again and, this time, concentrating very intently, made it out to the Yidderian side. He collapsed on the ground instantly.

"Adym, are you okay?" Raighn rushed over to the Myst and pounded on it, trying to make it allow him to leave and help Adym, but the Myst did not give.

"I am okay, but that hurt. I will need to feed. Where is the closest village to here so that I can get my strength back as soon as possible?" Adym sat up and held his head in his hands. His whole body ached in a way that felt as if he had fallen from a great distance.

"I have called Nicollete to you. She will come and guide you." Raighn sat down so that he was at eye level with Adym once more. "Adym? Do you think you will make it back home?"

"I will, and I will try to bring Nicollete with me, but after that, I will not try again unless I am in my shadow form. I will save my strength and my energy for the day that I need to leave to take the key to the one that is predicted to arrive and help us regain our freedom."

"Do you really think that she will be a Yidderian and born outside the Myst?" Raighn asked.

"I do. It is the only logical answer. She has to be Yidderian and born outside of the Myst if she is to bring us the key." He turned when he heard soft footsteps approaching.

"It is only me, Adym," Nicollete said as she came around a tree.

Adym looked at the lovely young woman. She was barely three hundred rotations of the sun, and she now had to live without her family. She was too young to be isolated from others like her.

"I will be okay, Adym. I look enough like the Yidderians that I can pass off as one of them." She turned toward her brother and placed her hand on the barrier across from where he had put his. "Raighn, Adym is here now. He will bring me home, and if he can't, I will be okay."

"There is a cave near here. Adym, I will take you there, and then I will bring someone back for you, but after that, you will have to teleport us to another village so that you can feed. If I have to live among the humans, I cannot be suspected of having a hand in any disappearances." She took Adym's hand in hers and, waving a quick goodbye to Raighn, led Adym to the cave.

Adym watched the young woman walk off in the direction of the Yidderian village. He made himself comfortable against the back wall of the cave, hating the necessity of hiding from those he thought of as prey. But he would hide if it meant protecting Nicollete from harm. Adym hoped he was able to take her back with him into the Myst; hell, he hoped he could make it back himself.

"Cousin, do not think that way. You will both be back before you know it. And thanks." Adym heard Raighn speaking softly in his head. His body still hurt from the force of the Myst, so he closed his eyes and slept for a while, waking up when he heard the sound of giggling at the entrance to the cave. He opened his eyes and saw that Nicollete was playfully leading a couple of young Yidderian men into the cave. He rolled his eyes at their thoughts and shook his head over Nicollete's flirty behavior.

Adym adjusted to a standing position, and his movement alerted the two men to his presence. One of them threw Nicollete behind him, trying to protect her from the stranger in the cave. He smiled at the small laugh that she let out.

"You will have to kill them, Adym," she said out loud. The two men turned to her in shock at her words.

"I know. I will need their strength." He froze the two men in place when they attempted to leave. Their fear started to spiral higher and higher. Adym took in a deep breath and felt his eyes begin to glow a brighter blue.

"And to keep my identity safe in case I do not make it back through the Myst with you." She said, and then she stepped out of the cave to give him the freedom to use the istotymir without needing to make sure it did not affect her.

Adym raised the fear of the two men to the point that the first one passed out in his terror. The second one watched with wide eyes as he started to be lifted off the ground. He found himself inside the rocks of the cave wall, his chest slowly being squeezed until he could barely breathe as his fear reached a point where he could not help but cry out. His fear increased exponentially until his last breath left him. The first man roused at the sound and found himself lying on the ground in front of one of the blue monsters that he had seen around the village. He looked at his friend implanted in the wall and felt his fear start to rise until, ultimately, his heart gave out.

Adym breathed in the sweet morsel of fear released at the time of death, and finally, his body began to quit hurting. He teleported the bodies to the middle of the desert so that they would not be found anytime soon, if at all.

"Thank you, Nicollete." He said as he walked out of the cave. "I made sure that the bodies were disposed of so that you can say that they left and you do not know where they went. There is no evidence that they were here." He hugged her and gave her a quick kiss. "I will be back before dark. I need to feed again and then find out some information. Will you be okay here by yourself?"

"I have been okay by myself since the Myst gates closed. A few more hours alone will be fine." She patted his back. "It is you who needs to be careful. You do not blend in as well as I do."

"Yes, but it is I who also can live here without needing to blend in." He said, and then he was gone from her sight.

Adym spent the day feeding at different villages and then finally found who he was looking for. Amalie was on Elynas. He entered her mind and searched for the key.

"Whoever you are, stay out of my head." Adym heard her say in her thoughts.

"I will leave when you tell me where you have taken the key," Adym replied back. He continued searching her mind and found that she did not know where it was. She had given the key to the Prophetess and did not know where it had been placed after that.

"Meet me at the falls?" Adym asked her.

"How are you at the falls? You cannot leave the Myst." She thought back.

"But yet here I am. Will you come and talk to me? I want to understand why." He asked her again.

Amalie laughed out loud and then thought back, "I am not stupid. The minute I go to the falls, you will kill me."

"No, I will not. That is for Tayin to do. I will not take that pleasure from him. I have never hurt you and will not now."

"No." She shouted out loud, and he could feel the fear in her mind and her unwillingness to meet with him despite her wish to be back in the Myst. He let her go and then moved his thoughts to the Prophetess.

Adym searched her mind but found a wall built that he could not penetrate. He knew that the location of the key was in there, but try as he might, he could not break through.

"Hello, Demon." A soft voice that he knew from his two visits with her spoke back to him.

"If you give me the key now, you and yours will not be harmed." He said.

"Both of us know that for the lie it is. I will not release you. I am not the one destined to, and I will hold the key in secret until the one who is meant to release you comes."

"Does Amalie know of this prophecy? Does she know that one day we will be free and coming for her?" Adym asked the woman whose mind was surprisingly strong.

"Not exactly. She knows one day you will be free but does not know how. Now go away, demon, and leave me in peace. I will not give you what is not mine to give. The chosen will hand it to you, and you alone, when she is ready to fulfill the prophecy. Until then, leave the people of Yiddera and me alone." Adym felt her push him out of her mind.

He sat in the cave behind the falls and let the blue water of his gift splash over him as he thought of what the prophetess had said. She had told him that the chosen one would hand the key to him. Did this mean that he would be able to leave the Myst again? Or did this imply that he would be unable to return to the Myst until she had given him the key? He sat there for a while pondering what the prophetess's words meant when he noticed the sun was beginning to set. He knew it was time to bring Nicollete back home. Adym teleported back to a village near Alendrot but on the opposite side of Lioleta from where Nicollete was staying. He called her to meet him at the cave and then took his fill of the fear he would need to take both him and Nicollete back into the Myst. He arrived at the cavern, and Nicollete wrapped her arm around his and, together, prepared to return home.

Adym knew something had gone wrong the minute he touched the Myst. It felt as if a hand had forcefully torn him and Nicollete apart and thrown her back to their starting point. He landed painfully within the Myst gates, and the first thing he saw was the disappointment and pain in Raighn's eyes.

Adym stood up shakily and tried once more to leave the Myst but felt Raighn grab his arm before he could go.

"Cousin, you cannot. I am afraid that trying to leave the Myst again so soon will kill you. I can feel the energy draining from your body." He released Adym and took a step toward the barrier. "Go see Kest, and we can try again at a later time."

Adym nodded his head and then turned toward Nicollete. "I am sorry. I tried."

"I know you did, my friend. I will be okay. Go take care of yourself."

"Before I go. There is a mine on the edge of Elynas down by the ocean that has an abundance of light stones. 'Discover' it, and you can live quite well among the Yidderians. What you make from their distribution will keep you for a few centuries. There is a little cabin built in the forest up the hill from the cave. Claim that as your home, and no one can argue that the mine is yours by right of ownership."

Nicollete nodded her head and then asked, "But how do I get there?"

"There is a shuttle that flies from the Yidderian villages every so often, and there are many ships that sail our oceans. Take one of these to get there. But you need to make sure that you are the one that discovers it, so go quickly."

Adym disappeared from Lioleta and went to Kest in search of sustenance.

For 27 long days, Nicollete did her best to try and blend in with the Yidderians on a daily basis. She had trouble explaining why she did not live in the village with the others and where she had actually come from, as no one seemed to have seen her other than occasionally since they first arrived. Nicollete answered their inquiries with made-up stories of how she kept to herself while on the ship and that now she liked the beach so much that she had made a home within one of the caves near the ocean.

Nicollete knew this was questioned, but Kian always seemed to corroborate her stories, and while she tried to find out why in his mind, she could never find an honest answer there. She left the village every day for long stretches of time to look for any Allurans that may also have been locked out of the Myst and had yet to find another. She would ask Raighn to talk with the Tarikan to see if any of them were on this side of the Myst and, if so, where they were staying so that she might join them. They looked different from the Yidderians, and she could help them get what they needed from the village.

For 27 days, she tried to fit in, and for 27 days, the looks sent her way became increasingly questioning. Nicollete relied on Kian more and more for things that she needed so that she did not have to leave the cave very often. She heard Raighn calling her to help Adym and leaving a note in the cave for Kian that she would be gone for the day; she headed out to visit her brother and see how she could help her cousin.

She did as Adym and Raighn asked of her and then waited for Adym to return from his quest. She took his arm and felt the nothingness of teleporting before coming against the solid barrier of the gates. She was thrown back out of the Myst and knew that it was not possible for her to re-enter her home.

Nicollete watched Adym disappear as he left to find Kest and turned to look at her brother. "I guess it is settled. I cannot get back into the Myst. I will miss you, brother." She said as tears rolled down her cheeks. She tried to hide them, but the finality of knowing she could not go home was a bit much for her.

"Ah, sis, don't cry. It is going to be okay. Do what Adym said, and you can survive this. We will see each other again soon, and before you know it, you will be back here for me to mess up your precious hats." Raighn said, trying to make things a bit lighter for them both.

Nicollete gave a slight smile and nodded her head. "Every year on my birthday, I will be at the Myst gates wherever on Yiddera I may be. We will meet, and I will tell you all of the news that I can. I will search for the key, and if I can find it, I will let you know."

Raighn smiled at Nicollete and put his hand against hers on the Myst. "More often if you can. I will be here whenever you need me to be." He removed his hand and turned to leave. "Now go and do as Adym suggested. Get established as someone important in their world but stay well hidden. In the bright sunlight, you can see that your hair is blue and that your eyes have a slight glow. Keep your hat on, little sister. I love you, and I will miss you." Raighn walked away, and Nicollete ran back to the cave to grieve and make plans for her departure from Lioleta.

For the next several weeks, Adym, Raighn, and Kest took turns sitting with Tayin in the quiet of his room of peace. It was in the third month after Tam's death that Tayin finally stood up and left the room. He was not healed, and he was not who he had once been, but he now knew that he would be able to keep his promise to live. Tayin walked outside to the gardens that he found to be peaceful and decided it was time to try and learn about his enhanced gift. He took a steadying breath and closed his eyes against the pain of these thoughts. He practiced for several hours, knowing he didn't have to, as the moment the two gifts melded, he had perfect control over it.

The wind picked up, the birds chirped a little louder, and things seemed to appear and reappear at random as the three men walked through the immaculately kept gardens. The men usually kept their gifts under tighter control, but today, their minds were focused on the man sitting alone on a bench under a canopy of bright red flowers. This would not have been unusual except that yesterday, that canopy did not exist where it stood today. For that matter, neither did the bench or the pond that the man was studiously watching.

Kest and Raighn sat on the ground, covered in soft, fragrant grass, while Adym sat on the bench next to Tayin. They sat silently for a few moments and looked at the flowers and the pond in wonder. Each one questioned how they came to be there.

"They are illusions," Tayin answered the unspoken questions.

"But they are so real that I can smell the flowers," Raighn replied as he picked one of the blooms. "It feels real."

"And I can feel the coolness of the bench beneath us," Adym stated. He shifted his weight on the solid bench and ran his hand over the smooth stone.

Tayin just shrugged his shoulders. He sat there in silence once again and watched as a fish jumped out of the water and then went back under. He then created some soft pink and purple irises to appear around the far end of the pond. The wind caused them to sway gently and waft their fragrance toward the four of them.

Kest adjusted his position to sit cross-legged and looked up at Tayin. "Tam never created illusions that were this real, and he had centuries of practice. How are you doing it?"

"I don't know. The moment that," Tayin paused and choked back his emotions, "the moment that Tam died and I received his gifts, I felt them meld with mine and have had a perfect understanding of how to use them. The two gifts act as if they were always one." He waved a hand, and the illusions disappeared instantly. Adym fell to the grass and received a sheepish apology from Tayin.

"What else can you do?" Adym asked as he straightened back up and found a comfortable spot on the grass.

"Everything, anything, watch." Tayin looked up at the sky, and the bright morning turned black as night instantly fell. Then he looked around and pointed out the nightmare creatures that started coming out of the shadows around them. The nightmares were ones that many of the humans had dreamt up, and several were from the nightmares of the Allurans. Fantastic bear-like beasts came at them, and the three men sitting around Tayin scooted closer together as the Kahru came closer.

"Adym, go to each of our houses and tell us what you see there," Tayin said.

Adym left, and they all heard an exclamation of "Oh," when he reached Elynas. He showed them that what he saw on Elynas was the same images that they were seeing. He then went to Kest's and then Raighn's house and again saw that it was night everywhere he went, and nightmare images were creeping through the darkness. He arrived back at Kofira and sat once again on the grass.

"How?" He asked again.

Tayin stopped the illusion, and once again, the birds chirped in the crisp morning air. "I can't explain it. I can make everyone, everywhere, see what I want them to. It is similar to how I can get them to dream the same dream. I can make the illusions so lifelike that you smell them, taste them, hear them, and feel them. They are all but real." Tayin lay down in the grass and stared at the cloudless blue sky. His grief over losing his brother and the guilt at mastering his brother's gift so quickly felt like a brick was pressing down on his chest. He concentrated on breathing through the pain and not spreading his emotions to his friends.

"Can you make it spread beyond the Myst? Can your illusions and your nightmares be given to the Yidderians while we are locked in here?" Kest asked.

"Yes, but the Myst grows stronger every day that we are locked in. Someday, nothing will make it through the barrier. Every time I make an illusion appear on the other side, I can feel the slight resistance getting stronger and stronger." He placed his hands underneath his head. "It doesn't matter anyway. We cannot feed on their fear while we are in here, so why bother with the effort."

The other three men looked at each other, knowing that this was true. They had all tried to leave the Myst or cause fear in the ones that were beyond it, and they had all felt that resistance and that inability to reap the rewards of their efforts. They all sat there in forlorn silence for several minutes, each thinking of what would happen if they did not figure out a way out of the Myst soon.

"Friends, we need to discuss our future." Adym began. "We need to decide what to do with the humans that are trapped in here with us and how to find the Yidderian-born Alluran who will release us."

"But first." Interrupted Raighn, "Tayin, could you make us a comfortable place to sit?"

Instantly, the red-flowered canopy was back, along with the beautiful pond. Four chairs with soft cushions appeared next to a round table. Again, the men marveled at their friend's new ability. After they sat and a Tarikan brought them hibiscus lemonade, they began their discussion.

"I do not want any of the Yidderians here," Tayin spoke gruffly. "At this time, I do not trust myself not to kill them all instantly."

Kest, the animal shifter, often thought 'in the moment' as many animals did, but he also had the preparation instincts of those same animals when it came to times of predicted famine. He knew that killing the humans today would cause them all to suffer and go hungry as time went by. Not knowing how long they would be trapped within their own Myst gates, he was more cautious in his ideas.

"I will take them. We will make them a village to live in, next to the LuZivot village on Geltahn. We can feed anytime we need to, but we must be careful not to kill any of them until they build up their numbers." Kest paused for a moment and took a drink. "After a while, we can build villages for them in each of our domains as they increase in numbers so that we each have a supply at hand."

"I can take some of them now," Raighn said. "We do not want to overcrowd you, Kest. Split their numbers in half and send them to me. Make sure there are a number of pretty women in the group you send me, and I will do my best to bring about a blue-haired Yidderian." He smiled wickedly.

The three others laughed out loud at this. As of yet, they had never heard of a woman, Alluran or Yidderian, saying no to him and were sure many would volunteer in his attempt to create the one destined to free them.

Adym, a smile still on his face, nodded his head no. "Cousin, as much as I am sure you would enjoy that, I do not think that the blue girl will come from within the Myst,"

"And why not?" Raighn replied.

"Because, as I told you before, the key is locked on the other side of the Myst from us. Someone out there has to be the one to bring us back the key, as we cannot leave to go get it." Adym paused for a minute, and his voice became quieter. "While you were in your room of meditation, Tayin, I tried several times to leave the Myst, and while I was able to once, it exhausted and drained me greatly. I searched Amalie's mind, but she did not know where the key had been hidden. I do know Amalie took the key to their prophetess, but I cannot find where she hid it." He saw Tayin's jaw clench at the use of Amalie's name. "I have searched her mind, but she is able to push me out of her head. The prophetess says she cannot give me the key as it is not hers to give. Only the one destined to find it and release us can give me the key."

"Maybe the girl born to release us will be able to leave the Myst, retrieve the key, and then bring it back to us," Kest said.

"I do not think so, Kest. I am positive she will be a Yidderian born outside of the Myst gates."

Tayin stood up, and the illusions once again collapsed, leaving the three others on the ground once more. "I do not care what happens with the filthy humans. And as for the one destined to free us, I want her found as soon as possible. I will be free of this cage, and I will get my revenge. Born inside the Myst or out, she will be the priority of every Alluran until she is found and the key is returned to me." He walked away from his friends, leaving them staring after him. His anger caused waves of nightmares to peak from the shadows and follow in his wake. Each of the three was amazed and, whether they wanted to admit it or not, a bit scared of Tayin's powers.

Amalie sat outside of the little chapel that she was using as her home for the time being. She had tried to stay in the room within the monastery that Alena had given her, but she found that the quiet of the chapel and the darkness of the surrounding forest were more calming to her tortured soul.

She sat in the bright light of day, drawing in the sketchbook, which was the only thing she had left, other than memories of her time in the Myst. Amalie only had that since she never went out without her backpack of drawing supplies. She remembered Tam laughing at her over this obsession, but Amalie had replied that she enjoyed drawing the many new plants that she came across when they went out together. He had then taken her to Geltahn to sketch the ghostly trees that grew along the swampy rivers there. She had spent the day deep in her drawings while Tam had visited with Kest.

Amalie drew in a breath and eased the squeezing sensation that always occurred when she thought of Tam. Today, she was trying to exercise the demons she loved from her mind by drawing each of their faces in her book. Maybe then she could begin to heal. Amalie began with Raighn. He was easy to draw, and as he had never expressed any ill feelings toward her, she found drawing him almost relaxing. She then decided to draw a little rain cloud with lightning coming from it. She was unsure why she felt the need to do this, except maybe it helped her remember what his gift was. As if she could ever forget what any of their gifts were.

She went on to draw Kest and then Adym. Amalie turned the page and stared at it blankly for several minutes before she began to sketch. She drew the two men who meant the most to her. First, she drew Tam smiling and with a hint of the love they shared in his eyes. She started softly crying as she drew the face of her love, but tears poured from her eyes as she drew Tayin. She couldn't get the image of his anger and grief out of her head, and so that was the way she drew him. She had wanted to show his kindness but could not. She saw that her tears blurred some of the lines but could not stop them from flowing. Amalie set the sketchbook aside while she tried to control her emotions.

She stood up from the table and walked through the monastery grounds and down into the village. She meandered the main street until she found herself at the edge of town and on the path that led to the falls. Amalie stood debating with herself whether or not to go there. Adym had already shown her that he could leave the locked Myst gates, and though he had promised not to kill her, she was not sure she could believe him. Did she dare go to the falls and sit with her feet in the red pool at the risk of meeting with an angry Adym, or did she turn around now and head back home? No, not home. This side of the Myst would never be home to her.

Amalie continued onto the falls and sat in the cave with her feet in the waters that had once belonged to her love. She saw the images dance in the vapors that formed from the warm waters meeting the cool air. Amalie sat there and thought of what she was supposed to do now. She knew that it was time to visit her son but felt guilty over doing the very thing that she had killed Tam for forbidding her from doing. It felt almost as if going back and hugging her son was dishonoring her love's last wishes.

She smiled in sorrow and knew that nothing she did now mattered to Tam; he was no longer around to fight her over anything. He was no longer around for anything. She laid her head against the cave floor and wept for the loss of such an exciting and vibrant being. She cried for all the pain that her act of anger had caused and would continue to cause. To keep her family safe, she would need to make sure that the Yidderians were terrified to go near the Myst in case they accidentally let the demons out. She had to impress upon them that those who lived in the Myst were demons from hell. She laughed ruefully at the idea that now she was the one causing fear in the Yidderian people in order to keep the Allurans from doing it.

The sun was starting to set in the evening sky, and Amalie walked back to the chapel. Tomorrow, she would let Alena know that she was leaving. It was time to go back to Kahlali. She would take one of the devotees of the Calling, the name Alena had given to the religion, with her so that a church could be set up in her village. She needed a church in every town situated near the Myst to stand as a visible reminder that the Calling taught against the evil of the demons. She needed a reverend to teach the people the need to stay away from the Myst. For someone who did not believe that Y'ddra was a Goddess, she found it ironic that she would be teaching others to view her as one.

The following day, Amalie walked over to the Monastery and found Alena at home playing with her little girl. Amalie sat on the couch and watched the two play for a bit before Alena came over and sat next to her. Amalie handed the sketchbook over to her friend.

"I want you to hold on to this. I have everything in it memorized, and I think that the information you find inside will be beneficial to the healers who come here to learn. There are a variety of plants described in this book that many of the healers will not get the chance to see unless they travel to the different continents or you have the plant brought here."

Alena leafed through the sketchbook and came to the drawings of the five men standing in a circle. She gazed at their faces and could tell Amalie was happy when she drew the picture. She turned the page and gasped at the beauty of the first of the solo drawing.

Amalie laughed at her friend. "Beautiful, isn't he?"

"Is this the one that you loved?" Alena asked.

"No. Though he is loved by many, he is not the one that took my heart." Amalie stood up, walked over to the cabinet that held a pitcher of cool water, and poured herself a drink.

"I have met this one," Alena said as she turned to the page that held the picture of Adym.

Amalie sat back down in a chair across from Alena. "Be careful of him. He is the only one that might be able to cross the barrier. He is the one that is the most concerning to our peace until the gates are opened then, my love's brother will be the demon to watch out for."

"Yes, this one has talked with me since the gates were locked. He has tried several times to find the memory in my head that will show him where the key is. I will be sure to be on guard against him." She looked up at Amalie, noticing the ever-present sorrow that now covered the face of her once-happy friend. "He is the one that lives in the Myst of Alenar, is he not?"

"He is," Amalie replied back.

Alena turned the page and saw the drawing of Kest. Turning another page, she saw two faces, each with a different expression on it. She saw the tear stains that marked the page and knew this was the one that Amalie had killed and loved. She did not comment on it directly but instead asked about the little pictures that she had drawn at the top of the page.

"They are just doodles," Amalie said, shrugging her shoulders. She knew that Alena did not believe her but accepted what she said anyway.

"When are you leaving?" Alena closed the book and placed it on the coffee table.

"I will be leaving tomorrow as that is when the shuttle leaves, which will get me to the boat in time to leave for Kahlali.

"I will miss you, my friend. Will you be back to see me soon?"

"No. This will be the last time that I visit Alenar. I am going to go back to Ethyn and try to make up for the time I was away from him. I am also going to do everything in my power to ensure his safety and that of my future generations."

"Is going back there the right thing for you? Being so close to where you lost everything may be hard for you. Have you thought of maybe moving Ethyn here?"

"I want to be close to my home and to where I can touch the Myst that holds the very essence of my love. I want, no, I need to be close to where my heart died." Amalie sat her glass down and stood up. "I will miss you, Alena. Thank you for all that you will be doing to help protect the Yidderians and my family from the," She felt her throat catch, "the demons that live in the Myst." She hugged her friend and then went back to the little chapel to gather her belongings and wait for tomorrow to come so that she could finally be near home once again.

The captain woke slowly from his fear-induced sleep to find that the strangers had disappeared. He sat up and looked around to see several of his crew making the rounds among the passengers to see if everyone was alright. He shook the last vestiges of night-mares from his eyes and gazed at the pile of children still sleeping peacefully under the shade of a tree. Again, he hoped that they were only sleeping.

"Captain Rais, what happened?" asked one of his bewildered crew members.

Captain Rais stood up and shook the sand off of his clothes. "I am not sure, son, but I think the blue Myst has closed us in here. I do not think that we will be able to leave it now." He walked over to the strange blue barrier and pushed against it. It gave somewhat but would not allow him to exit its boundary. He walked around the cove and tested several areas of the Myst but found it impossible to get through.

The people, bewildered by their recent experience, gathered around the captain, looking for guidance. He stood before them, unsure if he had any to give, but knew they needed him to be the strong one. He closed his eyes and took a deep, cleansing breath before speaking.

"First, I cannot explain what happened to us or why we were brought here, but we are here now and must make the most of it. The strangers were just as surprised as we were that the Myst closed us in. I think they are also locked in, as right before I passed out, I saw they looked shocked that they could not leave. Second, it seems we have been left here to fend for ourselves. We need to find shelter for the night, find food, and make sure the children survived this ordeal." Captain Rais paced in front of the crowd.

"After that, I am not sure. Let us take care of the necessities for now and devise a plan together for tomorrow." He then sent several men and women to bring back wood for a fire to keep them warm throughout the night. Others he sent out to look for fresh food. Several of his younger crew were gathering poles and nets from the ship to fish in the ocean with. And with relief, Rais saw that the children were beginning to stir and waken. They had survived whatever it was the blue-haired stranger had done to them.

The afternoon was fraught with tension as nightmares washed over them in waves. Monsters peeked out from behind trees and rocks, and the children cried in fear. The adults huddled together around the fires that burned brightly along the beach. Finally, after what felt like hours, the nightmares ceased, and the sun once again glowed in the evening sky. Never had the group experienced such fear and uncertainty. As the night fell, some of the party took the kids back to the ship to sleep while others stayed by the fire and tried to sleep on the beach. Unfortunately, every new sound seemed louder than it should have and made their rest fitful at best.

Days passed, and there were no signs of the blue-haired men returning. Captain Rais placed lookouts around the perimeter of the beach and further inland so that if they did return, he would be alerted immediately. They had not found any caves or other natural shelter, so they had constructed basic huts tucked away in the trees and a communal place where they could meet together and still be sheltered from the elements. It was no use hiding. The strangers knew they were there, and further away from the beach, other blue-marked people had been spotted. At this time, staying where they were seemed like the best solution.

Captain Rais set up an election so that four others besides himself could make decisions, and every week, a community meeting was held so that everyone could express their needs or concerns. Soon, the company of people created a working colony. Each person knew what role they played in helping out the settlement. Even the children were given tasks so that they felt useful.

The ship was used as a storage area. While they could have used it for shelter, it was too small to live in daily. The passengers had been bunked in tightly for the voyage as they had expected to create a colony on Lijiang. Much of the space was carrying necessities for their new home. Captain Rais knew they had reached Lijiang, but they had not docked where they had planned to. At this point, he did not want to unload the ship completely. Rais was hoping that soon they could find a piece of land that they could use to create their town, but this was not the spot. The shore was beautiful, but there was not enough room along the beach for growth, and pushing further inland put them too close to a village of the blue-haired people.

Three months passed before one of the fearsome men returned, leading a contingent of others with him. The bright blue-haired man silently pointed to a few of the human's belongings. The people with blue stripes down their faces and chests went to where he indicated and started gathering the items and taking them into the trees. Then, several of them began taking apart the ship. For a brief moment, Captain Rais watched in amazement at how quickly and efficiently they worked.

Rais stepped forward, inwardly shaking with discomfort, and faced the man he recognized. "What are you going to do with us?" He asked, getting right to the point.

He had the weird sensation of hearing a voice speak to him in his head. "I am taking you to my home so that we can build you and your people a settlement. It looks like you will be staying with us for a while." The man shook his head in bewilderment and bounced up and down on his feet like he couldn't stay still.

"I am Captain Rais. Who are you?" He spoke aloud, shaking off the headache that hearing the voice in his head had given him.

"My name is Kest." The man spoke aloud. Kest walked to the shore and looked out at the workers dismantling the boat.

Rais walked over and stood a few feet from him. "Why are we here?"

Kest gave a mirthless chuckle. "You were originally brought here to be fed on and for us to have some fun with, but." He stopped talking and then turned to face the human. "The Myst gates have been locked. There is no way for either of us to leave them. We cannot let you go as we had intended to, and we cannot get out to hunt others. So, our two populations will need to learn to live with each other. Of course, our ways differ from yours, but I think we will settle together quite well with time."

"To feed on?" Rais's eyebrows went up as he asked this. "You were going to eat us? Are you still going to eat us?"

"Not exactly. We feed on the energy of your fear. And yes, we will continue as your group is the only resource left to us, but you will still live, thrive, and grow as a community, and in time, you will come to accept your place in our world." Kest walked away from the beach and sat on one of the benches in the communal hut.

"You are the leader?" He asked and watched Rais nod his head. "Good. Explain to your people that we will work together to build them a new home. I need you to instruct them to gather as much as they can carry and follow the Tarikans to the place you call Malseka. You and I will then decide who will stay there and who will go on to Kruger, I think you call it. You will know best who works well together and who can be trusted to lead your people there. As time passes, we will split the groups again and place them on the three other continents so your village does not become crowded and you all have room to grow."

"And if I do not agree to this?" Rais asked.

"You will, as this is your only option. We can be very persuasive, and you would not like our methods. This is what is best
for you and yours." Kest said before he stood up and left the
building. Once outside its confines, he became a giant rex and
lumbered over to the Tarikan, standing in place as they loaded
him up with more supplies than he could have carried as a man.

Captain Rais sat on the bench, his mouth gaping at seeing
a man becoming a fearsome beast. He knew those around him
also watched the sight with fear and awe. Finally, Rais stood up
and directed his people to join in the task of taking apart their
makeshift homes and following Kest's directions. He was in the
first group to go through the strange nothingness that led to
their new homeland and was pleasantly surprised at the beautiful
area set for their use. He then returned to the beach, finished
helping the others clear the site, and waited until all of his people
were gone before once again stepping into the nothingness of the
Alluran form of travel.

Kest set the Tarikan to work on building a village for the
humans that now took up residence within the Myst. He wanted
to make sure that they were, if not happy, comfortable and had
what they needed to thrive. Like any hunter, he knew that while
it was easy to hunt his prey into extinction, he needed to ensure

they flourished so that he could eat for many years. The captain of the ship they had taken was helpful in letting him know what areas would work for them and how best to make the Yidderians feel at home. The captain, Rais, was very active in helping him build a place for the Yidderians and encouraged his people to aid the strange Tarikan in constructing their homes. As the captain suspected, this made the people feel more in control of their destiny.

Kest had talked with him, and though Captain Rais was obviously afraid of him, he understood that there was no leaving the Myst and that Kest was trying to give them a new home. Kest also knew that Rais was aware of the reason he wanted them to be happy, but neither man spoke aloud of this knowledge.

Captain Rais helped Kest divide the Yidderians into two groups and went with him into the nothing that took them to Kruger to help set up a village there for one of the groups. Kest worked with Raighn to decide where the town should go and found a nice spot adjacent to the LuZivot village. Together, the three men worked to find a way to have a semblance of peace between their different races. It was acknowledged by all that this was their new way of life, and none of the parties were happy about it, but they knew that peace had to occur for the happiness and well-being of all involved.

Over the next few years, both Yidderian villages were thriving, and new little ones were born. Kest looked at each baby to see if any of the infants had blue markings, and soon, it became a ritual for the Yidderians that when a child was born, they were presented to Kest to show that the child was not blue. Even those who lived on Kruger were taken to Malseka and presented, and every time, Kest was disappointed to see not even a blue freckle or highlight on any of the children.

Children born among the Yidderians were educated on the different Alluran races and were made aware of the needs of the SeiOrhii. It was hard to come to terms with at first, but the Yidderians soon learned that being fed on was something that they could not escape, and soon it too became just another part of life. They settled into their new homes, and while it was not what they had expected life to be on the new planet, they were learning to be content.

Nicollete gathered her belongings from the cave and headed out to the ocean. She sat her bag down and thought about how best to stage her death. She was leaving her homeland and heading to Alenar. How strange it was to think of Elynas as Alenar, but she must start calling the places by the Yidderian names if she wanted to blend in. She had said her temporary goodbyes to Raighn yesterday, and today, she was making sure that none of the Yidderians followed her. She was going to try to start life as a Yidderian on Alenar, as Adym had suggested. Nicollete had decided to stage her death to help with this so that she would not have to try and explain to Kian why she was leaving.

She walked out into the calm waves, took the hat she always wore off, and tore the brim. She unraveled part of the ribbon and snagged it upon the rocks so that it would look as if she had been swept out to sea. She watched the hat flutter lightly in the breeze and knew it would stay put until Kian came looking for her later on in the day.

Nicollete turned back toward the shore and saw Kian standing on the dry beach, looking out at her. She reached up to tie the ribbon of her hat more securely on her head before remembering that she had just placed the hat on the rocks. She held her chin up and walked out of the water, coming to stand in front of Kian.

"You were going to leave me thinking you were dead instead of saying goodbye?" He asked of her.

"I felt it would be easier this way." She calmly told him.

"It wouldn't be easier for me." He reached out and took the pins from her hair, causing it to tumble down her back.

"How long have you known?" She inquired as he held her dark blue hair in his hand.

"Always. I saw you walking in the village with who I would guess was your brother, as you two have similar features. I saw you smile at him when Andrew pulled you behind him to protect you from who he thought was trying to cause you harm." He pulled her into his arms.

"Nicollete, I have always known what you were, and I still have chosen to be with you. I know that some of your people mean harm, and I think your brother is one of them, but I know that you do not. I also know that the day you took off running, something big happened. Your face went so pale that I knew that you had not forgotten to do something as you told me you had." Kian walked with Nicollete, sat her down on a nearby rock, and then went out to retrieve her ruined hat. He sat the hat next to Nicollete and then sat down at her feet.

"I followed you and saw you try to reenter the Myst. I watched as you sat and cried, and somehow, I know that you were talking with someone you loved as you touched the Myst."

The two of them watched as the waves rolled across the beach. Nicollete was not sure how to respond, and Kian was trying to figure out how to keep her from leaving him.

"I have to leave here, Kian. I cannot stay. I must get to Alenar to establish a claim on something important so that I can live on this side of the Myst safely." Nicollete said as she ran her hand through his blonde hair and wished she didn't have to leave the one Yidderian she felt safe with.

"Let me come with you. I can help. You can claim whatever it is you need to, and I can get what we need from the Yidderians. Being seen with me will help with your disguise, as no Yidderian will expect one of your people and one of mine to be together. Most Yidderians have never even seen," He paused, "what do you call your people?"

"We as a people are called Allurans."

"Thank you. As I was saying, most Yidderians have never met or seen an Alluran, so they will only see what they expect to see. Please say that I can join you on your journey."

"Kian, as much as I would love to have you come, I want you to be sure that it is what you truly want. You will be putting yourself in danger if it becomes known that I am not Yidderian."

"I will follow you anywhere." He stood up, wiped the sand from his pants, and, taking her hand, led her back to the cave. "Stay here, and I will make the arrangements for our travel. I will get you a new hat and a new dress and meet you here in the morning. There is a ship that leaves tomorrow night for Kahlali, and from there, we can find a ship to Alenar."

Nicollete smiled the first genuine smile she had in days. She had been nervous about leaving on her own. How was she to make sure that she was not noticed on a ship by herself? Now, she would have someone to help her along the journey and in establishing herself as a Yidderian.

The two of them boarded the ship without any trouble and, after one month, finally made it to Alenar. She left Kian at the village hotel and then walked to the Myst on Alenar.

"Adym," Nicollete said and ran her hand over the Myst, making it shimmer and jingle to let him know that she was there.

She only waited a few minutes before both Adym and Raighn showed up. She knew she only had waited that long as Adym had called to Raighn and had waited for him to arrive before they met with her.

"Raighn." She said with a smile. She placed both hands on the Myst and felt Adym put a hand over one of hers while Raighn placed his on the other. Nicollete closed her eyes and leaned her head against the Myst, emotion making it hard for her to speak.

"It is good to see you have arrived on Elynas safely, little sister," Raighn stated.

"Among the Allurans, this place is called Alenar, after the prophetess. I have to start calling everything I have ever known by new names now. It is going to be an adjustment." She smiled. "It is so good to see you both."

Nicollete stepped back from the barrier and looked at both of the men who had arrived to welcome her from her journey. "I cannot stay long as Kian will get impatient and come looking for me."

"And who is Kian?" Raighn asked sternly.

"He is a Yidderian who knows that I am Alluran and is helping me to blend in. He is how I have survived out here so far, so do not get all uptight and big 'brothery' about it. He is safe."

"Nicollete, please take care, and if you feel you can trust him, do, but if he so much as makes you question your trust, get rid of him," Adym told her.

"I will. Now I called you to ask where the cave you were telling me of is exactly." Nicollete stated, getting to business.

"Circle the Myst, and you will find a hidden trail that leads down to the ocean. Continue following the Myst, and you will come across a valley of pine trees. In that valley is the cabin I told you about, and a bit of a walk from there, heading back up the mountain, is the cave." He thought of the directions, and Nicollete saw where she was to go. He pointed out landmarks that would help her and then told her that if she got lost, to call out, and he would show her the way again.

She had him walk through the memory once more and then told him that she would be able to find it. She sat with her brother and her cousin for another hour to talk and catch up on current events before reluctantly reminding them and herself that she had to get back to Kian.

"I expect you back here often so that I can make sure you are safe, dear sister," Raighn told her firmly and then, smiling, sent a raincloud her way and soaked her flimsy dress.

She laughed and then, wringing out her dress, headed back into the village to get changed. Once she had dry clothes on, she told Kian that they were leaving the next day and to please go out and get enough supplies to last them a week or two. She also gave him a list of seeds to buy if they were available. She kissed him and watched as he left to run their errands. Tonight, she would go out with him for dinner, but in the bright light of day, she tried not to walk in the village as her hair, if the sun caught it just right, was more noticeable as being blue than the black most people thought it was.

Kian and Nicollete set out the next morning and walked for half a day, during which Nicollete ran her hand against the Myst gates as long as she could while Kian cringed at having to walk so close to it. He did not complain as he knew she was trying to bring herself comfort. She did not yet realize the fear it elicited in him. They made it to their destination in the early afternoon and found the cabin that Adym had told them about to be quite large and comfortable.

Nicollete could tell the Tarikan had decorated with Adym in mind as it was done in yellows, whites, and dark blues. The colors mimicked those that graced his house in the Myst. She walked into the open living area and found a light stone sitting on the table near the couch. Running her hand across it, the rock lit up with the soft yellow of the stone it lived in.

"How did you do that?" Kian asked, hurrying over to where she stood.

Nicollete handed the stone to him to look at. "It is a light stone and produces light when touched. It will turn itself off after a while. Each stone is different in how long it stays lit depending on its size and color." She watched as Kian ran his hand over the stone and was surprised that it brightened.

"This is amazing." He said as he carefully sat the stone back down on the table and went over to another one that sat on the table by a chair. This emitted a soft blue light and had a calming hum to it.

Nicollete joined him by the chair and wrapped her arms around his waist, resting her chin on his shoulder. "There is a cave not far from here that holds several thousand of these stones. I came here to claim this land because of them. Since Raighn," She saw a look of confusion on Kian's face in the reflection of the window, "My brother." She qualified. "Since Raighn knocked out the resources on the ship you traveled on, we decided that it might be lucrative for me to 'find' the light stones. It will help set me up for the time I am locked out of the

Myst. It will keep me financially sound for several centuries if I am out here that long."

Kian stepped out of her arms and sat on the couch, not quite sure that he had heard her correctly. "Centuries?"

Nicollete stayed looking out the window and realized how much he did not know of her.

"Yes, centuries. I am 314 rotations of the sun and will live to be around 5,000 rotations, give or take a hundred or so." She turned to him and saw that he was surprised but not repelled by her age.

"Okay, so that is something I had not expected to hear." He patted the couch seat next to him, and Nicollete went over and sat against him.

"And your brother is the one that ruined our ship? How? I thought a freak lightning storm did that."

"Raighn controls the weather. He can produce lightning at will," She left it at that, knowing that she had years with him to discuss her family and to learn of his.

"Come, let's look around the house and put away our supplies. Tomorrow, I will show you where the cave is, and then we will need to start building a fence around it and the cabin to claim it as ours. Once I show you the cave, I will head back to the Myst as I have a question for Adym. If any of the Tarikan are locked out of the Myst with me, I would appreciate their help in building the fence." She took his hand, and together, they explored the house while Kian tried to process everything she had told him.

The two put the supplies away and then went into the bathroom to shower. Kian was surprised at the warmth of the water that came from the spout since it was so cold up here in the mountains. Nicollete explained that the water was warmed by thermal heat produced by the many hot springs in the area. After their leisurely shower, the two slept in the big, clean bed that lay in the center of a large master bedroom. Nicollete took all of these things for granted as she was used to living in luxury with her brother, but Kian was overwhelmed at the grandeur and all the foreign-looking amenities that came with the cabin.

The following day, Nicollete took Kian to the caves, and together, they wandered in the cave's brilliance for a while and then went to look at the surrounding area. They decided together where they would like the boundaries of their property to be in relation to the cave and then, hand in hand, walked to the Myst.

Nicollete had not wanted to bring Kian with her, but he had insisted and stated that he wanted to meet her family if he could.

Nicollete had agreed, and now, having run her hand across the Myst, causing Kian to shiver in fear, they waited for Adym to arrive.

Kian could not see through the Myst but knew that someone had arrived on the other side. Nicollete smiled, walked forward, and touched the Myst with a gesture of greeting.

"I am glad that you made it to the cabin, Nicollete. How do you like it?" Adym asked as he appeared at the gates.

"It is lovely. Thank you for its use." She replied. "This is Kian." She turned toward Kian, pointed, and then looked back at the barrier.

"What brings you back here so soon, li uhra," Adym asked her.

Nicollete smiled at being called little one and then went on to explain to Adym that she needed to know if any others had been caught outside the Myst gates.

"There is one Chosin that I know of and a few Tarikan. Should I send them to you?"

Nicollete scrunched up her face, "Not sure I want the Chosin here. He or she?" She looked at Adym in question.

"He."

"He will try to rule us all, and I don't want to have to deal with that at this time. Send him to me in a few years once I am established, but in the meantime, I could really use the help and companionship of the Tarikan." She answered him.

Adym nodded his head and sent a message out to the Tarikan, saying that they were to find a way to Elynas, where a safe haven was waiting for them. Nicollete saw that a few Tarikans were here on Elynas already and were in the process of finding their way to her.

She then spoke out loud for Kian to understand and participate in the conversation.

"How many of the Tarikan can I expect within the next few days?'

"Ten or so," Adym replied, still in her head.

"Kian, can you go into the village and pick up a few bolts of the material that is for sale there? Any color will do, but we will have to make outfits that can hide the Tarikan, as they do not look like any Yidderian and could never pass for one."

Kian nodded his head yes. "I will leave first thing tomorrow morning and be back within a day or two."

Kian winced as he felt Adym enter his mind and then speak to him. "Keep her safe, or I will come for you. I now know your mind and can find you and your fears."

"Adym, for goodness' sake, stop. I am perfectly safe with Kian. I have told you that." Nicollete frowned at her cousin.

"It is alright, Nicollete. He cares for you and is only looking out for your well-being." Kian replied through gritted teeth.

"Adym, let him go, now," Nicollete said sternly.

Kian's shoulders relaxed, and he was able to take a step back further from the Myst and from the one on the other side. He then went over and sat in the trees while Nicollete continued her conversation with the demon on the other side. Kian understood now why the Prophetess preached that the ones in the Myst were demons and why there was a need to stay away from the Myst itself. He did not have any plans to come back should Nicollete choose to visit with her family again. He shuddered to think how it would be to live in a house with more of them.

"They are not as I am. You need not fear the Tarikan. It is the Chosin that might eventually join you that you will need to fear. I will keep him away from you as long as I can, but at some point, he will seek Nicollete out as she is currently the only LuZivot outside of the Myst gates, and he will want her companionship."

Adym said in his mind, causing Kian to stumble backward over a fallen log in his effort to put even more distance between him and Adym.

"Distance will not keep me out now that I know your mind. But I will respect Nicollete's wishes." Adym left Kian's mind.

"Nicollete, if you need me, let me know. I can still leave through the gates if you are in absolute need of assistance."

"I know, but I will not put you through that again. I will let you know when or if I find the key."

"Let me know when the Yidderians produce an Alluran daughter. She is the one who will find the key." Adym pressed his hand to hers and then left back to his house, leaving Nicollete and Kian to walk back to theirs.

Kian took Nicollete's hand and held it tightly to help ease his anxiety over the meeting.

"I told you to stay behind. Though Adym was displaying remarkable effort in not scaring you, I knew that you would not be comfortable with meeting him." She reprimanded him gently.

"That was control?" He asked her.

Nicollete squeezed his hand and smiled. "Yes. You would not be standing if he wasn't trying to make you comfortable."

Within two days, the Tarikan started arriving, and Kian stared at their differences. First, they had a blue stripe that went down their faces, which was obviously why they could not blend in with the Yidderians. The second most noticeable difference was their inability to talk out loud. He had tried to engage them in conversation but found their silence deafening. Nicollete explained that they, in fact, were not very silent, but as they could only communicate telepathically, he could not hear them; she, on the other hand, could and had to work hard to tune them out.

Thirdly, he found that he had no fear of them. Despite their strange looks, they were not scary in any way. They were very polite and helpful and quickly started constructing a fence around their property. Their ability to instantly communicate with each other made it possible for them to coordinate their building with each other while on opposite sides of the intended property lines.

As the days turned into weeks, a total of 32 Tarikan arrived, and within one month, the fence was built. It was not just a plain fence that marked the property lines but a wall that was indeed a work of art. He had never seen such intricate work on such a solid and sturdy piece. He was highly impressed with their abilities.

Kian had brought back the material that Nicollete had requested, and two of the Tarikan made robes and veils out of it. This allowed them to work freely outside without being seen for who they were should a Yidderian pass by. Kian had come up with the idea that might be a way to explain away their inability to talk to the Yidderians. He decided to let it be known that they were a sect of the Calling that had taken a vow of silence in Y'ddra's name. Thus, if anyone came to visit, and he knew that someday they would, the Yidderians would not find it odd that no one but him and Nicollete would speak to them.

YEAR 6

Amalie stood at the beginning of the path that led to where she had once lived. The sky was dark with rain clouds, and Amalie knew they would open soon, but still, she stood there. It had been almost three years since she had walked through that door, three years since she had hugged anyone that now lived inside. While part of her was excited to see her Yidderian family, she was also hesitant. As much as she loved those she was aching to see, the price to see them had been too high. Amalie would reverse time if she could.

She sighed deeply as the clouds poured forth their contents. Still, Amalie stood there and watched the people in the glowing window. They looked happy as they settled down to eat. Amalie watched the happy little family for a few more minutes. Then, knowing she could not hold off this reunion forever, she walked down the path, opened the wooden gate, and knocked on the front door. Amalie waited a few seconds before the door was open, nervous about what to say to them once they answered her knock. She stood there staring into her best friend's face before being gathered up into his arms.

"Amalie. How, when?" He squeezed her tightly, the two of them becoming soaked as the storm strengthened. She let the tears flow down her face and let him hold her as if he never wanted to let her go.

"John, who is at the door?" Amalie saw a very pregnant Micksie walking around the corner to see who had come to visit during such a fierce storm.

John finally let her go and ushered her into the house. Micksie dropped the dishrag she was holding and gave Amalie a big hug. Amalie hugged her back awkwardly.

Micksie led Amalie into the kitchen and set a plate of food in front of her. "You look like you could use a good meal. Would you like something to drink? Coffee, perhaps?" Micksie bustled around the kitchen, gathering a mug and pouring fresh hot coffee into it. "Milk?"

Amalie took the cup from her. "No, thank you." Amalie took a sip of the hot vanilla-scented drink and felt her shoulders relax. Amalie stared at the young boy sitting across from her and marveled at how much he looked like John but with her hair color. Ethyn had gotten so big. When she had last held him, he was barely crawling, and now here he sat, feeding himself and looking like a little boy instead of the baby she had left behind.

"Momma, who is that." Ethyn looked at Micksie and pointed a stubby finger at Amalie.

Amalie felt heartbroken at hearing him call someone else momma, but what could she expect? Micksie had been his momma for far longer than she had. Tears streaming down her face once more, she answered him.

"Hi, Ethyn. I am," she hesitated and came to a hard decision. "I am Amalie, a friend of your mom and dad."

"Are you sure, Amalie?" John asked her, knowing her heart was breaking as she decided not to tell Ethyn who she was to him.

"Very. We will talk about it later." Amalie smiled weakly and continued eating the delicious food that Micksie had sat before her. John nodded his head. They finished their meal in silence.

Ethyn let out a big yawn, and Micksie scooted her chair out to help him down from his and then took him to get ready for bed. She hesitated momentarily and looked at Amalie, "Do you want to help him get ready for bed?"

Amalie stared at her son and knew all she wanted to do was hold him tight, but she also realized that he did not know her and so told Micksie no. John and Amalie watched the two of them leave the room.

"I thought it would be easier on him, so I never corrected Ethyn when he called Micksie momma. We will tell him tomorrow who you are." John sipped his drink and then sat it back down on the table.

"No, it is best that he thinks she is his mother. I have much to tell you, but I am not sure exactly where to begin." Amalie stood up and walked into the living room. The couch had been moved, and a different blanket was thrown across its back. The curtains that framed the picture window were a bit frilly and reflected Micksie's personality, yet were a soft brown and green plaid that fit John's. She smiled as she stood by the window, looking out at the garden and what had once been her greenhouse.

"Here." John handed her a thick robe. "You remember where the bathroom is. Take off those wet clothes and put this on. You will be more comfortable. I will take your bag and leave it in the room next to Ethyn's."

Amalie took the robe and wandered down the hallway, looking at the many changes that had been made to the décor. She would have to find a place to live starting tomorrow. She could not stay here where everything reminded her of the past and yet looked so different. Amalie wanted something that looked out onto the beauty of the Myst. She took a quick shower and changed into the soft robe before returning to the living room.

Seated on the couch, John and Micksie were cuddled together, talking quietly. When they noticed Amalie walk into the room, they scooted slightly away from each other.

"Please don't. It makes me happy to see you two so happy together." Amalie stated as she sat down on the chair underneath the window. "When are you due?" She asked Micksie.

"In a couple of weeks," Micksie replied. "Amalie I."

Amalie interrupted her by putting up her hand and shaking her head no. "Micksie, there is no apology to make. I have known for many years now that you have always loved John. And John, I heard you that day talking outside of the Myst. The following year, I returned to that spot and saw you two with Ethyn. Thank you for bringing him to that spot. It was wonderful to see him after so long. With what John said and seeing you all as a family, I knew that you two were always meant to be together." She tucked her legs underneath the robe and on the chair beside her. "I cannot honestly say that it didn't bother me at first, but I, too, found the love of my life, and I understood." A look of sadness spread across Amalie's face, and she closed her eyes to try and keep her composure.

She breathed out slowly and then continued. "I am not here to try to get back what once was. I am here to see Ethyn and to make sure that he and his future children stay safe. I am here because there is no way for me to get back into the Myst, and even if there was, I would not be welcomed there anymore." Her voice hitched, and she took another deep breath, exhaling slowly.

"You would want to go back?" John asked.

"If I could rewind time, I would run through the Myst as fast as I could and never look back. But I can't. I will not go into the details, but we need to discuss Ethyn's future. Tonight, I am too tired to make plans. I came here tonight because I have nowhere else to go."

"You are welcome here anytime," John stated, ignoring the slight frown that flitted across Micksie's face.

"Thank you, but we would all be more comfortable if I stayed elsewhere." Amalie stood up, "Are any of my herbs and other research tools still in the greenhouse?"

"Yes, we placed the equipment in the cabinet at the back of the building, and the herbs are still growing in their pots where you left them. They are well marked as we are unsure what some of them are used for, and we did not want to confuse them with Micksie's cooking herbs."

"Is the cot still in there?" Amalie asked.

"Yes, but you do not have to sleep in there. You can use the guest room for as long as you need." John replied.

Amalie headed toward the guest room to get her bag. "No, I will stay in the greenhouse. I will keep you awake if I stay in here. It would be unfair to put you through the nightmares that my mistake cost me."

"Nightmares?" Micksie asked.

"They are a gift and a curse from my love's brother." She answered, knowing they would not understand. She grabbed her bag and then left through the back door to the greenhouse. Memories assailed her senses as she entered the building. While it smelled different, the table and the small daybed were still in the same place. Amalie sat her bag on it and then gathered a few of the herbs growing in one of the pots. She mixed two of them together, crushing them so their juices would blend, then swallowed the mixture, washing the bitter taste away with some water. Hopefully, she would get a few hours of sleep with their help before Tayin began her nightly torture.

Amalie woke up to a little face peering over her. Ethyn's face was like a balm to her tortured mind, so she stayed very still, hoping the angel above her would not disappear.

"Are you awake?" He whispered.

"Yes." She whispered back.

"I have a picture of you in my room." He stated matter-of-factly.

"You do?" Amalie said with excitement in her voice.

Ethyn crawled up on the edge of the twin bed and waited for her to sit up before he finished getting comfortable next to her.

The little boy nodded his head. "Yes, and I was told it was my first mommy but that she went away. I forgot about my first mommy until I saw you. Are you?" He inquired.

"Micksie is your mommy, honey," Amalie stated as a non-answer.

"Oh." Ethyn leaned against her, "Well, you look like my first mommy. Can I hug you?"

Amalie blinked back the tears and smiled down at her precious angel. "I would like that very much." Ethyn scooted up in her lap and gave her a big hug. Amalie had to keep herself from squeezing too tightly as she held the one she had lost everything for.

Micksie walked in, and Ethyn gave Amalie a quick kiss. Then he jumped up and went running to his mom. "Momma, she says she is not my first mommy, but she looks like her, huh?"

Micksie scooped the child up and gave him a quick snuggle before setting him back down. "She does. Run along outside and help dad with the chickens and then wash up for breakfast." She ruffled his hair and watched as he went running out the door.

Amalie watched the scene, and instead of feeling jealous, her heart seemed to ease. "You are a great mother, Micksie. Ethyn is lucky to have you." She stood up from the bed and began folding the blankets to put them back in the drawers she had taken them out of last night.

"Why did you tell him that you were not his first mommy?" Micksie said as she leaned her belly against the table.

"It is best that he not know that he is related to me. And besides, I do not want to cause him any confusion. You are his mother now and have been since I went into the Myst." Amalie carried the blankets over to the chest and placed them inside.

"Why did you go into the Myst?"

"I was tricked by a very clever demon." She smiled a sad smile at the memory.

"Did he trap you in there?"

"Yes and no. I was not allowed to leave, but then I never really tried hard to. I did not want to leave him."

Micksie shifted positions and watched Amalie tug on her shoes. "If you did not want to leave him, then why did you?"

"He died, and I found myself no longer welcome in the Myst." She said more curtly than she had intended to. "I am sorry, Micksie. I didn't mean to be rude. It is just hard for me to talk of."

Micksie nodded her head in understanding. "Well, let's not talk of it then. Come, let's make breakfast, and then we can discuss what to do next." She slid off the chair and walked out of the expansive greenhouse, stopping to pick a few fresh basil leaves first.

The two women went into the house, and Amalie sat at the table while Micksie whipped up fluffy waffles, eggs flavored with basil, and hot orange spiced tea. While she watched Micksie cook, she thought about how much she should tell them about her time in the Myst. Amalie decided that she would tell just enough to make them understand the importance of Ethyn not knowing he was related to her. She realized that Tayin knew he did, but she was hoping that Ethyn's children and grandchildren would grow up not knowing, and eventually, there would be no one left alive who knew they were descended from her. If they did not know, then Tayin could not see the relationship to her in their minds, and so her descendants might be spared his pain.

John and Ethyn came in from the barn and, after washing up, sat down at the table laden with delicious food. They ate in relative silence, with Ethyn taking surreptitious glances at Amalie and smiling shyly at her. She smiled back at him often and felt joy fill her heart at seeing him once again. This little boy had cost her so very much, and while it was wonderful to see him again, she cried inside at her loss, once again wishing she could turn back time. It hurt to know that because of Tayin's promise, she must disown the very one she had so wanted to see.

After breakfast, Micksie took Ethyn with her to the bakery in town, leaving her and John alone to talk.

Amalie toyed with her glass, not sure where to start, when John told her to stop fidgeting and just tell him what she needed to say. She smiled in remembrance of how well he knew her.

"Okay then. I made a mistake while in the Myst that has put Ethyn in danger." She began.

"Start at the beginning. Tell me what the mistake was and how it endangers him, and then we will figure out how to resolve the problem." John, ever the pragmatist, replied.

"I fell in love with one of the," She hesitated, knowing that it was important for everyone to think the worst of those in the Myst but hated it at the same time. "Demons." She finished.

"What made you fall in love with someone that you think of as a demon?'

"He was everything to me and more. I will not go into the details of how and why I fell for him." Amalie said quietly.

John sat his cup down and looked over at the woman he had loved for most of his life, crying over another man. He loved Micksie, but part of him would still always love Amalie, and it hurt him to watch her cry over a man she called a demon and know she had chosen that demon over him.

"Did you miss me at all?" He asked her.

Amalie looked into his serious eyes and frowned. "Very much. John, you are and always will be my best friend. It was not easy being away from you, but." She held up a finger to silence him when he started to interrupt. "We both know now that we were not meant for each other. I do love you, and I missed you while in the Myst."

"And if I feel that we are meant to be together?" He fingered the rim of his cup in agitation.

"You don't. I see how you are with Micksie. She is the one that you are in love with."

"You are right, I am. She is who my heart belongs to." He leaned back in his chair, "But sometimes I wonder what it would be like now if you had not wandered off into the Myst."

"I did not wander willingly. I thought I was following a child and did not want him to get too close to the gates. But that is neither here nor there. I entered the Myst, and I lived there for over two incredible years. I would be there still if it were possible, but it isn't."

She took a calming sip of her tea. "I will tell you why I call them demons so that you can understand the seriousness of the rest of what I have to say."

"They feed on the fear of other species. The demons gain strength and power from our fear and pain. They also enjoy the torture of our kind. They do not have to kill us, but they do, as they find it amusing. They do not have to make us crazy with fear, but they do so because it is fun for them."

"And you loved one of these evil creatures?" He asked, a look of revulsion crossing his face.

"Head over heels." She said simply before continuing. "The more that you fear, the more they grow in strength. It keeps them immortal."

John looked up at her with a worried expression. "They are immortal?"

Amalie nodded. "Not all of them, but the demons are."

"And the one you loved is immortal?" John asked.

"Yes, he was immortal." She smiled sadly.

"Was?"

"Yes. I killed him, but I didn't mean to. We were arguing, and I hit him with the claw I held in my hand. How was I to know that it would kill him? Nothing I had ever done had hurt him before. I still don't understand how it could have hurt him." Tears flowed quietly down her cheeks. She wiped them away and continued.

"His brother has sworn revenge against me and my future generations. He swore he would kill all of those within my bloodline once he was out of the Myst. John, he is the most powerful of them all, and when my love died, he received his brother's gift, making him even more dangerous than he was previously." Amalie stood up and walked over to the kitchen window, which looked out in the direction of the Myst.

"Someday, they will find the key that I stole, and they will be free. Someday, the demon in the forest will come for us, and he cannot be stopped. It is best that no one knows that Ethyn and I are related. Ethyn must never know that I am his true mother. If it is lost to time that I am related to him, then maybe his future children will survive the wrath of the demon that I fear the most."

"I do not understand the compassion I hear in your voice for a being that has threatened to hurt you and our son. I do understand the need to keep Ethyn safe, though. There is a clearing on the other side of the village, deep in the woods, that I think will suit you. The townspeople will help you build there if you choose to stay. Being across town will put distance between you and Ethyn, and this may help them forget who he was born to. Most people here think Ethyn is Micksie's, and those that know he is not will forget as time passes." John pushed away from the table and stood next to Amalie at the window.

"I will gather some of my farm hands, and we will begin clearing the area to build today." He placed his hand around her waist and gave her a little squeeze. "You will like it there. It has a clear view of the Myst." He released her and left her standing alone at the kitchen window.

Amalie slipped off her shoes and walked out onto her back patio. She stepped off the stairs and onto the grass, feeling the dampness of dew seep between her toes. She smiled up at the morning sun, then set out across the yard and out of the far gate. Amalie thought of Tam with each step that she took. It was exactly one year since he had died. It had been the hardest year that she had ever lived through.

The act of anger that had changed so many lives had also kept her from the person that she had done it for. Her desire to see Ethyn in person had led her to the impulsive act, and now she had to stay away from him and not let him know who she was in order to protect him. While hard, Amalie could live with the consequence of her reckless action because it kept her little one safe.

What she could not live with was knowing she would continue to wake up alone for the rest of her life. Tam had said she was his Korsyon in all ways that mattered, and Amalie knew this to be true. Every single day, she felt as if she was slipping away. Her heart broke anew every morning that she woke up and realized that the nightmares Tayin sent her were not just nightmares. Amalie was not sure how much more she could take.

She arrived at the barrier between where her heart had died and where her body now stood. Amalie reached up a hand and ran it along the Myst. For the first time, she felt not the tingle of excitement but of fear run up her arm. Amalie knew that Yidderians felt fear when close to the wall, and if they touched it, their fears flooded their minds, causing them to back away, but she had never experienced it. She touched it again and, gritting her teeth, pulled her hand away. It still held the feel of Tam, but Tayin's anger was the stronger feeling she got when touching it.

"What do you want?" growled Tayin as he stepped toward her.

Amalie noticed that she could not see through the Myst as clearly as when she had first exited it.

"Stop the nightmares." Amalie blinked her eyes to rid them of the creepers that ran the edge of her vision.

Tayin pulled in his illusions, and Amalie saw that the images were still there but not as noticeable.

"What do you want, Amalie?" Tayin asked again.

She placed a hand on the Myst and managed to keep it there, and the longer she held it against the barrier, the more the fear began to dissipate, and she once again felt the warm tingle she had come to expect. She sighed in pleasure and thought briefly of the first time she had stepped through the barrier and found Tam waiting for her.

"I wanted to once again tell you how sorry I am. I know that you will never believe me, but I didn't mean to hurt him. I would do anything to change the outcome if I could."

An angry laugh escaped Tayin. "Anything? Nothing you can do will ever make what you did okay. Nothing you can do will change anything. I have to live every day knowing that he is not coming back. His gift now is mine, and it is a painful reminder of both you and him. You murdered the one that you claim to have loved, and for what? Nothing."

"Not nothing. I was angry because of his unfounded jealousy. He threatened my son's life." She yelled back.

"But you know that you could have come to me, and I would have fixed things for you. Instead, you killed him. You took the most important person to me away." Tayin laid his head against the blue shimmer, and Amalie saw tears flowing down his face.

Amalie stepped away from the Myst. "I came here today not to argue but to share in your grief. I did an unforgivable thing, and I cannot undo it, though I wish that I could. I mourn him with every fiber of my being, and I needed to be with someone today who mourned as deeply as I do."

"We do not mourn the same." Tayin looked up at her, and hate glimmered in his eyes. The nightmare illusions that he held at bay broke free and surrounded Amalie, causing her to fall to her knees and wrap her arms around her head, trying to keep them away.

"Tayin, stop. Please," She cried.

"Bring me the key, and I will spare your young one. You will die, and it will not be pleasant, but bring me the key, and I will make sure he does not see the nightmares."

Amalie looked up at him and knew that what he said was partly true. He would not hurt Ethyn while he was young. Amalie could see in Tayin's eyes that once Ethyn was an adult, he would be the victim of revenge against her.

"I do not know where it is, and I cannot give it to you." Amalie trembled as the visions became stronger. She looked at the body of Tam lying in front of her. She could feel the stickiness of his blood as it covered her and could smell its metallic tang.

She could hear him gasping for breath like a sadistic soundtrack playing over and over again.

Tayin had so much more control over the illusions that were once Tam's. Tam could make them visually real, but you could not touch or feel them, nor did his illusion smell. Everything about the ones Tayin created felt real to her senses.

"Do not bother me again unless it is to release me from the prison that you have locked me in." Tayin left her sitting there crying. He vanished the nightmares and left her in the bright sunshine, the birds singing as if nothing was wrong in the world.

She sat there and cried for all that she had lost, for all that Tayin had lost. Amalie knew that today would be hard, but she had hoped that Tayin would have realized by now that what had happened had been an accident. She had hoped he would look inside her mind and find her love for Tam and know that she was in as much agony as he was.

Amalie stopped her tears and thought of pleasant memories of their time together, and she smiled at many of the ones that crowded in her mind. She remembered the day that they had gone to the Rainbow Falls together. They had taken a picnic lunch with them and swam in the lake below the falling water.

It had been a cold winter day, but the warmth of the water made swimming pleasant.

"No." she heard from inside her head, and the pleasant memory vanished to be replaced by the memory that was never far away. And so Amalie once again was subject to Tayin's torture. He was always in her mind, never allowing her peace. Never allowing her to remember anything about her time in the Myst without showing her Tam's death. As if she needed his help remembering that particular memory. It was a vision that would never go away.

YEAR 7

THE MYST HAD BEEN closed for two years, and in that time, Nicollete had turned herself into a highly respected member of the Yidderian world. With Kian's help, she opened a store in the village just outside of the Monastery grounds. It was there that they sold the light stones that they "found." Since there was no other light source at this time, these became highly sought after and made Nicollete very rich.

Now, she was sitting outside the Monastery with the Prophetess and discussing how the building was coming along. Nicollete, as always when she left her house, was wearing what had become her signature large hat. She had it tied just below her chin with an elaborate orange bow. She had found that the orange tamed the color of the blue and made her hair look darker and blacker. After this long living in the Yidderian world, she knew that she passed easily as one of them, but she still did not want to slip up.

"Do you think that the light stones will work in the Monastery as a type of main lighting?" Prophetess Alena asked her.

"I do, but they will need to be of the larger yellow variety to light up the bigger rooms. I would still keep trying to figure out a way to use the sunlight to help light up the building where possible. Many of the smaller stones will work well in the sleeping quarters and hallways." Nicollete replied.

"I was thinking of using the top floor as the artists' rooms. This will allow them to have natural light since we can put glass in the ceiling to allow the sun to shine through. I also thought the bigger yellow or white stones could be used there in case of overcast days." Alena commented back.

Nicollete put a hand up to shade her eyes as she looked toward the massive building. "The spot you chose for your new home is perfect, and the glass roof will allow an abundance of natural light in. I think that you may want to continue using candles for a while until you adjust to using the stones. They take a while to learn to use, and we are finding new applications for them daily. One of their downfalls is that they do need complete darkness to recharge periodically." Nicollete looked back at the Prophetess and smiled. "It seems odd that the sun does not charge them, but having found them shining in a dark cave led me to experiment, and without a doubt, they replenish their, "battery," if you will, best in complete darkness."

"Thank you for your advice, Nicollete. I will let you know how many we will need for the first-floor rooms, and then as we continue building, I will put in an order for the rest."

"Prophetess, are you sure you will not take them as a donation? I am happy to be of service to the Calling."

Alena laughed a light, airy laugh. "Heavens, no, I would not consider it. You have already discounted them very generously for me, and I do not expect or want more."

The two women continued walking along the building until they came to the hedges, about chest height, that outlined the maze. Nicollete looked at the path and saw a beautiful fountain placed in the middle of the labyrinth. She pointed at it and asked the Prophetess why they had chosen that particular design. It was a sculpture of a man with long hair, and from his outstretched hands, lightning seemed to flash. The water splashed up from small points along his arms and head, making it look like it rained down on top of the artwork. Then, it fell into a round pond that held brightly colored fish.

"It represents an old Earth god that was supposed to have the power of lightning. I liked the idea that it also represented the strange lightning that made it impossible for us to leave Yiddera. The sculptor that created it is fascinated with old Earth mythology." The Prophetess shrugged her shoulders. "I liked the way it looked and had it turned into a fountain. Do you like it?" She inquired of Nicollete.

"Very much." She replied a bit sadly.

Prophetess Alena looked at her, "And, yet, it saddens you?"

Nicollete nodded. "It reminds me of my brother." She made her way along the hedges and came to sit on the wide lip of the fountain pond. Nicollete ran her hand in the water, which was made warm by the many underground hot springs.

Prophetess Alena sat down next to her. "He is gone? Did the demons take him from you?"

"In a manner of speaking." Nicollete smiled ruefully. "I know that you do not want to accept any more donations from me, but I would like to donate a few of the rare blue and purple lightstones to shine up at the rain caster. It would bring me joy if you would allow me to do this."

"I think that would be a great idea. It will honor your brother while making the sculpture even more magnificent." Alena paused. "But why the blue? A few of the yellow ones would make it look as if sunshine was coming through the rain."

"My brother is partial to the blue and purple colors. And I would like to see them shining in the rain."

"May I ask how he died?" Alena adjusted her position to look more fully at Nicollete.

Nicollete smiled again and, laughing softly, splashed the water once more. "He disappeared the day the Myst gates closed." She said evasively.

"Ah, he was one of 'The Lost.' Do you think that the ship was destroyed upon reaching Lijiang, or do you believe, as a few others do, that they became trapped in the Myst once it locked?"

"The Myst was impenetrable to the Yidderians prior to the Myst closing. What makes you think that they could possibly be locked in there with the Allurans?"

"I do not believe they are. I believe they were capsized before they reached Lijiang once the darkness covered the world on that fateful day."

"Yes, that makes sense. I think that is a good explanation as to what happened to them. The SeiOrhii that caused the darkness and the nightmares to occur caused much destruction that day in his grief." Nicollete, usually cautious with her words, said.

"In his grief?" Repeated the Prophetess softly. "I have only heard one other person use the term SeiOrhii. Why do you use it?"

Nicollete realized her mistake and made to rectify it. "I met one of them years ago, and he said he was a SeiOrhii. It was a strange word, so I remembered it."

"And why do you think the darkness was caused by the grief of one of them?" Alena looked at Nicollete in speculation.

"The darkness felt sad to me." She stated simply. Nicollete stood up and walked toward the labyrinth's exit. "I thank you for the conversation and the order of so many light stones. I will add the purple and blue ones to the shipment and have them delivered to you by the end of the week. Now I must hurry back home. If you need anything else, just let me know." Nicollete left the Prophetess sitting on the fountain bench and knew that she was mulling over their conversation. What conclusions the Prophetess drew from it, Nicollete could not help.

YEAR 10

IT HAD BEEN FIVE long years. Five long years in which every day, she felt that her heart no longer beat. Five long years of making sure that no one would ever open the Myst gates. That no one would ever suffer the demons again. Five long years in which she wished every day that she had died with him. No, five long years in which she regretted her impulsive action, the action that led to his death. Five very long years.

But today, it would be all over. She had one thing left to do, and then she could join him. She had done everything she could to make sure that Ethyn and his future children stayed safe. Amalie had worked hard to get the village to fear the Myst and those it contained. She made up stories of their evil so that no one would be inclined to release those within. She made sure that the Demons were the stuff of nightmares. The only thing that she had done that was honest to her true feelings was to create a fountain in the center of town that was a replica of the

Rainbow Falls, and on the stones next to the red crystal pond, she had engraved the words *"My heart is forever entwined with yours."* No one but herself and John knew that this was written there or what it meant.

The SeiOrhii talked of the Korsyon, the bond in which two of their own became one and loved for all eternity. Each felt the other's heartbeat next to their own, and this entwining of hearts meant that if one died, so did the other. While she had never shared the Korsyon with Tam in the way the Allurans thought the Korsyon worked, she knew that she had bonded with him forever. It was true that if bonded when one died, so did the other. It just happened that her death took five years. Every day of that five years away from him had left her dying a little more than the last, but she knew today would be her last. She could not go on any longer.

Amalie made it to the barrier that separated her from where her heart longed to be. She laid a hand on the warm Myst and felt the magic of the Allurans tingle her palm. She closed her eyes and enjoyed the sensation for a few moments, remembering the happiness and the pain she had experienced on the other side of this wall. It was this exact spot where Tam had first appeared to her and this same spot where he had tricked her into following him into the Myst. It was at this very spot that her heart quit being her own.

She shook her head and ran her hand along the Myst, her other hand holding tightly to the little glass bottle in her pocket. She watched as waves shimmered along the Myst as she touched it. Amalie knew that Tayin would come. He always did. After a few minutes of waiting, she began to pound on the Myst. She started panicking. This could not be the day that he chose to ignore her. She needed to see him on this day, on this anniversary of her love's death.

"Tayin." She called and waited again. When no answer occurred, she started pacing the area, running her hand continuously on the barrier, knowing it would annoy Tayin.

"Tayin, I know you can hear me. You owe me this visit." Her yell frightened a few birds out of the surrounding trees. She watched them fly away, squawking at her for disturbing them.

"Damn you, Tayin, answer me." Tears started flowing down her cheeks as she called out for him. Amalie had to see him today because she needed to see his face one more time. She needed to see the face that so matched that of Tam. It had to be today since she was losing her ability to see through the light blue Myst. This was the last chance she had to see his beautiful face.

She screamed louder and pounded again on the barrier. "Tayin, get your ass down here. After years of being haunted by you, of having nightmares every night, you owe me one more visit." She watched as he suddenly appeared and she knew that he had been there the whole time. He had used Tam's illusions to hide himself. She stared at him for a few seconds before looking away.

His face, identical to her love, was filled with hate, anger, and grief. She felt shame to have put that look on Tayin's face. He was the friendly one, the happy one, the one SeiOrhii who cared for everyone, even the Yidderians. He was the one who went out of his way to make her feel more at home with the SeiOrhii. He was the one quick to laugh and slow to anger. In his fury, he looked more like his brother than ever, except for the grief. Tam's face had never expressed despair. Often anger, a few times hate, but never grief. He was the fiery twin, the one her heart cried for.

"What do you want, Amalie?" Hate filled the deep voice.

She looked into his eyes once again, eyes the perfect blue of the Alluran moon, eyes that looked at her in hate. She took a deep breath and answered his question.

"Take my life. You swore that once you were free of the Myst, you would take my life and that of my family." She stepped closer to the barrier and placed both hands on it.

"Take my life right now and then swear to me that you will not hurt my family, that you will forget about them, and I will give the key back to you." She braced herself and tried to bury the lie and make it seem like it was true. She felt him enter her mind to find the truth behind her words, and try as she might, she could not keep him from seeing that they were a lie. She did not intend to free the SeiOrhii.

Tayin stepped closer to her. "Why do you bother lying? You were never able to hide your thoughts from me. From Tam, yes, but never from me. No one can hide their thoughts from me. You know that. So why try?" His voice was genuinely curious.

She chose not to answer him, though she was sure he would find the answer on his own. He was still in her head. Instead, she reached into her pocket and took out the small vial she held.

"Will you take my life or not, Tayin?" She asked forcefully.

"No." Was his simple yet devastating reply.

She opened the bottle and quickly drank the contents, knowing she only had a few minutes before the poison inside would do what Tayin was refusing to.

"Stay with me and take the fear at the end of my death. I do not want to die alone." She sat on the grass and folded her legs up underneath her.

Tayin looked down at the woman who ruined his life and sneered at her pretty face. "You ask this favor of me after what you have done? Can you not see that what you did has damaged me, too? That I am unraveling and losing control? Your pain is nothing compared to what I suffer and will continue to suffer." He watched her face start to turn white, and her breathing grew ragged.

"No, I will not stay and watch you die. I will not take the fear that you offer. You deserve nothing from me." He walked as close to the Myst barrier as he could and entered her mind one last time.

"I will be free once more. I do not know when or how I will be released, but I will, and when that day comes, I will hunt everyone in your bloodline down, and I will kill them. I will torture them as slowly and painfully as you have tortured me. Every day for all eternity, I must live with the memory of what you did. I now live with the gifts belonging to Tam that you so painfully gave me. No, I will not ease your death or your conscience." He paused for a moment before continuing.

"Know that I count the days until I can eradicate every last one of your descendants from Yiddera. Die knowing that you can do nothing to stop this." He turned his back to her and began walking away.

"Tayin, please, stay. I do not want to die alone." She laid her head down on the grass and cried. She knew that she deserved his scorn, his anger, but she wanted his forgiveness.

"You will never get my forgiveness. I do not care that you are in pain over your thoughtless act. I do not care that you do not want to die alone. You have sentenced me to an eternity of pain, and so in your last moments, you deserve to feel that same pain. That same sorrow. That same feeling of being alone." He walked away and never looked back.

Amalie lay on the grass, looked up at the bright sky, and watched the birds as she took her last few breaths. Her heart slowed, and her mind became fuzzy, and in the last moment of life, she saw Tam's face. She knew that whether he had wanted to give her this memory or not, Tayin had given her a gift. His thoughts of Tam, on this day marking the fifth anniversary of his death, flooded her mind. She was not dying alone.

Ten years, Amalie had been on this planet for only ten years. Alena cried over the news of her friend's suicide. Despite knowing that Amalie's life since leaving the Myst had been a living nightmare, Alena had never thought that Amalie would choose death. She wondered how John was taking the news and knew that it was probably not well. She needed to send him a letter reminding him not to tell Ethyn that he was related to Amalie. It was Amalie's wish that he and his future children remained safe should the time come that the demons were set free.

Alena sat at her desk and wiped the tears away. She reread the missive that was sent to her by the emissary who lived at the priory in Kluane. Amalie was found lying next to the Myst, a vial of poison in her hand. The note included the vial so that Alena could have the contents analyzed, as they could not figure out what was in it at the priory. Knowing the monastery had a wide variety of plants from around the world, they hoped that the botanists and healers on Alenar could identify the contents. A small fabric bag that contained a handful of seeds was included in the missive. Alena, having read Amalie's notebook, knew what they were and why Amalie had written her name on the bag to make sure that she got them. They were a last resort.

Alena set the small bottle, the bag, and the letter aside and pulled out a fresh page to begin writing her condolences to John.

My dearest friend,

I am so sorry to hear of your loss, of our mutual loss. Amalie was our friend for so long it is hard to think of her as being gone. Even while in the Myst, she was still with us, and we knew that one day we would see her again. Today, I have learned that she has chosen to no longer live on Yiddera. I know that you were closer to her than any of the rest of us were, and I cannot begin to imagine your pain. Cry for her, grieve for her, but I implore you to remember her wishes.

Amalie died because she was being tortured nightly by the demons in the Myst and by her own dreadful memories. She worked hard to ensure that those of us on this side of the Myst were safe from the demons within, and I want to remind you that Ethyn is the one that she wants most protected.

Ethyn is the one who will be hunted by those within now that Amalie is gone. Keep him safe, John. Do not let him know that he is Amalie's son. He must forget so that his children and grandchildren will not know. It is only by keeping them ignorant of their lineage that they will be safe. The demons will penetrate their minds and search for every tiny clue they can find to see if they are of Amalie's bloodline. The demons have sworn to wipe them out. But how can they if they do not know who they are looking for?

John. I know you. I know that right now, you are contemplating telling him as you feel he has the right to know, but you are wrong. Telling him would be signing his death warrant. Honor Amalie by keeping this secret for her. You know that this is what she would want.

I will always be here for you should you need me. I grieve with you, and my heart wishes that things had been different.

My love and prayers,

~ Alena

Alena reread her letter, and though it didn't quite express what she wished it to, she folded it and then sealed it into an envelope. She pulled the bell rope, and an acolyte came in. Taking the letter from her, he promised he would take it into the village immediately so that it could go out in the mail right away. Alena told him to have the shuttle take it immediately and not wait for the boat to take it to Kahlali. She watched the letter leave her office and hoped that the three weeks it would take to get to John was not too late. She hoped that he had not already told the young boy who he was. She hoped that John would be clearheaded enough to know that Ethyn was in danger and that telling him Amalie was his mother would increase that danger.

Alena's letter reached John, and he respected both Alena's and Amalie's wishes until Ethyn turned 21. At the time of his son's birthday, John took him to the spot where Amalie had died and told Ethyn the story of his birth and of his mother. John felt that Ethyn should know and be allowed to decide what he wanted to do with the information. He warned his son that if he did not keep who his true mother was a secret, then if the Myst gates were ever opened, his children and grandchildren may not be safe. Once Ethyn's son was 21, the story was passed down, and eventually, it became known by all his descendent, who, while they believed in the story and even believed the Prophetess that a blue girl would set the demons free, they did not believe that the demon would hunt them down after all this time.

Tayin listened to the minds of Amalie's blood and smiled at their willful ignorance. He kept careful watch over those who stayed in Kluane and those who moved away. He bided his time planning their deaths and his revenge against those born of the one that took the life of Tam and locked him in the Myst. Their disbelief that someone would eventually let him out would be what sealed their fate.

YEAR 43

Nicollete heard a sound from behind that startled her. Realizing who it was, she relaxed her shoulders, stood up from her garden, and turned to face the Chosin who had just arrived. She knew he would appear at some point and knew it would be soon since he had just a few weeks left before he would need to be guided into the blue waters by Adym to feed Y'ddra. Nicollete shook the dirt off her dress and pulled off her gloves, placing them gently in the basket next to her.

"So, you have arrived." She stated.

"Yes, I find that in the few weeks that I have left, I require the companionship of my own kind." His voice was weary and a little rough, and it did not match the boyish look of his face.

Nicollete looked him up and down and then waved her hand for him to follow her.

"I understand. While Yidderians are amusing, it is hard to live among them and not those of our kind." She smiled at him. "I get tired of having to talk out loud."

He nodded and accepted the glass of snowfruit juice Nicollete handed him.

"Does Adym know that you have arrived on Alenar?"

"He does, and he will be arriving in a few days. He has asked that we have a few Yidderians waiting for him in anticipation of making it through the gate. I understand that the last time he tried, it was very draining for him."

"It was. I have been preparing for weeks for this time to come. I will show you my preparations after you have finished your drink, but only if you promise not to wipe out the entire stock of food that I have prepared for Adym. While you are welcome to one or two, please remember that he will need strength to guide you to your destination and to get back home." Nicollete refilled his glass as she spoke.

"I will not overindulge." He looked at her from over his glass. "At least not in that aspect. I might in another." He looked her over, and Nicollete could feel the warmth of his gaze as it traveled down her body.

"It is your right as a Chosin, but I warn you I have been without for several years, and I might wear you out." She laughed seductively as she caressed his bare shoulders. "It has been a very long time since I have been with an Alluran, and while Kian was a perfect mate in many ways, he lacked the roughness of Alluran males that I enjoy."

"Roughness, such an inadequate term, but, Yes, the Yidderians are too soft." He stood up and took her in his arms and kissed her passionately, biting her lips and pulling her closer at her response. "As you pointed out, it is my right to take you, and I find that preparations for my death can wait. My need for you cannot."

Nicollete took his hand and guided him into the bedroom, and together, they spent a few very enjoyable hours. They showered and then dressed before Nicollete led the Chosin down the path to a large bunkhouse hidden in a thick stand of evergreens at the edge of her property. She opened the door, and several Tarikans were standing watch over 30 plus Yidderians.

"How long have you been collecting?" The Chosin asked as he walked around the room, pausing to breathe in the sweet smell of the Yidderian's fear as he passed them.

"Since Kian died four years ago. I did not feel comfortable collecting while he was still here, but I knew I needed to begin as I could not gather this many all at once without being suspect." Nicollete followed behind him as they spoke. She knew that their silence was increasing the fear of those around her because she could see the eyes of the Chosin start glowing brighter. "Come, we must leave here before you lose your control."

They left the building and together walked back to her house. Nicollete let him kiss her and then watched as he departed down the path leading to a tiny fishing village a few miles from her. She walked into her house and sat down on the couch, tucking her feet up under her. She sighed in relief, knowing that he would be reasonable at this point. The Chosin had the right to do what they wanted, when they wanted, in the last year of their life. They fed indiscriminately to have the strength Y'ddra required in her feeding. They often would not listen to reason when there was famine at their time of sacrifice. This Chosin was understanding and knew he might be the last sacrifice for a long time. He also knew that Adym, being stuck on the other side of the gates, would need sustenance to get through the barrier so that he might do his duty. Without Adym, the Chosin could not fulfill his destiny.

Nicollete hoped he would not decimate the fishing village, but if he did, well, the Yidderians would eventually repopulate, and they were nowhere near as important as his duty to Y'ddra was. She would try to make sure that the Chosin got what he needed and what he wanted while still making sure that Adym would have what he required as well. The next few weeks would take strength on her part. Nicollete made herself a light snack and then prepared for bed. Tomorrow, she would gather a few more Yidderians and then let Adym know he was welcome to arrive at any time. It would be nice to see him again.

The next few days were exhausting. Between active nights and trying to keep the Chosin occupied and out of the shed while she gathered a few more Yidderians for Adym, Nicollete had not gotten very much sleep. Finally, Nicollete felt it was time to summon Adym. He would need a week or so to recover his strength and another to prepare for the ritual. She had wanted to go up to the Myst and call to him herself, but the Chosin insisted that he go with her, and so bright and early one morning, the two walked the few miles it took to get to the Myst.

In the end, it was good that the Chosin came with her as Adym had trouble getting past the barrier and needed help standing once he appeared. Nicollete led the Chosin away as

Adym fed on the Yidderian they had brought for him. Nicollete did not want to be hit with the istotymir and did not want the Chosin to interfere with Adym's meal. Nicollete heard Adym call out to her when he was finished, and with the help of the Chosin, they carried the body, threw it over the cliffs, and then left for the house.

Nicollete guided Adym to the bunkhouse, left him there to regain his strength, and told him that she would have drinks and food available in the main house when he was finished. She walked back down the forest path and enjoyed the moment's peace. Nicollete smiled as she could still hear some of the thoughts of Adym and the Chosin in her moment of peace. For the first time since the Myst gates closed, she felt almost as if she was home.

Adym sat in the chair across from Nicollete and just stared at her. She looked healthy but tired, and looking into her mind, he saw she was lonely. He had been with her for two days, but this was the first opportunity they had had to talk alone.

"Are you doing all right out here?" He inquired.

"Yes. I have an active business thanks to you." She nodded her head in appreciation. "And I have the Tarikan. Without them, I would be much more homesick than I am, but I hope the sadness of not being with my family will ease somewhat in time." She smiled gently at Adym.

"Raighn asked me to make sure the Chosin was treating you well. What is his name? I didn't catch it."

"I have never bothered to ask. Tell my brother I am fine and that the Chosin is tolerable. Also, tell him I will meet him at the Myst in just under two months, and we can have a nice long chat then. And tell him I love him."

"I will," Adym replied.

"Adym?" Nicollete began.

"Yes?" Adym could hear the worry in her voice.

"Is he doing okay? The last time I talked to him, he seemed different. Raighn thinks he has to be the strong one and the big brother, so he will not always tell me the truth about how he is doing. Will you?" Nicollete leaned forward in anticipation of Adym's answer.

"He is okay, but he misses you terribly. He feels it is his fault that you got caught outside the Myst when it became locked.

Though you and I know that is not true. If you had listened to him, you would not be here now." Adym raised an eyebrow at her.

"Yes, I know." She sat back in the chair and felt guilt wash over her.

"Li uhra. There is no need to let guilt eat at you. What is done is done, but Raighn is taking it hard. He has started using the entasi leaf more and more, and I worry that he is letting it take control of him. I am not sure how to help him." Adym said, worry for his cousin was evident in his voice.

Nicollete let out a little laugh. "You can't, Adym. Let Kest help him, but you stay away. He will not listen to you, and you know it. You tend to get all bossy and condescending, and then he bristles and does the opposite of what you say just to piss you off. Express your concern to Kest and then leave things alone."

Nicollete laughed again at the scowl that crossed Adym's face. She knew that he did not like to be told what to do. He considered himself the protector of the SeiOrhii leaders as he was the eldest, and while most of the time his advice was sound, Raighn, the youngest of them, rebelled despite it. Many times, the group reminded Adym that they did not always have to do as he suggested. Still, Adym was stubborn and usually found a way to make his wishes happen, except with Raighn. Raighn rarely went along with anything that Adym proposed. The two, in many ways, were alike but also very different from each other. They both liked to have their way and had a stubbornness that was hard to penetrate. But, Adym was rigid and wanted everything to be organized and done very well. At the same time, Raighn was very laid back and often went with the flow. Their differences drove each other nuts.

"Thank you for telling me the truth, Adym. I can always count on you to do so. When I next see Raighn, I will talk with him and see what I can do to help ease his pain." Nicollete got up and lit the fire in the hearth as the night was becoming chilly, and she lit the pale purple light stone on the table next to her before sitting back down.

"What are you going to do over the next few years? The Yidderians are sure to start noticing that you are not aging." Adym picked up the cool glass of water and took a sip, then helped himself to a piece of the fruit from the tray before him.

"I have been thinking of that. I have been here for 38 rotations of the sun, and I should look much older by now. I have been wearing a veil so that my face is obscured, but I know I will soon have to leave here. I have begun to set up my affairs to maintain my holdings until I can move back. I think that in a few years, I will plan my death and then move to start somewhere new. Any suggestions?"

"Move back home to Lioleta. Raighn will appreciate having you near him for a while. There, you can live close to the Myst in the town that is just beginning to be built. Set up a shop selling the light stones. The sun is brutal there, and you could possibly make a living selling the cream that you LuZivot use to protect your skin from it. Build an amphitheater and hold plays and dances there. Raighn would like that."

"I would like that. I will move back to Kruger, which is what the Yidderians call Lioleta, so I can be closer to my brother. I will set up a light stone shop and claim to be my own granddaughter." Nicollete laughed lightheartedly. "Adym, thank you."

"Li uhra, you are family. No thanks are needed." He stood up. "Now I must get some sleep and then be up early to feed. I am still quite weak from traveling through the Myst barrier. I do not think that I will be making this journey again. The Myst is pushing back too hard in its efforts to keep me in." He leaned down and kissed Nicollete on the cheek. "Goodnight, little cousin."

Nicollete watched Adym slip into the guest bedroom before she began to tidy up. Tomorrow, she would make the journey to the Rainbow Falls and the village to ensure that the Prophetess's laws were being followed. She did not want a Yidderian to interfere in this crucial event, and as a witness was needed, she did not want to be seen by any of them. For a while, at least, she still needed her masquerade to be believed.

Three weeks had passed, and the trio of Allurans teleported to the cave behind the falls. She sat back on the stones to the side of the cave and watched as the Chosin bathed for the last time in the yellow pools of his gifts. She chanted the words of comfort and praise that thanked him for his sacrifice and prepared his mind for death. She watched as Adym opened a portal in the ground under the blue falls and escorted the Chosin down to his fate.

Nicollete waited several minutes in silence and then saw that Adym was back. He closed the portal and waited beside her. Together, they felt the Chosin's pain and torture as he was eaten by Y'ddra, and together, they repeated the ritual words to guide his soul and his strength to Y'ddra. His death would take hours, and with each passing one, the colored crystals became brighter and more vibrant. By nightfall, the waters glowed with the brilliance of the stones. The sacrifice had been accepted, and

Y'ddra was fed. The two took a few more minutes to gaze in awe at the beauty of the sacrifice and then teleported back to the house where they stayed. Tonight, Adym would feed on what was left of the Yidderians Nicollete had gathered, and tomorrow she would be with him as he tried to make the perilous journey back into the Myst. They had a last meal together, and then Nicollete left him to gather the fear he needed.

The Myst glowed a brilliant blue, renewed by the sacrifice, which worried Nicollete. With the strengthening of Y'ddra, would the Myst gates now be passable? She called Tayin and asked him to be at the gates in preparation for Adym's arrival through them. She was surprised to find that Kest and Raighn joined Tayin but was glad to see all of them there to welcome him home and help him through the ordeal.

She placed her hand on the Myst and felt the three inside place theirs next to hers. The tingle of unity ran through her hand, making tears flow down her face. She took her hand from the Myst, hugged Adym, wishing him a safe journey, and stepped aside as he disappeared. She waited a few long moments before she saw him appear on the other side. It had taken him far too long to cross this time, and she could see that he was near death and shaking from pain.

Nicollete longed to help him but knew that she could not. She touched the gates one last time and felt Raighn place his hand on hers before returning to the path that would take her away from her family. They needed to concentrate on healing Adym now; she would only be a distraction. She felt their minds fade from hers as they gathered Adym and took him to his home, where sustenance was waiting for him.

Once back at the house, she took out a paper and made her will. She left the house and the business to her future descendants. She left it in the care of her followers until one of her children came back to claim it. Nicollete had told many Yidderians that she had a child who had stayed on Kruger when she moved to Alenar. Many times, a Tarikan had come to visit her in the guise of her child. The ruse was necessary if she wanted to keep up the belief that she was Yidderian and wanted to maintain her holdings. Nicollete then began planning her demise. She would develop a sickness and then pass in her sleep. Once she had "passed," she would dress as a silent follower of the Calling and make the trip to Kruger with a few of the Tarikan. She would send a few of them ahead of her so that they could start building what she would need to survive there. She gave herself four years to plan and prepare, and within a few months of Adym's visit, she had sent a group with designs for the home she wanted to be built and plans for the store she hoped to open. By the time she arrived, they would have everything done, and her transition to Kruger would be smooth.

It was in the year 47 that Nicollete stepped off the boat and made her way onto the shores of her native land. The heat warmed her bones, chilled from the years of living on Alenar, and filled her with a new excitement for life. Instead of just trying to survive, she would begin living and planning. Nicollete realized that she could help shape the Yidderian world. She could make it into a place that genuinely feared the Allurans. A place that, once the Myst gates opened, would be idyllic for the SeiOrhii, or she could make the Yidderians feel that the Allurans were a harmless myth. She smiled at this idea. Suppose she encouraged the belief that the stories of the demons in the Myst were just stories. They would not be prepared for the SeiOrhii once they were released. It would also make it easier for the one destined to open the gates to decide to unlock them if she thought the stories were mere fables.

Life was not going as she had once dreamt it would, but she had a new dream now and a world to help shape. Nicollete smiled, adjusted her hat, and walked to the waiting carriage. It was time to go see her new home.

YEAR 47

RAIGHN WAITED IN ANTICIPATION of Nicollete's arrival. Today, she was to meet him at the edge of the Myst by the ocean.
He had missed her quick laughter and her witty sarcasm. He had
missed her annoying hats and their arguments. Now that she
was back on Lioleta, they could visit more often. The Tarikan
on the outside of the Myst had built her a beautiful home, and
just looking at the design, he knew that Nicollete herself had
designed most of it. It was very feminine and opulent, and the
Tarikan had done her justice in their efforts to bring her dream
to life. He, of course, had not seen it in person but had seen the
drawings presented to him by the Tarikan inside the Myst. Even
separated, the Tarikans shared their minds as no other Alluran
did.

Raighn could hear her thoughts as she approached their designated meeting spot and frowned at their faintness. The longer

she was outside the Myst, the harder it became to communicate with her.

"Hello, big brother." Nicollete smiled as she put her hand out to touch the Myst and felt his touch against hers.

"Hello, little sis. How was your trip?" Raighn sat down in the sand and watched her mirror his movements.

"It was long, but I am glad to return to Lioleta. I missed the heat. I do not understand how Adym can prefer the cold." She shuddered in memory of the years she spent in that cold.

"It is so good to see you. You missed our date on your last birthday." He scolded gently.

Nicollete adjusted her skirts around her and took off her hat, laying it on her lap so it would not get sandy. "Well, I was attending my funeral then and couldn't make the date. But I am here now, and we can meet as often as we like. How are you doing?" She inquired.

"I am as good as can be expected. I miss hunting, and I miss the beach that we used to go to for picnics. But I am adjusting to the confinement."

"Are you really? I have heard that you have turned to the entasi leaf to while away the time."

Raighn frowned at her. "You have been talking with Adym. How I choose to spend my time is none of his concern or yours."

"Don't get upset at me. It is perfectly fine if you use the drug. It is a delightful way to pass the time, but I worry that you will let it control you, and it makes you aggressive and not very nice. Just please do not let it overwhelm you." She said with concern in her voice.

"Again, it is not any of your concern. What is of concern is what you will do while on." Raighn paused, trying to search for the word he wanted but not finding it, asked, "What do the Yidderians call Lioleta?"

"Kruger, after the ship's captain that landed them here." She replied.

"Kruger." Raighn rolled the name around on his tongue and frowned. "It is harsh. Anyway, what are your plans while here?"

"I plan to open a store that sells the light stones and maybe a few other items. I would also like to build an amphitheater as I do enjoy the theater, and there is not one here yet. I plan to become an important pillar of this society so that I can start shaping the Yidderian culture to fit our needs once you are freed."

"You have always been ambitious." Raighn paused, "You look well. Yidderian life seems to agree with you."

"It does, and it doesn't. I will never understand why they do not just do things for the good of everyone and why money is so important to them. I do not understand their need to turn Y'ddra into a Goddess." She laughed lightly. "And I do not completely comprehend how they can be so kind and caring one moment and inflict pain on each other the next."

"They have not hurt you, have they?" Raighn asked with concern.

"Oh no. I have always been treated with great respect. I think this is because I have something they need and want, and to disrespect me could possibly hurt them. You see, if not respected, I can always make the light stones unaffordable or deny access to them to whomever I choose to."

The two sat silently for a few minutes, enjoying each other's company. The sun began to set, and the ocean waves rose further on the shore, lapping against Nicollete's feet.

"The Myst is getting hard to see into. I am beginning to lose the ability to see you through it, Raighn. I do not know what to do when I can no longer see into the Myst and gaze at my home. I do not know what to do if your voice becomes faint in my head." Nicollete whispered.

"I will always be able to communicate with you. Someway. Somehow. We will not let this separation take that from us. The one prophesied to unlock the gates will come soon. Y'ddra will not let us stay locked in here forever. I wouldn't be surprised if they were opened in just a few short rotations of the sun. Surely, we will not be here for even a full year." Raighn said as a way to try and comfort her.

"You, dear brother, are being overly optimistic, but I will go along with it. It has been around 42 rotations so far, so another 60 or so to reach your year should go quickly." She stood up and retied her hat. "I must go. I will meet you again in a week or so. I have set up several meetings and dinners with the leaders here and hope to situate as one of them. Who knows, maybe I will find a new partner amongst them." Nicollete placed her hand again on the barrier, "Be well, big brother. I am doing okay out here; please see that you do okay in there."

"When the gates are unlocked, I will be okay. Until then, I will try to adjust to being confined. Take care, little sis, and I will see you again soon." Raighn dropped his hand from the gates and returned to his home in Alendrot.

YEAR 78

Eliana sat at her great-grandmother's bed and held the dying woman's hand. She softly cried as she sat there. She looked into the fading eyes of the first Prophetess. Alena was a great woman and would be mourned worldwide upon her death. Eliana had been named for her. She hiccupped and wiped away a tear that threatened to fall on her great-grandmother. Neither her grandmother, Luka, nor her mother, Mina, had the gift of prophecy, and many thought that it would die with Alena. But it had not. Eliana had been born with the gift and had been instructed most of her life in how to live with it. She had been taught meditation, how to keep others from entering her mind, how to interpret what she saw, and also how to rule the world.

The responsibility of being the second Prophetess weighed heavily upon her, and she wondered if she had what it took to walk in her great-grandmother's shoes. Eliana was not sure how to do all that was expected of her.

"You will do great. You have to believe in yourself and do what Y'ddra requests of you. She would not have allowed my gift to be passed to you if you could not handle it." Alena whispered through her dry lips. "I am so proud of you, and I know that I leave the people of Yiddera in good hands. Remember that your number one responsibility is to keep the key safe and allow no one to find it." She gasped, and Eliana could hear death coming closer to the frail old woman.

"Shh. Rest now." Elaina held the hand to her face and brushed the hair from Alena's wrinkled face.

"I will rest when I am dead, child." She frowned in reprimand. "Now, I have left you a few things that no other should see. They are for the Prophetess's eyes only. You will pass them down when the time comes for you, too, but until then, they are to remain in your possession only. I put them in a trunk at the foot of my bed, and when I am gone, you will open it and read the letter I have left for you. This room is yours now. It is important that you occupy it and do not let anyone else lay claim. I explain why in the letter." She closed her eyes, took a deep breath, and then squeezed Eliana's hand. "Do not mourn for me. I am going to meet Luke. I have missed him."

Eliana felt the old hand go slack and heard the last breath leave the Prophetess's body and knew that she was no more. She cried and cuddled up against her great-grandmother's body, not yet willing to accept that she was gone. She lay there for almost an hour and then, pulling herself together, left the room to confront those waiting in the living room. The minute she emerged from the bedroom, the family that waited for her knew that the once-great woman was now gone. Grief filled the room, and many went in to pay their respects to the matriarch of the family.

Eliana left the apartment and had a servant gather her followers into the ballroom, where she let them know that the Prophetess had died. They all sat in a moment of silence out of respect for the first Prophetess, and then another moment was given in respect to the second. As planned, several of the followers left the room and set about spreading the news of Alena's death to the rest of the world.

One week after her grandmother's death, Eliana took over her apartment and, late one evening finally opened the trunk at the foot of the bed. Inside were a couple of sketchbooks, an intricately carved box that held a pink crystal in it, and the letter that her grandmother had told her to read. The trunk also contained a few other personal items, such as a locket that held a picture of both her grandmother and grandfather. Eliana slipped this on over her neck and held it close to her heart. Her eyes closed in grief over the loss of the woman she had felt the closest to.

Eliana took a deep breath and opened the letter that had her name on it. Her eyes widened in shock as she read the letter. It told of Amalie's story and how the Calling had been changed to keep the Yidderians from trying to open the Myst gates. It was on page six that Eliana came across what she knew her grandmother had wanted to keep quiet.

My dear, you must make sure that the blue girls that will start arriving are kept away from the Myst. One of them is destined to open it and let the demons out. I do not know when or which one, but they must all be taught that they can be used by the demons to help them achieve their freedom, and if they are let loose, the Yidderians will never know true peace again. There is a notebook that should be passed from Prophetess to Prophetess as it contains useful information that can help us have a fighting chance against them should the demons become free of their chains.

Eliana, I must impress on you the importance of studying this book and learning all that you can about the demons. Many things this book contains look innocent but are not. The symbols above the pictures are the gifts of the demons. At least, that is what I believe they mean. Beware the one who lives on Alenar, as he may be able to break free from their prison.

Now, the flora that is described in the book holds the key to helping us permanently get rid of the demons. Be careful with them as they can hurt us as well. Amalie poisoned herself with one of the tisanes described in this book. It is the one she called Love. There is an ingredient it calls for that can only be found in the Myst and in my meditation garden. It is a beautiful white flower, and it must be nurtured and cared for, as it cannot be replaced if it is allowed to die.

My child, this room must not be allowed to go to any other but the Prophetess. Behind the window curtains is a hidden door. It is hard to see, and there is a trick to opening it. I showed this to you once when you were first coming into your gift. Open the door and go down the stairs, and you will find a vast room full of old Earth treasures. While important to our history, they have no consequences if lost. In the furthest corner is a pedestal that holds a small round stone with a crescent moon-shaped hole in it. This is the key to the Myst. This is what must be guarded with your and every other Prophetess's life. This is what the blue girl will one day look for and find. This key will open the Myst and let the Demons go free. Should the day come that one finds this most precious item and tries to use it, you will need to have Love brewed so that it can be used to stop her.

Eliana read the rest of the letter and then opened the book that it talked about. Inside, she saw the herbs and the tincture that her grandmother wrote of. She looked at the plants so intricately drawn and knew that the artist had loved her work. She read the recipes that were scribbled next to the pictures and knew that a few of them were currently being used by the healers and a couple of them by the chefs.

She turned the pages and saw the faces of four men and wondered how they could be the demons she was told of all her life. Yes, their coloring was different, but the artist drew them in a way that made her feel as if she could like these men and maybe even trust them, except the last face. It was drawn twice. One face was looking at the artist with love, and the other with anger, grief, and hatred. This twisting of such a handsome face showed Eliana that the other drawings were deceptive. Handsomeness did not equal kindness. She shut the book and tucked it back in the footlocker and then went outside into the enclosed garden.

Eliana had sat here often with her grandmother, meditating and learning how to interpret the visions she received from Y'ddra. She saw the white flower that held such importance and smiled at its health and beauty. She now understood why her grandmother had always warned her to stay away from it and not pick the flowers. The words under the sketch depicting this flower said that once picked, a liquid could be squeezed from its stem, which could lower the immune system and stop healing in all beings on Yiddera. The flower petals held a poison that was slow and painless but fatal to all that ingested it if taken with the nectar from the stem. She found it interesting that this beautiful and delicate plant could be so deadly.

Eliana decided that one plant was not sufficient. If a drought or a hard winter came, it could potentially kill this one specimen, so she decided that once it seeded, she would plant several in a row and each year harvest the seeds and keep them safe in case one of the plants did not survive. It was always best to be prepared for everything.

YEAR 105
ONE HUNDRED YEARS AFTER THE GATES CLOSED

Kest flew in and landed on the beach, his talons sinking into the wet sand. He shook his wings out before folding them against him and then let out a loud shriek. Raighn jumped at the sound as Kest laughed and shifted back into his Alluran form.

"Dammit Kest. I hate that noise." Raighn picked up the sheers he had dropped and continued pruning the grapefruit-scented nictina vine that ran up the pillar on the right side of the garden room.

"I know," Kest said with laughter still in his voice. He climbed the steps that led up to the covered patio, opened the gate, and sat on the divan that was placed in the center of the enclosed garden.

Raighn finished his pruning and put his tools away in the trunk that lay under the divan. He went into his room, washed up, and then rejoined Kest on the terrace. He called a Tarikan to bring some wine out to his guest, and within moments, the two men were sipping on the light white wine that Kest preferred. Raighn popped a leaf from the entasi plant onto his tongue and let it dissolve before taking a deep drink of his wine.

"You are partaking more often of the drug than usual. Is everything okay?" Kest inquired, waving away Raighn's offer of the plant to him.

"I like the way it makes me feel, and it helps me forget that I am trapped in here. So, what if I use it often, it is enjoyable." Raighn shrugged his shoulders and enjoyed the sensation the plant induced. Every sense was enhanced as the drug took effect. Smells were better; touch was more sensual, colors were brighter, and emotions were more intense. Entasi was a drug that helped you live in the moment and not worry about anything else, past or present. It made him feel as if he was one with the world.

"Whatever. Do you want to go hunting with me?"

"Where? And who?" Raighn asked.

"I have placed a few Yidderians in the swamps of Geltahn, and I thought we could make their journey through them fun." Kest, being an animal shifter, liked to track those he hunted. Raighn's ability to control the weather could make the hunted more fearful as the elements went against them.

"Sounds fun. Do you want to fly back to Geltahn or walk there?" Raighn asked. Kest replied that he would walk with Raighn as it would be faster. The two men entered the Hall of Myst and walked through the bright yellow/orange door that took them instantly to Geltahn and Kest's gracious home.

The air was crisp with the freshness of the new dawning day, and the sun was just peeking out from the horizon when the hunters spied the hunted. The five Yidderians were walking along a narrow path between two patches of murky water. Raighn watched as the bodies of water grew deeper as he surrounded the Yidderians with the quagmire. Kest turned into a caiman, his electric blue markings making the animal even more dangerous looking, and swam around the humans, keeping them trapped on the small island that Raighn had left for them.

Their prey's mounting fear fueled the SeiOrhii, and their gifts became stronger as they fed. Kest made his way onto the island, causing those on it to back up into the water. His tail lashed back and forth, and his sharp teeth gleamed brightly in the light that was beginning to shine through the trees. He moved slowly toward the group, anticipating the catch.

"Run." Shouted the eldest of the quintet. The Yidderians ran through the waist-deep water and made it to dry land before Kest could reach them. Kest became a man once more and frowned at Raighn.

"You let them get away." He said as he sat on one of the rocks that Raighn had put in his path.

"Of course I did. You were about to catch them too easily, and I want them filled with fear before we quit the game."

Kest and Raighn watched as the group ran, and Raighn laughed as one of them pointed to the trees and told the others to climb. The humans climbed the tree and visibly relaxed once they reached a point high enough that the caiman could not get to them. They believed, wrongly, that they were safe now that they were on higher ground.

"Let them think they are safe for a few minutes," Kest suggested.

Raighn nodded and leaned against one of the ghostly-looking trees and watched the hunted cross the swamp by jumping from tree to tree.

"What are you doing for the rest of the day?" Kest asked in casual conversation to pass the time.

"It depends on how well this hunt goes. Later this evening, I do have a field to water for the Elders. You?"

"I have nothing planned. The Yidderian village is getting a bit too small for their growth. I might head over to Adym's and see if he is willing to host a village near him." Kest said, shifting in anticipation of the continued hunt they were on.

"Ready?" Raighn inquired of Kest a few minutes later, and the Yidderians were once again out of sight.

With a nod, Kest turned into the giant bird once more and flew high above the tree line, and Raighn caused the wind to pick up and make the trees more treacherous than they were moments before. Raighn walked along the ground, firm dirt formed under his feet with each step he took.

They found the five huddled on the branch of a particularly large tree, holding on for life as the wind increased and caused the tree to sway dangerously. Already slippery with moss, the branches were much harder to hold onto once the wind started.

"I did not know that such a beauty was among those you chose for today's entertainment," Raighn said, still leaning against the tree's trunk, looking at the group overhead. A woman with long reddish-brown hair and a body that showed softly rounded muscles clung tightly to the branch directly above him.

"I chose her for you. I figured you would like dessert." Kest laughed as he saw Raighn cause the girl to fall from the branch.

The girl squealed first in fright as she fell and then again with surprise as she was caught by Raighn.

"She is delightful and afraid of heights. Thank you." Raighn pulled the girl closer to his chest and started walking back toward Kest's house. "I think my game is over here. Which one did you choose for yourself?"

"Unlike you, I do not enjoy playing with Yidderian women. They do not appreciate it when I grow claws while we play. I will stick with Alluran women. They do not mind when I am part animal." Kest flew over and snagged up one of the men in the tree. The man screamed in fear as Kest dropped him and then caught him again before he fell too far.

"Enjoy your hunt, my friend," Raighn called to Kest and then took his catch back to Lioleta. The girl, looking up at him in lust, had lost some of her terror from the fall; she wrongly assumed that someone who looked as Raighn did would not cause her any more fear.

Kest arrived on Alenar to find Adym pacing the area of Myst that bordered the Rainbow Falls. He walked beside Adym for several minutes in silence, knowing that Adym was deep in thought over what to do should the gates not be opened soon. It was several years past time for a sacrifice to be given to Y'ddra. As this was Adym's primary job, Kest was sure that Adym was trying to figure a way out of the Myst with a Chosin in tow.

"You are right, but I can barely leave without much pain, and every time I have tried to take someone with me, I have failed." Adym finally spoke to Kest.

"Are there any other Chosin outside of the Myst?" Kest asked, knowing that the answer didn't matter. They could not be sacrificed without Adym taking them through the stone floor of the waterfall and into the hidden chamber beneath.

"No. I have already escorted the only Chosin, who was locked on the other side, into the chamber. Y'ddra's colors have begun to dim, and there is nothing that I can do about it." Adym shook his head in frustration and stared out of the Myst for a moment longer before inquiring into what had brought Kest to visit him.

"Both Raighn and I have hosted Yidderian villages for the last one hundred rotations, and now we need another one." Kest walked with Adym back to his home and then toward the LuZivot village nearby. "Would you be willing to build one here?"

"I would. I have been thinking that the Southeast clearing between those mountain ranges would be a good place to build. It is protected from the wind and is quite big. I think there is plenty of room for them to spread out." Adym pointed to the break in between the two peaks.

"I will explore it later and start the planning with the Tarikan." Kest stopped in front of a café and ordered a hot spiced cider for himself and for Adym. Used to the muggy heat of Geltahn, Kest needed the warmth of the drink. The two men sat at one of the many tables placed outside of the café.

"I am surprised at how well the Yidderians are adapting to our culture," Adym said. "They have incorporated their own customs in with those of the LuZivot and have even begun to accept being fed upon as a way of life."

"They have, but they still do not like it. There is talk among the younger generation every so often of revolting against it, but then one of their elders reminds them that they cannot defeat us. They are a spirited people."

"The day will come when we are free of the Myst. What do you plan for the Yidderians who will be free at that time as well?" Adym sipped his drink.

"I will decide at that time, but I am of the mind that just because we are free to leave the Myst, that does not have to mean that they are. I would like to keep them inside with us in the unlikely event that we are locked in again."

"Once free, we will make sure that we are never in this predicament again," Adym stated.

"Ah, but we never thought this predicament would happen in the first place. We cannot be sure it will not occur again. I prefer to prepare for the worst and hope for the best." Kest finished his cider and handed the cup to the café owner, who passed by. He stood up and tucked the chair underneath the table. "Are you still looking for the blue Yidderian?"

"I scan the minds of those nearby and shadow-walk Yiddera every few rotations. I will find her, and I will get the key from her."

"Still think she will be born outside?"

"I am sure of it. The original Prophetess told me that the one who will free us will hand me the key. She cannot do that if she is born within the Myst." Adym told Kest.

"But if not inside the Myst, how can she hand you the key?"

"I am the only Alluran that can leave. I anticipate the need to leave the Myst to retrieve the key from the Yidderian born."

Kest nodded his head, told Adym he would be by tomorrow to begin building the village, and then running down the road, grew wings, and took flight.

YEAR 825

TAYIN PAUSED IN HIS narrative, and the illusion he had cast disappeared, and once again, Yiddera held the look of desolation and death. The air once more smelled of grief and sorrow. His heart clenched as he braced for another wave of her anger to pass over him and watched as the land grew more arid. A solitary tear fell down his face as he stared out at the wasteland that he once took such pride in keeping beautiful. He was pulled out of his darkness by the Prophetess once more, patting his hand.

"And the long years until the gates opened? What happened to you and yours?" She inquired.

"You are actually interested in what happened to the Allurans, aren't you?" He asked in surprise.

"I am. Knowing Teffin, the Dimoni, who is not very talkative about the time she lived amongst your people, sparked my interest. Then, I met Kassel, who further

piqued my curiosity about the Alluran people. However, it is becoming friends with Cay that made me realize that we, Yidderians, have a biased view of who you are." She patted his hand once more. "Now, do not get me wrong, we have good reason to be, but after conversing with those of you who were once one of us, it made me curious as to our similarities and our differences."

"We tried to continue on as before, but it wasn't possible. Too much had changed. So, I wallowed in self-pity and grief until the need for revenge ate at my very soul. I felt like a caged animal waiting to be let out so that I could kill every last one of those who had imprisoned me in the first place. I watched and kept careful track of Amalie's descendants so that I could make sure that I was successful in my revenge." He chuckled without mirth, knowing how unsuccessful he was in this and thankful that he had been.

"I fell deeper and deeper into a hole of my own making." He looked thoughtful for a moment. "I felt I was the only one that had lost anything with the closing of the gates, but in truth, Raighn was going through something a bit similar to what I was. While his sister did not die, nor was she his twin, he was kept from her, and the two

were almost inseparable before the Myst gates kept them apart."

"Raighn also fell into the darkness, but instead of focusing on revenge, he became more and more dependent on the entasi drug. It made him feel more intensely, and his anger was not something any of us wanted to be around, but it also kept him from caring. He could watch the time pass without caring about anything around him. Always one for the women, he became more so, and between sex and the drug, he self-isolated. We all did to some degree."

Tayin stood up and kicked a stone in his path, pacing back and forth in front of the Prophetess, who still sat on the rock he had just vacated. "Kest and Adym became obsessed with finding the blue Yidderian who would free us. Kest searched every child born amongst the Yidderians who lived in the Myst with us, and Adym shadow walked the outside world every few rotations looking for her. Both argued fiercely with each other on where she would be born, and yet both accepted the others' need to find her."

The Prophetess watched the man pacing in front of her and shuddered at the slight tingle of fear that ran down her spine each time he passed her. She took a deep breath and asked, "And the others?"

Tayin sat back down and reigned in the istotymir he was unconsciously releasing in his agitation. "The Elders quit trying to guide us and let us go our own ways. Which was probably for the best, as the more they tried to get us to focus on what we should actually be doing, the more we spiraled. The Chosin that missed their time of sacrifice were left bewildered and wondering as to their purpose if they could not die for Y'ddra. They felt her calling to them to heal her, but without the ability to leave the Myst, they were helpless to answer her cries."

The two sat silently for several minutes, each thinking their own thoughts.

"And then Diem came." Tayin once again made the world in front of them beautiful and full of life.

The Prophetess knew by the landscape that they were now on Malseka.

YEAR 345

DIEM SAT IN THE shade of a stand of trees, watching the other kids playing a game of kickball. She did not like to be dirty, and so when invited to play, she told them no. Now, she laid down her book and watched as one of the boys kicked the ball over the river. Then, she saw the ball bounce across the bank toward her. The blond kid ran across the bridge and skidded to a halt in front of her.

"Hey, you wanna come play?' He asked her.

Diem frowned at him and wiped the dirt off her skirt. "No."

He ran over, scooped up the ball, and threw it back across the river before he sat down in front of her. "Why not?"

"Because I do not like to get dirty, and I prefer to read." She said.

"Oh." He said, staring intently at the girl. He saw that in the shade, her eyes glowed a bright turquoise blue. "My name is Jack." He held out a dusty hand to her, and seeing her frown, he smiled as he wiped his hand on his pants and held it out for her to shake once again.

Diem tentatively took his hand in hers and then just as quickly let go. "My name is Diem."

"Are you LuZivot?" Jack inquired.

"No, why do you ask?" Diem asked as she raised her hand to make sure her silk head scarf was still properly placed.

"Because your eyes glow like theirs do." He looked back at the game being played and stood back up. "Are you sure that you don't want to come and play?"

"I am sure." She said, looking up at the tall boy.

He smiled at her and then took off running back over the bridge, stopping just on the other side. "Hey, do you want to be friends?"

Diem stared at the boy in his torn jeans and messy hair, and while she wasn't sure why, she found herself smiling and yelling "Yes" back to him. He smiled again and then left her sitting there as he rejoined the game.

Over the next few years, Diem and Jack became inseparable. He often messed up her dress to irritate her, and she would tell him stories in the quiet of the woods. Jack eventually got her to play games with the other kids and even to swim in the river with him. She taught him how to dress more neatly and to speak Alluran, a language she picked up quite easily from the LuZivot children who sometimes joined them in their games. At around age ten, Diem showed Jack her biggest secret. They were hidden in the small clearing in the middle of a stand of large trees when she took off her head scarf and showed him the blue streaks in her hair. She told him that it had to be a secret, or the SeiOrhii would take her, and he vowed never to tell. The sharing of her secret bonded the two of them together, and afterward, one was rarely seen without the other.

When Diem was 13 and Jack was 14, he tried to kiss her, and she pushed him away, telling him that she was his friend, not his girlfriend. He smiled his cheeky smile and told her that he would change her mind someday. Then he leaned in and stole a quick kiss anyway. It never occurred to Diem that he was serious about wanting to be more than friends, so she just laughed at him as she wiped the kiss from her cheek, and then, grabbing his hand, the two ran off to join their friends who were gathered in the village park.

Two years later, Jack saw Diem kissing one of the other boys, and the two of them had their first real fight. Jack did not understand why she did not like him as he liked her, and despite

Diem trying to explain that she saw him as just a friend, he stubbornly insisted that she not kiss another boy as she was his. Diem left him standing outside the schoolyard after he made that statement and would not talk to him for several weeks.

"Diem, you have a visitor." Cressida, Diem's mother, called to her.

Diem rolled her eyes, knowing that it was Jack, yet again, trying to get her to talk to him. She turned up the music in her music box and opened her book. She told her mother that she did not want to see him until she was ready, but her mother kept insisting that Diem should relent and just talk to him. Diem was not ready to talk to him again. She heard a noise behind her and looked around to see Jack standing at the door to her room.

She slammed her book closed and turned off her music. "What do you want?"

"I want my friend back." He said, walking into her room and sitting on the chair by her vanity.

She eyed him warily. "As long as a friend is all you want."

"For right now." He stood up and went and sat on the bed next to her. "I miss talking with you. I am sorry that I got mad about you kissing Joe."

"And if I do it again?" She asked.

"I guess I don't have a say in who you date, but I don't like that you don't see me that way."

Diem heard the sadness in his voice and, for the first time, looked at him as a girl would look at a boy she might be interested in. He was her height, but then she was very tall for a girl, had dark blond hair and light brown eyes. He had a ready smile and had a nice muscly build to him. And yet, given that she could see why other girls would find him attractive, she just didn't. All Diem saw when she looked at Jack was her best friend. The friend that she told her secrets to, the friend that she knew, was afraid of spiders and hated the smell of fish. He held no mystery for her. She knew everything about him, and maybe this was why she could not see him as he wanted her to.

"Jack. You are my best friend, and I wish you would try and understand that. I am not mad at you anymore. I am glad you came over today."

"You are?"

"Yes." Diem stood up and slipped on her shoes. "I am leaving tomorrow to visit with my aunt Annalisha for a while, and I would have hated to go without seeing you again." She walked into the hallway. "I am going swimming. Are you coming?"

Jack jumped off the bed and followed her out the door. "Yes." She took his hand in hers and pulled him out of the house and into the jungle in search of their favorite swimming pond. Shouting to their friends as they passed, inviting them to join them in swimming. Soon, quite a few boys and girls joined them, and they spent the evening in laughter and companionship. As the night stars came out and they all headed home, Jack asked her when she was leaving tomorrow.

"I leave pretty early in the morning. Not sure exactly when, though." Diem had decided to leave to visit her aunt just to get away from Jack for a while, to see what life without his always being around was like, and still had not asked either her mother or her aunt's permission. Not wanting to tell him that, she decided not to give him an exact time.

"I will come and see you off." He said.

"No need to get up early. I won't be gone long, and before you can even start missing me, I will be back to annoy you." She gave him a big hug once they reached her door and watched him walk down the street to his house. She let herself in and went in search of her mother.

"Mom, can I go and visit Auntie tomorrow?" Diem asked as she sat down on the rattan couch under the cooling breeze of the open window.

"I don't see why not. I am sure she would love to have you for a visit." Her mother sat on the couch next to her and pulled her into a hug. "I am glad you patched things up with Jack. He is such a nice boy."

"He is my friend, and I am glad we are not fighting anymore, too." Diem snuggled against her mother, and the two sat there watching the second moon ascend until it was almost as high in the sky as the first.

"I want to leave early tomorrow morning, so I am going to start packing tonight." Diem leaned down and kissed her mom on her cheek. "Good night."

"Good night, my dear. Don't stay up too late, and I will see you in the morning."

Diem was just about to step through the red door when she saw Jack running up to her, a package in his hands. She hesitated with one foot already through the door for Jack to come to a halt in front of her.

"I told you not to bother getting up so early." Diem scolded him gently.

"I know, but when have I ever listened when you have told me not to do something? Here." He handed her the package.

"What is it?" She inquired as she unwrapped it.

"Just a little something I have been meaning to give you. I know you won't be gone long, but I wanted you to have something to remember me by."

Diem held up a pretty little pendant of two entwined hearts hanging from a thin gold chain. "It is beautiful, Jack." Diem let him clasp the necklace around her neck.

"It is my heart entwined with yours."

Diem turned around and frowned at him. "Jack, I am not your girlfriend." She reached up to unhook the clasp and felt his hand close over hers.

"It is whatever you want it to mean. My heart will always be yours regardless of whether we are a couple or forever remain only friends. Please wear it."

Diem let go of the clasp and dropped her hands to her side. "I will see you soon." With that, she stepped through the gate to Kofira and left Jack on Geltahn.

Diem stayed on Kofira for over a year. Her aunt was happy to have her, and while her parents were a bit reluctant, they decided it would do her some good to meet new people and have new experiences while under the supervision of someone they trusted. The only warning they gave her was to keep her blue markings secret so that she was not taken away from them by the SeiOrhii, who were looking for a Yidderian-born Alluran. She promised to keep her hair hidden and to stay out of the view of those who might question her eyes.

It was on the last weekend that she would be staying with her aunt that she found her way to the red pool on Tayin's property. Diem was out with several friends when they dared her to sneak onto his property and take a crystal from the red pool. At first, she protested and stated that she could not possibly do that because he was sure to catch her, but after much ribbing, she relented and said she would do it. The group walked with her until they came to the edge of his gardens, and then they left her to go the rest of the way alone.

Diem stayed in the tree line, and when she was out of sight of the others, she untucked a strand of her turquoise blue hair from her head scarf. She decided that if she was caught, it might be better to be mistaken for a LuZivot than a Yidderian. She walked boldly out of the tree line and then across the garden and sat at the edge of the red waters. She stared into their depths and found herself seeing dreamlike images spiral out from the warm waters and then fade away in the cool air. This water both drew her to it and repelled her.

Hesitantly, she placed a hand on the edge and then quickly grabbed a rock that poked out from the water. A tingle of awareness shot up her hand as she touched the crystal, and it kept pulsing as she held it tightly in her fist. Diem felt her mind being pulled even harder toward the water and found an almost irresistible urge to plunge herself into its depths but managed to ignore the temptation. She deposited the crystal into her pocket, and once it no longer touched her skin, the waters became less compelling.

Diem ran to the tree line and, tucking her hair back under her scarf, she made it back to her friends' unseen. She held out the rock to them, and with much excitement and awe at her bravery, they passed the stone to one another and then gave it back to her. Laughing, she walked with them back to their village and then left them to head back to her aunt's house.

She placed the red crystal on her nightstand and wondered why none of the others felt the same pulsing sensation from it that she had. Diem briefly wondered if it was because of her hair color but dismissed that notion. She crawled into bed for the night and found herself amid the most pleasant dream she had ever experienced. She woke the next morning feeling like she was

finally ready to go home.

YEAR 363

KEST CIRCLED HIS HOUSE for what seemed like the hundredth time when he came to a stop in front of his veranda and changed back into his Alluran form. He walked up the steps, sat in one of the chairs, and looked out across the valley toward the Kirod river. He was becoming increasingly more frustrated as the years passed. This confinement was not natural for him or any of the Allurans, and he had thought that by now, they would all be free. It had been over three hundred and fifty rotations of the sun, and Kest still had not found a single blue-haired child born amongst the Yidderians held in captivity with them.

He stood up and leaned against the railing and watched as the marsh birds flew over the river searching for prey. He had thought that the blue-haired child they waited for would have been born by now. Kest had arrived home today to find that, at last, one had been born but had died soon after childbirth. For some reason, he could not fathom children born during the time that Allura was in the sky did not survive. The one born today had survived for less than 15 minutes.

How would the prophecy come true if all the children born with the markings died? Maybe the one that would finally find the key would not be born during the blue moon. He changed once more into an Ageetah and raced across the valley, trying to run out his restless energy. Kest thought about his last conversation with Adym and wondered if Adym might be correct. The girl they waited for might be born outside of the Myst. However, Kest thought he would still keep looking here. Someday, one of the children might live, and when that day came, he would snatch her up and make her go find the key. He was tired of such a limited hunting ground and wanted to run or fly across the whole of Yiddera, not just the space in the Myst that he was currently relegated to.

The concert was loud and full of energy. The beat of the drums entered Diem, and she danced along with their rhythm, as did many of the other attendees. Drinks were being offered by one of the Tarikan as they passed through the crowd, many of which carried the juice of the entasi flower, which made the people drinking it feel as if they were in tune with the world. Everything looked brighter and felt better, and all the user wanted to do was to live in the now.

Jack handed Diem one of the flavorful drinks, and Diem could taste the sweetness of the drug on her tongue. Laughing, she downed the rest and continued dancing to the intoxicating music. She felt Jack take her hand and pull her close, and together they danced, and when she felt his lips on hers, she did not pull away as she usually did. He was her best friend, and while she still did not want anything more, thanks to the drug, the feel of his lips on hers erased all thoughts other than what was happening at the moment. His hands on her back pushed the silk of her shirt against her skin, and the texture was soft and cool.

Jack leaned down and whispered in her ear, and looking up into his eyes, she saw his want of her and, with just a small moment of hesitation, shook her head yes. The two ran out of the throbbing crowd and into the surrounding jungle. They made it to their secret place before Jack took off her shirt, music still loud enough to be heard in the distance and filled the hollow with its melody. He laid her on the slightly damp grass and once again took her in his arms. The drug coursing through Diem's body caused her to push away her common sense. She knew that Jack would assume this meant they were together, but her mind told her she could figure out that tomorrow because tonight his body called to hers.

Two weeks later, Diem sat on her bed with concern on her face. She was counting days in her mind and on her fingers, and she kept coming up with the same number. She counted once more and finally gave in to the truth. Shoulders sagging, she let the truth sink in. Diem was two days late for her monthly cycle. She went over to the dresser, opened a small red box, and counted the leaves that lay inside.

She was puzzled at the amount that she counted. She had not missed taking a single one of the leaves, so how could she be pregnant? Or maybe she wasn't; she was only two days late. Diem picked up one of the leaves to recount and noticed that the veining that ran up the leaf was curvy and not as straight as it should be. She sniffed it and found it to have a sweet scent similar to the honeysuckle vine that grew in Kofira. Diem gave it a little nibble and found it also tasted sweeter than it should. It did not have the slight tang she expected the Op to have. She examined each of the leaves and found that all of her birth control leaves had been replaced with the Capol leaf.

Diem thought about when she had last filled the container and knew that she had filled it with the Op leaf. She was diligent about taking her birth control as she did not want children and, at only 28, did not expect to want children for many more years, if ever. She had replaced the leaves at the beginning of her last cycle as she always did, and Diem was always regular. It never wavered. She placed the leaves back into their box and took it out to her mother.

"Mom?" She started

"Yes, dear." Her mother looked at the box that she held, and a pink blush spread across her cheeks.

"Mom, last month I asked you to pick me up a new supply of Op."

"And I did." Her mother interrupted her and then went back to busily wiping down the table.

"Mom. These are Capol leaves, not Op leaves. You know the difference, and I also know that you had to go to a different shop to get these leaves as the two are not sold at the same store." Diem placed the box on the table and tipped the leaves out. "Why?"

"What do you mean, dear? I made a mistake, but it shouldn't matter, should it?" Her mother looked at her with anticipation in her eyes.

"Mom, how could you? You know that I do not want children, and for hell's sake, I am only twenty-eight, and now you have helped ruin my life." Diem sat down on the chair in anger.

"Honey, I only did it for your sake. It is about time you settled down with Jack. I know that he asked you to marry him, and I know that you told him no. I don't understand why, as it is only a matter of time before you come to your senses and say yes. I decided to give you a little push."

"A little push? You pushed me right into parenthood, something I never wanted. And as for Jack, this doesn't change anything. I do not love him." Diem got up from her chair and glared at her mother, "And besides, how can you be sure that it is Jack's baby that I might carry? He is not the only one that I have had sex with." With that, she left the house and headed out to walk around the river that bordered the Animal Shifters house. Today, she needed the peace that the river afforded, even at the risk of being seen by the SeiOrhii that lived there.

Diem sat at the river's edge under a stand of tall ghostly trees and watched the water flow over her bare feet. Her life had just changed, and she was not ready for it too. She sat there pondering what she wanted to do. Diem was deep in thought when she felt someone sit down next to her. She looked over at Jack and scowled at him, scooting a bit away from him.

"Your mom just told me." Jack began with a big smile on his face. "Now, you will have to marry me." He said as he moved over to sit closer to her.

"Fuck you, Jack." Diem stood up and walked away from Jack and further up the river, dangerously close to the SeiOrhii's well-groomed yard.

"Diem. We are going to be parents. Aren't you happy?" Jack said as he ran to catch up to her.

She stopped and frowned at him again. "If you knew me as well as I thought you did, then you would know that the answer is no. I don't want children. And you know that I do not love you in that way. I will not marry you. I have already told you that."

"But the night of the concert." He began.

"Was a combination of the music, the drugs, and the moment. Nothing more. It was one night, not a lifelong commitment." She turned away and headed back down the river toward home.

"But Diem, I love you."

She stopped and looked at him in sympathy. "I know, but that doesn't change anything. You and my mother have changed my life in a way that I never wanted." She saw him stick out his chin and knew instantly that he had planned this with her mother. "Leave me alone for a while, Jack. I am mad enough at the both of you that I want to scream." She turned down a path that led her into the LuZivot village and out of sight of Jack. Diem walked straight into the building that housed the colored doors and, opening the red door, stepped out into Kofira. She needed time away to think, and she knew that her aunt would give her the privacy and support that she needed.

Diem bundled up her new daughter and picked up the bag that she had packed the night before. She had been on Zeljani for the duration of her pregnancy after leaving her aunt's, and now it was time to go home and introduce her parents to their new granddaughter and Jack to his little girl. She walked the short distance to the door that would take her to the LuZivot village on Geltahn and home.

She arrived quickly at the village and sat down for a fresh glass of iced mint tea at the outdoor cafe. Diem had sent a message to her parents telling them she was on her way and to please have Jack with them when she arrived. Diem now waited, giving them time to do as she wished. Her daughter started fussing, and she knew the little one was getting hungry. She gathered up the small bundle and fed her, gazing down at the soft brown eyes, and while she did love her child, all she could think about was the fact that she still did not want children.

Diem finished her tea and then headed to her parent's house. She knocked on the door, and an excited Jack picked her up and twirled her around once he had opened the door.

"Jack, put me down." Diem straightened her dress once he had complied, and then she picked up the basket that contained her sleeping baby and went into the house. She hugged everyone and then introduced them to the little girl.

"Mom, Dad, Jack, this is Louella. I call her Lela for short." Diem handed the baby to Jack and then stood up. "Everything that you will need for her is in the basket and the two small bags by the front door." She walked over to the door and out onto the walkway. "Jack, you wanted a child, and now you have one." Diem then left up the path that would take her back to Zeljani.

Jack grabbed her arm and brought her to a stop. "Why? How can you have left me for so long and then come back and just give me our child as if you don't even want her?"

"Because Jack," Diem started, as she took his hand from her arm, "I never did want her. You knew that. I had an offer from the school on Zeljani to learn about Alluran history and work as one of their teachers teaching a class on Yidderian history, and because you and my mother interfered, I had to decline it. I recently reapplied and received the offer again, and this time, I am going to take it. I will visit when I can, but Lela is your responsibility now, not mine." She kissed his cheek and left him standing behind her, knowing he was staring at her in frustration.

Diem enjoyed her classes and enjoyed teaching the history of her people to the young Allurans who came to learn. And over the course of the next six years, she felt she had found her calling. She adored teaching. About once or twice a year, she did go back to Geltahn and visit with Lela and her family. She came to forgive Jack and renewed her friendship with him. He truly was the best friend she could ask for, and he was a fantastic father. The only downfall to their relationship was that every time she visited, he asked her to marry him, and every year, she told him no. She hoped that, in time, he would stop asking but knew that he wouldn't.

YEAR 368

ADYM WALKED THE YIDDERIAN village enclosed in the Myst of Elynas and found two that would suit his needs. He bade them follow him, and once he had taken his fill of their fear, he released them to go back home. Adym was not sure if the two would be enough to sustain him as with each year that past, it became harder and harder to pass through the gates, even in just shadow form. He walked to the edge of the Myst, sat down, and, taking a deep breath, closed his eyes in concentration and then felt his shadow cross the barrier. He shuddered with the amount of energy it took to get through.

Adym walked around the Yidderian village, listening to the gossip and entering the minds of any that said something that sounded promising. Nowhere could he find a hint of a living child born during the time of Allura. It was two days after the moon's cycle, and Allura no longer filled the sky. If a girl had been born, there would have been talk of it. He entered the monastery grounds and went in search of the current Prophetess. He found an older woman talking with a young girl of seven, who he soon learned was to be the next prophetess. He searched both of their minds and again found no hint of a blue girl being born.

Leaving the monastery, Adym went back into the village and gathered a little more fear so that he could teleport to the monasteries on each of the continents. In both Kofira and Geltahn, a woman had given birth, but neither child had survived. Adym then left the Yidderian world and reentered his body back on Elynas. Frustrated, he stood up and headed back into his house. Maybe Kest was correct that the one would be born in the Myst with them, but he didn't think so. Prophetess Alena had told him that the one would hand him the key, and he believed that she was telling him that meant that their release would be brought about by someone outside of the Myst. And, of course, the key was outside of the Myst, so it only made sense that she would be as well, but maybe he was wrong.

Adym called Kest and asked him to bring someone that was afraid of heights and meet him at the top of the highest peak on Elynas. Adym teleported to the top of the mountain peak and soon saw Kest flying across the sky, his talons clutching the snack he had brought for Adym. Kest landed, and Adym replenished his strength and then thanked Kest for the Yidderian.

"Have any Allurmonuhra's been born this cycle of Allura?" He asked Kest.

"Not that I can find. All those that are do not tend to live. I am unsure why the Yidderian's offspring cannot survive the pull of Allura. I find it strange and frustrating, but I also wonder if maybe the one will not be born at this time of the year. Maybe we are assuming wrongly. Just because the first was delivered under the influence of the moon doesn't mean they all will." Kest sat down next to Adym and shook a feather out of his hair.

"I have thought of that, but even outside of the Myst, the only girls born that fit the prophecy are delivered under the moon." Adym looked out over the mountains and smiled at the beauty of the land before he turned his attention back to Kest. "I think that the one we are waiting for will be, and I believe she will be able to talk with us telepathically."

"What makes you think that?" Kest asked curiously.

"Because how else are we to know that she is the one? What if, as time goes on, the daughters begin to live through birth? Wouldn't the Prophetess just kill her so that she cannot set us free?" He paused in his thoughts, "But let's say the Prophetess doesn't kill them, and several of them actually grew up? If the one we await can talk with us in our minds, maybe that is how we will know she is the girl we are looking for. She is supposed to hand me the key, and while I can leave the Myst, I do not plan to until I am positive she has the key. If she can speak with us, then I will be able to ask her and hear the answer in my head."

Kest nodded his head in agreement. "That is a sound idea. If she is to set us free, she has to be more like us than just having our blue markings. I will ask my father what he thinks and see if he can give us more of an answer from Y'ddra than she has given us so far." Kest stood up, and his arms transformed into giant-sized wings. "I will go ask him now. See you soon." He took a running leap off the cliff, and Adym saw the bird that was Kest fly toward the village, where he knew that he would become himself once more and then walk through the green door that led to the Elders.

Kest arrived at his father's home and entered, giving his sister a brief hug before entering Brecher's hobby room. Kest smiled as he saw his father diligently working on one of the models that he was so fascinated with. Brecher was making a miniature version of Yiddera. He had all of Zeljani done and was now working on Geltahn. The intricacy of the buildings, as well as the flora and fauna, were amazing. Kest would never understand how his father could sit still long enough to create the miniatures. He knew that he could not.

Kest sat down across from his father and waited impatiently for him to come to a stopping point. He saw his father smile at him as he placed the small brush he had been working with down.

"It must be important if you felt you had to wait to interrupt me. Usually, you come into a room telling me what you want." Brecher smiled again at his son.

Kest laughed and then began telling his father of the conversation that he and Adym had. "We both would like you to talk with Y'ddra to see if she will give you any more details on the girl we are waiting for. If she knows any more, that is. Adym tells me that her colors are fading, and the rainbow lake is now clear and holds no color. I am sure that Y'ddra is tired, but if there is anything she can do to help us identify the one, it would be appreciated." Kest, no longer able to sit still, jumped up and paced in front of the model.

"I will ask her." Brecher watched his son pace the room. "Sit down. You are making me anxious."

Kest sheepishly did as his father asked. He knew that Brecher could no longer shift into an animal, and Kest's energy reminded him of what he was no longer capable of. "Sorry, but you know how it is."

"I do. Once we are done with our conversation, take a run for me." Brecher replied wistfully.

"Will do. Dad? Why do none of the Yidderian children survive birth when born under the Alluran moon?"

"I am not sure. I will see if Y'ddra can shed any light on that as well." Brecher stood up and went over to Kest, giving him a big hug and asking him to stay for dinner. Kest accepted and said that he would be back in time but was going to take that run that Brecher had suggested.

Once Kest left the room, Brecher reached out to Y'ddra. He sat in repose and concentrated on his conversation with her. After a long discussion, he left her mind with many more questions than he had gone to her with.

At the dinner table, Kest was surprised to find that the Elders and the SeiOrhii house leaders were all there. He sat in the chair next to Daija, and though he enjoyed the food and the company, he couldn't help but wonder why his father had gathered everyone here tonight. Whatever Y'ddra had to say must have been rather important to call an impromptu meeting of the council.

Brecher finished his last bite and took a sip of his wine before letting anyone know why he had called them all here.

"Kest arrived earlier today asking me to talk with Y'ddra about the blue girls. I spoke with her and found that she is very tired and weak and unable to influence the world as easily as she has in the past. This length of time without nourishment has been hard on her."

"She should have thought of that when she created a key that would lock us in with no way to get out except upon the arrival of some stinking Yidderian." Daija interrupted.

"Daija, show some respect." Her father barked at her.

"Sorry."

"She does have a point, and while I understand that she created the key to keep us safe from the Kahru, it should never have been created to lock us in permanently." Tayin scowled.

Elder Elcrys smiled gently at Tayin. "Tayin, as a history keeper, surely you remember why it was created to keep us in the Myst. Y'ddra did not want any of us wandering out and felt that this was the way to keep us in. I am sure she did not ever expect the pieces to become separated on different sides of the Myst gates. And as much as I do not want to anger you further, Tam should never have let Amalie into the Hall of Memories. We did warn him that she might be the one that locked us in."

Adym placed a hand on Tayin's shoulder to calm him. He could feel Tayin shaking in anger, which he fought to control. "Let us not dwell on the past. Brecher what did Y'ddra tell you?"

Brecher put down his glass and began again. "She stated that the one who will set us free will indeed have the ability to speak to one of us telepathically. And while she is not sure who she will speak to, I do believe it will be to you, Adym, she reaches out to."

Adym nodded his head. "I wondered that myself, as the Yidderian Prophetess, told me that I would be the one the key was handed to."

"Now she told me something I find intriguing. She stated that she was unsure of why the Yidderians could not have children during Allura and wondered, herself, if it was because she grows weak as the pull of the moon strengthens. But then, as the time for the prophecy grows nearer, more blue girls are destined to be born, so she is not sure of the real answer. Y'ddra also said that we need to look harder as a child has survived the blue moon, and because one has, she knows that more will soon be able to. She states that the Prophecy said that Allurmonuhra would increase in numbers the closer to the time of the prophetic fulfillment."

Eyes grew wide, and voices whispered around the table. After years of careful searching, how could a blue girl have escaped their notice? Ever the pragmatic one, Adym raised his hands to get everyone to quiet down and then asked if the girl was outside the Myst or inside and if she was the one they were waiting for or not.

"She did not give me any more details than that," Brecher stated. "I suppose we must look very carefully in both places and see who we missed. Also, I believe that as the prophecy said, the numbers would increase closer to the opening of the gates, that the first girl born may not be the one, but as I am not sure, we must continue searching."

Elder Saniel spoke up, "I know that we are all tired of waiting, but if one allurmonuhra has already survived, then we have hope that another and another will and that soon we will once again be free to range the whole of Yiddera. Let us not despair but rejoice that the prophecy looks like it will soon come to pass."

The meeting went on for a few more minutes while they discussed ideas on where the girl might be hidden and how before they all left for their respective homes.

YEAR 369

It had been six years since she had left Geltahn and given Lela to Jack, and now Diem was headed back home. Diem was going to be teaching at the school in the Yidderian village and would be able to live closer to her daughter, whom she had never wanted but had come to love. She looked forward to seeing her every day and introducing Lela to all of her favorite spots. Diem looked forward to family gatherings, watching her daughter grow, and teaching the children in her new classroom about the history of the Alluran people.

Diem stepped out of the forest of weeping willows and smiled at the thriving village that she had grown up in. It was the oldest of all the Yidderian villages and had the eclectic look of one that had refused to let go of the past but also could not resist embracing the new.

She embraced her family warmly and gave her daughter the dress that she had brought for her and then settled down to a home-cooked meal on the first night back with her family. It was an enjoyable evening with everyone talking over each other, trying to catch her up on the events that she had missed.

"I am going to be teaching at your school, Lela," Diem told her young daughter, who would be starting first grade this year. Excitedly, Lela bounced up and down in her chair and told her mother that she was happy she would get to see her every day. Diem smiled in pleasure and listened as her daughter told her all about what she had been doing since they had last been together.

The evening ended, and over the next month, Diem prepared her classroom, renewed old acquaintances, and became part of the town once more. She and Jack picked up their friendship, and they were together often. Diem had missed this closeness between them, and she enjoyed going out with him and Lela and learning more about their lives. She knew that coming home had been the right decision.

Diem kissed her daughter on her forehead and handed her the small orange bag that held her daughter's overnight things. She had been home only one month when a LuZivot had seen her walking by and summoned her and four others standing nearby to present themselves to Kest tomorrow afternoon. She shook her head, knowing that her daughter would not understand, but the summons had come, and Diem must go. She knew that, at some point, she might be chosen but had not expected it to be this soon after her arrival. This was part of life for a Yidderian.

"Mom, this was supposed to be our weekend together." The 6-year-old Lela whined. "I haven't seen you in forever, and now you are leaving me again."

Diem smiled as she replied, "Lela, honey, this was not my plan either. I wanted to spend the weekend with you, but I was chosen, which means I have to go. I will only be gone for a few days, and then we will catch up." She ushered her daughter out of the room and handed her over to her father.

"Sorry for this." She said as she walked with the two to their living quarters about a block from where she was staying.

"Mom, stay safe." Lela gave her mother a big hug and then entered her house. Diem stood outside in the hot, humid air before shrugging her shoulders at Jack, who smiled ruefully at her.

"Only one month since you moved back here, and already you are leaving me again."

"Only for a few days and not by choice. Take care of yourself and Lela. I will be back soon." She headed to the gates of the village to wait for the escort. Pausing, she looked back at Jack, "You have done well with her. She is a beautiful little girl."

"She is." Jack turned away from Diem and headed into the house after their daughter.

Diem met up with four other villagers and followed the LuZivot sent to escort them to Kest's domain. They entered the Hall of Myst and stepped through the bright yellow door that led to where they were going. The group entered a hall significantly cooler than it was outside and waited as patiently as possible for the feeding to begin.

This was the first time Diem had been among those gathered to be presented to Kest for feeding. However, she was not afraid of being chosen as she knew this was an inevitable part of life. She would recover, and life would continue as it always had.

She tapped her foot in impatience and watched as those next to her fidgeted as well. Diem turned her head toward the sound of voices coming down the hallway and watched as a group of people entered the room across from where she stood. One of the men caught her eye, and Diem felt her heart flutter unexpectedly. She did not know who he was, but given the deference the others offered him, she suspected he must be Kest. Diem, despite growing up in Geltahn, had never seen the animal shifter before.

Diem saw the man glance at her and then enter the room. Seconds later, he walked back out the door and headed straight for her. He stopped directly in front of her and, without asking her permission, pulled her head down to his. She had never been kissed as this man was kissing her now. Diem found herself being lifted and instinctively wrapped her legs around him, never breaking the kiss.

She lifted her head from his when she heard the sniggers of laughter from those around them. Diem looked into the eyes of the animal shifter and saw not a man to fear or the god some of her people thought he was; she saw only a man who she knew intuitively was her future. Diem saw an inquiring look in his eyes and nodded yes to his unspoken question. Then, still wrapped around him, they took off, running down the hall and out into the jungle that surrounded the house.

Kest walked into the hall with several of his staff, heading toward his office to discuss the coming week's duties, when he caught a scent of something different in the air. He knew that there were

LOUELLA RANES

Yidderians in the hall waiting for his attention, but one of them was different. There was always fear and unease in the air when they waited, but today, in one of their minds was the feeling of boredom and the desire to just get this over with. This mind did not have a fear of what was to come. He paused in his discussion and looked at those waiting for him.

The one at the end caught his attention. He entered the room absentmindedly with the others and then headed right back out. Hers was the mind he sensed, and her lack of regard for why she was there intrigued him, but it was her beauty that drew him to her. He could not help himself as he walked over to her. Kest felt her heart speed up, again not in the fear he expected but with desire, as his did. He pulled her head down to meet his and was surprised by her enthusiastic response. Kest felt her legs wrap around his waist, and he laughed softly in her mind, and without needing to ask, he knew that she would go with him. He held her tightly and, to the sound of Yidderian and Alluran's laughter, ran with her out into the jungle to a spot hidden from view that lay just along the river banks. The sun was beginning to set when the two unwrapped their limbs from around each other.

"What is your name?"

"Diem." She replied, "And yours?"

He laughed a barking kind of laugh, "Kest."

"I thought so." She sat up and pulled her shirt back over her head. "I should go."

"Stay with me." He stood up and slipped his pants on before taking her hand and helping her tie the strings that held her skirt in place.

"I know you need to feed, and I have kept you." She stepped into her sandals and started walking back to where they had come from.

"What makes you think that I won't feed right now?" He asked as he pushed her back against a tree.

She laughed at him and tipped her head down slightly to look at him. "That is, of course, within your right, but," she paused and squinched her eyes a bit. "I can see that is not your intent." She said in his mind.

Kest stepped back from her and stared with open mouth, fascination, at the woman in front of him. "You can talk to me telepathically?" He took off the headscarf that she had managed to keep on during their play. "You are not fully Yidderian? I should have guessed, as your eyes have a slight glow. Why have I not seen you before? I have looked for a blue-eyed and blue-haired

Yidderian and did not find you. Who are your parents? Are there others like you?"

Diem pushed away from him and, holding his hand, started walking once again. "My parents are the owners of the clothing store in the village, and I was born during the summer rising of Allura. As I am sure you are aware, most children born at the rising of both the winter and summer Alluran moon are stillborn. I am the first that I know of that has lived. My parents were unsure why my hair had blue in it or why my eyes somewhat glowed." She laughed. "They had many arguments over my mom's fidelity until they remembered hearing of a prophecy which spoke of one such as I being born to a Yidderian." She stopped walking and sat on a fallen log.

"You have never seen me before because I was kept a closely guarded secret. Only a handful of people know that I have the blue markings of an Alluran. My parents did not want you to take me away from them, so they never presented me at birth."

Diem saw Kest's eyes harden and patted the log next to her. "Come, sit by me." She waited until he did and took his hand in hers. "They did not want to lose me to the SeiOrhii. It is known that you looked for a blue-haired Yidderian, but no one knows exactly why. My parents love me and were afraid of why the Allurans would want me, so they kept my identity a secret. Do not hate them or seek them out for punishment. It is what any parent would do in the face of the unknown."

"I guess I did not realize that the Yidderians had not heard the full content of the prophecy, and so, therefore, could not know why we looked for you. It is said that a girl, such as you, would be born and release us from the Myst." He realized who she might be as he spoke, and jumping, he grabbed her hand and pulled her up with him.

"You. You are the one we have been waiting for. Come, we must see if you can open the gates." Without slowing down, he ran with her through the green door, and together, they appeared in the council hall. She heard him call the Elders and other SeiOrhii leaders. His bright, electric blue hair and eyes seem to crackle with life in his excitement. He grabbed her hand, leading her into the council room, where she was surrounded by all the men that her people feared for the first time in her life. She held her head high as she stood there next to Kest.

"What do you mean you have found the one?'

"How can this be?"

"Where did she come from?'

The many questions were asked simultaneously, and Diem smiled at the confusion on the many faces surrounding her.

The SeiOrhii named Adym held up his hand to quiet the group of excited Allurans.

"Kest, she cannot be the one we are waiting for." He stated, as the room settled into nervous quietness and seats were taken by the Elders.

"Why not? She is an Allurmonuhra. She has to be the one."

"She does not fit the prophecy." Was Adym's calm reply.

"How does she not? She can see into my mind and read my thoughts. She just needs to learn to hear the music and follow it to the key." Kest replied in excitement.

"The one we search for must be born outside of the Myst to find the key that is hidden out there," Adym stated.

"That is what you have always said, but I have always questioned. Is it not possible that maybe she can leave the Myst as you do Adym and therefore be able to find it once on the outside?" Kest asked.

Everyone turned toward Adym and waited for his reply.

"Maybe, but I do not think so." He turned toward Elder Brecher, "What does Y'ddra say about this."

Brecher cocked his head to one side and listened quietly for a few minutes. "She laughs, and that is all I can get from her." He said in frustration.

"Sorry to interrupt, but have any of you thought that maybe you should ask me if I can do this or not." Diem stood regally next to Kest's chair. She was determined not to show her slight fear of those seated around the large table as she spoke.

"Well, can you?" Asked Tayin.

Diem stared at this SeiOrhii. She had moved from his lands on Kofira to Geltahn. She knew this man was the most powerful of those seated at the table. He was also the one who had the most reason to hate the humans and the one with the greatest desire to leave the Myst. He was the bringer of nightmares, and she had been on the receiving end of many of these.

"No, I cannot." She said, still staring at Tayin.

He frowned at her and then turned to the rest of the council, "I suggest we take her to the blue springs and see if she is attracted to it. Though I doubt she will be. She is human, after all. But if she is the one, as Kest suggests, maybe she will be attracted to the blue waters and be able to leave as Adym does."

Adym shook his head again. "You can try, but you will not succeed. The one we are waiting for will not be locked in with us."

Kest jumped up at Tayin's idea. "We will leave now and see if your theory is sound." He again threw Diem on his back, and she experienced him changing forms underneath her. Finally, he arrived on Elynas and stood her before the Myst.

"Why are we here? Kest, I cannot get through the Myst barrier. I have tried, and it is just as impassable to me as it is to everyone." Diem tried to get him to listen to her.

"Try to leave anyway." Kest scooted her closer to the gates.

"I just told you that I can't. I have tried before. Everyone has." She replied.

"Try again." He demanded.

Sighing, she reached out and tried to do as he requested. But, as she knew it would, her hand met the solid barrier, and nothing she tried could make it move. She looked at him with an "I told you so" expression.

Kest and Diem walked back to where the others now gathered, and Kest stood her before the blue springs that bordered the Myst before it disappeared under the rocks only to reappear again, pouring down the rock wall behind the Rainbow Falls outside of the Myst gates.

Nervously, Diem walked to the water's edge. She looked at those around her, waiting impatiently for something to happen.

"I don't feel anything. It is just water."

"Dip your hand in it." Suggested Kest.

She did as he asked and felt the warm water caress her hand. The water flowed through her opened fingers, and she lifted her hand back out of the water. Diem dried her hand with her skirt and turned back to Kest.

"Nothing. I am sorry." She said in response to the disappointment she felt coming from the group.

"I told you." Said Adym as he left the waters to head into his house.

Elder Brecher patted his son on the shoulder, "Sorry, Kest. She isn't the one."

Kest hugged his dad before heading back to Geltahn with Diem. Once they reached the moist heat of Geltahn, Diem suggested that she leave to head back to her home. Kest shook his head no and led her into his apartments and onto the veranda. He sat her down and had a servant bring them a light repast and some mint tea.

"It is late, and I would like you to stay." He said as he sat in one of the low-slung chairs lining the deck.

"I would like that too." She replied as she sipped her tea. "I am sorry I am not the one you hoped for."

Kest got up and knelt in front of Diem. "You may not be the one that will open the Myst gates, but you are the one I hoped for." He took her head in his hands and kissed her.

It was a bright, beautiful morning when Kest woke up to Diem slipping her shoes on. He rolled over in the bed and watched as she tried to quietly open the door so as not to wake him.

"Where are you going, my pet." He asked.

Diem jumped at the sound of his voice and turned back to see him awake and watching her. She leaned against the door jamb, admiring the man's physique for a moment before she answered him.

"It is time that I went home."

"Stay with me."

She sighed with longing. "I would love to, but I need to get back home. My daughter will be worried about me."

Kest sat up in the bed. "And her father?"

"He will be worried too. After all, I was brought here for you to gather strength from. My family will assume that I have lived these last few days in terror, not in the delightful way that I have." Diem walked over to Kest and kissed him lingeringly. "Call me when you get hungry again." She laughed.

"I will always be hungry for you. I want you to stay here with me." He pulled her down in the bed with him and nuzzled her neck. "There is no need to leave. I will send someone to your family to let them know that you are safe and that you are now living here."

"Kest, let me up." She slapped his bare backside and sidled out from under him. "Do you really want me here?"

"Very much so."

Diem saw that he was sincere. She sat down on the edge of the bed and looked out the window, gazing at the jungle still covered in the last shadows of the night.

"I need to go home first and explain things to my family and get my daughter settled. It is going to take some effort on my part to get them to understand that this is something that I want to do."

"Two days, I will let you have two days, my pet, and if you are not back by then, I will come for you."

"I will not keep you waiting." She kissed him again and then left to walk back to the village.

Diem was not sure how she was going to explain this turn of events to everyone. She was not sure how it came about herself. One look at Kest had been enough to know she wanted him. One kiss had confirmed there was something happening between them. Four days of ecstasy had shown her that she needed to be careful not to lose her heart.

She had never been in love. Lust, yes, but not love. She knew that Kest could make her fall in love, and she knew that, with him, falling in love, if he reciprocated the feeling, would change her life forever. She made a vow to herself that she would never admit to loving him, should that day occur, because of the consequences that would come with it. She was Yidderian, a mortal, and he was SeiOrhii, an immortal. The SeiOrhii bonded with their mates for eternity. Diem did not have eternity; if she was lucky, she would have a couple of hundred years with him, and she would not shorten his lifespan to hers.

Once at the edge of her village, she looked around at the hustle and bustle of the people going about their daily lives. She smiled as she saw the children running around playing until they had to head to school. Watching the kids made Diem realize that she would also have to decide on her job. Could she continue teaching while living with Kest? She watched as people headed to work and shop signs were turned to open. She hurried over to the clothing shop, where she could see her father preparing to open for the day. Diem walked inside the tiny store and hugged her dad before stepping behind the counter to see if her mother was there yet. She was not.

"Dad, is Mother coming in today? I need to talk with you both about something important." She said, leaning over the counter.

"No, she is taking the day off. It is good to have you back." He looked over at her in concern, "Are you okay? He didn't hurt you, did he?"

Diem smiled. "I am fine. He definitely didn't hurt me, but I do need to talk to you about my time with Kest. Can you close a bit early today, around lunchtime, and meet up with Mom and me for lunch?"

She saw her dad frown and knew what he was thinking. "I promise I will not cook. I will let Mom handle all that, or I will go get something from Pips Place. You know you like their sandwiches. Your choice."

"I will pick up the sandwiches and meet you at home for lunch." He leaned over and kissed her on the cheek. "Glad to have you home, bug."

Diem grabbed her bag from where she had dropped it by the door and headed home.

Lunchtime arrived, and after the food had been plated and everyone was seated at the table, Diem's parents looked at her to start the conversation.

She took a bite and chewed slowly for a minute, trying to decide where to start. Finally, she set her sandwich down and just blurted it out.

"Kest has asked me to move in with him, and I am going to."

Her father choked on his food, and her mother looked as if she was going to faint. Once things settled down, she continued. "The first day that I was there, I met Kest, and let's just say that I spent the next four days with him, not in fear. I know this is hard to believe, but I am not in any way afraid of him. I enjoy his company."

"But Diem, what if he decides that he does want to feed on you? If you are living with him, he will always have you there when he needs your fear." Her mother asked with concern in her breathy voice.

"If that happens, which I know it will not, but if it does, then so be it. It was my purpose in going there in the first place. Besides, if he has me for that purpose, then he won't need any of my family or friends." She placed a hand on each of her parents. "Mom, Dad, it is going to be okay. I am happy about this. Do not fear for me. There is no need."

"What are you going to do with Lela? Are you taking her with you?" Her dad asked.

"No. I am leaving her with Jack. She has lived with him her whole life, and that will not change. I will visit her when I can, but she will be staying with her dad." Diem released her parent's hands and finished her sandwich before speaking again.

Sitting his half-eaten sandwich down, her dad asked, "And Jack?"

Diem looked back at her dad. "What about him?"

"He has asked you to marry him. Are you just going to leave him?" He asked reproachfully.

"I have told him no, just like every time he asks me. Despite what both of our families want and expect me to do, I will not marry Jack." She sipped her lemonade. "I have never loved Jack in that way and will never marry him."

"But you have a daughter together." Said her mother.

"Only because I did not realize that my birth control had been switched with something else. This matter is closed. I have made my decision, and you will have to learn to respect that decision because it will not change." She took another drink and then continued telling her parents of her plans.

"I will be spending the evening with Lela, but I will be back later tonight to pack what I want to take with me. Tomorrow, I will keep Lela out of school and spend the day with her before I leave tomorrow night."

Her mother looked at her in surprise. "Why so soon? You just moved back here. Can't you stay for a few days?"

"I told Kest I would be there in two days, and so I will be." She kissed her parents on the cheek and excused herself so they could finish lunch and discuss her amongst themselves.

Diem walked out of the kitchen and into the small room she was currently occupying. She had planned to stay with her parents until she had found a small place for herself, but now it looked as if the hunt for new living quarters was over. She smiled to herself as she thought of where she would soon be living. Diem hummed happily to herself as she packed the few belongings she had.

"I am happy too." Diem heard Kest in her head as clearly as if he was standing right next to her.

"I did not realize that you could communicate with me when I am so far from you," Diem said back.

"I did not either, but then your ability to hear me and answer me telepathically was a surprise as well."

"The view in front of you is beautiful. I have always loved the Kirod River. Every time I have visited Geltahn, I have made it a priority to see the sunrise at least once by it."

"You can tell where I am?" Diem heard the surprise in Kest's voice.

Laughing, she replied, "Yes, and I can tell you are drinking that delicious mint tea that I like so well." She latched her bag and sat it on the table next to the door. "As much as I enjoy our conversation, I need to go find Lela,"

"Who is that?" Kest interrupted

"My daughter. I told you about her. I will be spending the rest of the day with her, and I do not need you distracting me." She headed out the door and waved bye to her parents, who were still sitting at the table whispering with each other. She left the house and headed toward the school.

"I will not bother you today. Do not leave me waiting long." Diem could feel him fading from her thoughts. It felt so natural to have him in her head with her that it was a bit shocking now that he was gone. She knew that this was something the Allurans lived with, but as a Yidderian, she had never had anyone else's thoughts in her head but her own. It was odd to think that she had an ability that her race of people did not.

She made it to the school and checked Lela out, and hand in hand, they walked into the jungle and came to their favorite spot.

"It is good to have you back, Mom."

"It is good to be back and see you, Lela." Diem squeezed her daughter's hand in her own. Excited as she was about moving in with Kest, she would miss Lela when she left her again. She loved her daughter, but she also knew that she was not a great mother and that Lela was better with Jack than she would be with her. She squeezed Lela's hand once more.

"I have something I want to discuss with you, sweetheart."

"You are leaving again, aren't you?" Lela asked, her shoulders drooping in sadness.

"Yes, but I am not going far. I will still be on Geltahn, and I promise I will visit often." Diem replied.

"If you are staying on Geltahn, then why not stay here with me and Dad?" Lela questioned.

Diem let go of Lela's hand and scooted down the tree branch that she was sitting on so that she could look Lela in the eyes.

"I love you, Lela, but I do not want to live with you and your father. You are six now, and you should know that this is never going to happen." She stood up and went over to lean against the tree across from where the girl sat, looking up at her.

"I am going to live with Kest."

"You are going to live with the Animal Shifter? But why? Aren't you scared?" Lela's eyes widened in fear for her mother.

"I am not scared. In fact, I am very excited and happy to be moving in with Kest." Diem went over and gathered Lela up in her arms. "I love you very much, and I promise I will see you often. I will always be here for you; you know that, don't you?"

"I do." Lela gave her mother a big hug and then dragged her down to the river's edge, and together, the two spent a couple of delightful hours swimming. They dried off, and as they put their dresses back on, Diem marveled at how much Lela reminded her of Jack. She had his sense of adventure and his total disregard for looking neat. Smiling at this thought, she ran her fingers through Lela's hair to loosen the tangles and then retied her dress bow so that it was even. Once she had finished fussing, the two walked out of the jungle hand in hand.

Before they had reached the edge of town, Diem knew that Kest was waiting for her by the bench that sat in the middle of the town square park. She felt her heart race in anticipation of seeing him but also wondered why he had chosen to appear earlier than they had discussed.

"Because I found that I did not want to be away from you for two days. I want you next to me tonight."

Diem laughed out loud, and Lela asked her what was so funny.

"Nothing, my dear. There is someone waiting for me in the park that I would like you to meet." She turned the direction they were heading toward the middle of town and soon came upon Kest sitting on the bench, calmly waiting for her. Just seeing him sitting there took her breath away. Diem smiled and introduced her daughter to him and then invited him to dinner with her and her family.

Kest accepted, and the three of them walked the short distance to her mother's house. Lela was quiet the whole way and clutched her mother's hand tightly. Diem could feel her daughter trembling as all Yidderians seemed to do when around one of the SeiOrhii, but as she was unsure what to do about it, she just reassured Lela that everything was going to be alright. The table had already been set for five people, and Diem knew that Jack would be there tonight. She frowned slightly and then decided that he, too, needed to know that she was serious about her decision to live with Kest, so she silently added another place setting next to hers.

Dinner was very awkward at first, with no one talking much and Diem trying to keep up the stilted conversation until she had finally had enough. She pushed her plate aside, put down her fork, and then glared at each of her family members in turn.

"I understand that this situation is unique, but the least you could all do is treat him as you would any guest that sits at our table," Diem stated angrily. "I would have expected good manners to prevail at the very least."

"It is okay, my pet," Kest told her as he placed a hand over hers.

Diem visibly relaxed at his touch, and this shocked her family more than her outburst did. Cressida, Diem's mother, picked up a pitcher of the cool lemonade and rose from the table.

"Would you like some more lemonade?" She hesitated over his name.

"Yes, please, and you can call me Kest." He smiled at her and held his glass up for her to pour into it more easily. Cressida filled the glass, only spilling a little in her nervousness, and then hurried back to her seat.

"Thank you, mom." Diem smiled at her, and her mother smiled back.

The conversation centered around the town and what was going on that week, and after a while, those seated at the table felt more at ease with the unexpected guest. Dessert was served, and for the first time that evening, Jack spoke.

"What are your plans with Diem?" Jack asked Kest. Everyone stopped eating and watched the interaction between the two men.

"What business is it of yours?" Kest asked. At the same time, Diem said, "Jack" in exasperation.

"She is the woman I plan to marry, and I do not understand your interest in her. Again, I ask what are your plans for her?"

"Jack. That is enough. You know very well that we are nothing more than friends."

"I plan to keep her with me for all time, and what we choose to do in that time is for us to decide," Kest stated calmly.

Diem looked at him with wide eyes. "For all time? Do you mean it?"

He looked back at her just as seriously. "I do. And as you know, this is not a topic that we speak lightly of."

Diem smiled again and took another bite of the strawberry shortcake. Kest finished his dessert and then excused himself. "I thank you for dinner, but it is time for me to go." He held out his hand for Diem. "I know it is a day sooner than we planned, but?" He raised his eyebrow in question.

"If you will wait outside, I will be there shortly. I have a few things left to say to my family." Kest leaned down and kissed Diem and then walked out of the house.

"How can you, Diem? How can you leave me and our daughter for that man, that monster? He feeds on our people? How can you be okay with that." Jack asked.

"I am not okay with that, Jack, but there is something about him that calls to me and tells me that he is where I belong. I am not leaving anyone for him. I will still be in Geltahn, and I will visit often, more often than I did before."

"But what about me?" He asked with loss evident in his voice.

"Jack." Diem went over and knelt by his chair. "You will always be my best friend, my partner in crime, my child's father, but that is it. You need to accept that." She kissed his forehead. "Take care of Lela for me, and I will see you both soon."

Diem went over and gave her daughter big hugs, promising to see her later in the week. Then, Diem hugged each of her parents before grabbing her bag and leaving with Kest. She was halfway down the path when she looked back at her family, still standing in the doorway watching her. Their faces were full of concern and unwilling acceptance of her decision.

"Thank you, Kest, for being so understanding."

"I do not like that man." He said in reply.

"Jack is harmless. He and I grew up together, and he still thinks, despite how often I have told him otherwise, that we will marry someday."

Kest just grunted and then, throwing her on his back, changed into the Ageetah and raced with her through the jungle until he came to the vast grounds that surrounded his home. He changed back into his Alluran form and, scooping Diem up in his arms, walked her into his house. "Welcome home, my pet."

YEAR 370

DIEM AND KEST HAD lived together for one year when she decided it was time to talk with Brecher. She had met the Elder a couple of times and knew that he was Kest's father. He had always been quite nice to her and made her feel welcome in the family. This could not be said of Kest's sister, Daija. While she was nice enough, she had no interest in treating Diem like part of the family. She often reminded everyone that Diem was only a Yidderian who happened to be born with blue markings, not a SeiOrhii. Because of this, Daija felt that she did not have to take much notice of Diem as she wouldn't be around for long anyway.

It was this sentiment that caused Diem some concern. She knew that Kest would form the Korsyon with her, but her unwillingness to enter into the bond prevented this from happening. She was, as Daija often pointed out, not SeiOrhii. Kest was one of the Allurans who could live forever and Diem could not imagine a world without him in it. She was simply a Yidderian, and this meant that, at most, she would live to be a couple of hundred years old, and she would not be the one to shorten her love's life. She shook her head and begged Y'ddra not to take her words for an acceptance of the bond. All it took was for Kest and herself to admit their love to each other for the Korsyon to form.

Diem stepped through the door that led to Zeljani, down the hallway, and out into the crisp, fresh air. She walked along the cobbled street and, coming to a relatively modest dwelling, knocked on the door. Since Brecher could not hear her coming, she had asked one of the Tarikan who lived with the Elder to let him know that she was on her way. Brecher answered her knock and, smiling, bid her welcome.

Diem stepped into the living room and followed Brecher out into his lovely gardens. She sat on a well-padded chair next to a table that looked out onto a pond that had a school of purple and red-colored fish swimming peacefully in its depths. She thanked the Tarikan, who brought her a light white wine and, after having enjoyed the first sip of her beverage, began to tell Brecher why she was there.

"I can ask Y'ddra for this favor, but she is fickle and may not honor the request," Brecher replied as he, too, enjoyed his drink.

"Oh, but please try. Surely, she can understand that I do not want to do anything that may cause Kest harm. I know that Kest is ready to accept the bond, but I cannot. Please ask her to wait. I have to be sure that I can live eternally with him before I can accept the Korsyon." She pleaded.

"My dear, you do know that if he has decided that you are the one and Y'ddra agrees, he will not mind a shortened life. He loves you just the way you are, and I am sure that he has thought of the consequences of bonding with someone who is not SeiOrhii. Have you never told him that you love him?" Questioned Brecher.

"I cannot and will not say the words if it means shortening his life. Please understand and please help Y'ddra to understand as well."

Brecher stood up from his chair and patted the young woman's shoulder. "I will go and commune with her and see if she is willing to talk today. Please stay and enjoy my gardens. I will be back after a while."

Diem watched the handsome man stride through the patio and into the house. She had never asked why he was the only one who could talk to Y'ddra and why, as far as she knew, he was the only Alluran who was not telepathic. Kest had told her that he had the gift that his father had once had, but where Brecher could only become one or two animals and control only a few more, Kest was able to become whatever animal he chose to, and he could control and talk with them all. He had mentioned that since the war with the Kahru, his father was no longer telepathic and could no longer communicate with animals or become one. Diem decided that she would ask Brecher today, and if he would care to tell her, she would appreciate the story.

She finished her wine, and the Tarikan refilled it and brought out a small plate of fruits and cheeses for her to enjoy. She nibbled on a slice of cheese, and then, taking a plum in her hand, she got up and meandered the grounds. Brecher was fond of animals, and many of his topiaries were in their shape. He also had several ponds scattered about the garden in which a large variety of fish swam. Diem wandered around the yard for about an hour before Brecher returned to her.

"She has agreed, but she says to be very careful of your thoughts as she may take them as a confirmation of the Korsy-on." Brecher smiled as Diem threw her arms around him at his words. She kissed his cheek and then sat back down in the chair across from where he stood.

"Brecher, do you mind if I ask you a personal question?" She began.

"Go ahead. I will answer if I can." He leaned back in his chair, curious as to what it might be that she would ask.

"I was wondering how you came upon the scar across your face and how it is that you no longer have your gift. I thought that once a SeiOrhii was given his gift he kept it forever."

Brecher chuckled. "I would have thought Kest would have told you the story by now. It is a long story, but if you have time, I do not mind telling it."

"I have time." Diem tucked her feet up under her and straightened her dress around her, preparing for the story.

"It was during the War of the Kahru. You have heard of them, haven't you?" He inquired.

"Yes. Kest told me that many lost their lives and that Y'ddra created the Myst key to protect the Allurans from the creatures."

Brecher nodded his head and then, with a faraway look, began his tale. Diem could see that he was back in time and reliving the events of his past.

The violence of the war shattered the still morning air. Brecher could hear the roars of the Kahru echo across the valley and, as all

Allurans could, the screams of those who were being attacked. He could also hear the plans being made by different groups across Yiddera. He looked around him and saw that one of the Kahru had come sniffing around for the group that he was trying to help protect. The Kahru were unstoppable in their hunt for the Allurans.

Brecher laughed inwardly at the irony of this whole situation. The Kahru, brought here by Y'ddra to feed the SeiOrhii, could not be scared, and so while they could not be fed upon by the SeiOrhii, the Kahru could devour Allurans. They went after the women and children first; this was the bear-like creatures' favorite food here on Yiddera. Next, the SeiOrhii. They seemed to have a taste for the immortals. This was the only creature that they had ever encountered that could kill them. The Kahru liked to rip out their insides and feast as the SeiOrhii lay bleeding, unable to heal fast enough to get away. Something in the claws of the monsters poisoned them, making it impossible for them to heal. It was a painful but relatively quick way to die.

The only Kema among their race was his responsibility to protect. She was the only one who could lessen the potency of the poison spread through a swipe of the alien's long claws. Brecher was with his son Kest and his daughter Daija, along with the Kema and several women and children. Syler was also with them as he refused to leave Daija's side. Brecher briefly wondered if the two would someday form the Korsyon but brushed aside this thought in his need to concentrate on the matters at hand.

Brecher and Kest, as animal shifters, might be able to communicate with the Kahru but so far, all attempts had failed. Daija, as an illusionist, though weak, might be of use, and Syler was their teleporter. He took them from one place to another to keep them one step ahead of the Kahru, but he could only take two or three at a time, and they were a company of 23.

"Daija, when I tell you to, I want you to cast a mirror illusion so that the Kahru will not see us easily. Kest and I will transform into Kahru so that they will think they have just stumbled on a group of their own. Syler start taking the children and the women to the Falls. We need to get to the Myst as soon as we can." Everyone nodded their acceptance of this plan, and once the Kahru noticed the group, Daija sent up the wall of illusion. She was having trouble keeping it from wavering but it was enough to cause the Kahru to stop their advance. Kest and Brecher stepped outside the illusion, their forms those of the Kahru but with electric blue running through their fur, marking them as slightly different from the all-brown Kahru in front of them. They knew the differences in

coloration could cause their plan to backfire, but in their growing knowledge of the Kahru was the questionable idea that the Kahru could not see a full range of colors, making it hard for them to differentiate between the blue and the brown.

While distracting the beasts, Syler whisked away the vulnerable in their group to relative safety. Once at the falls, they would be escorted by another band of SeiOrhii into the Myst of Elynas. Y'ddra had told everyone to get into the Myst as quickly as possible as she had made a way to lock the Kahru out, but it would also lock out those left outside the Myst when activated.

Syler came back for Daija and Tove, the Kema, leaving Kest and Brecher without a healer temporarily.

"I am going to try and enter their minds once more. I will try to get them to leave the area if possible." Brecher told Kest. "If something goes wrong, run."

"I will not leave you, Dad," Kest argued back.

"I want to make sure that you are safe, and if that means leaving me behind, then so be it. Son, I need to know that you are safe. Now stand back in case I piss one of these creatures off."

Kest reluctantly took a few steps back from his father and went into an attack stance in case he needed to save his father.

Brecher tried entering the mind filled with hunger and rage and could not find any way to communicate with the great Kahru. He could not find an ounce of fear within their minds and knew that it was useless to continue trying. He exited the angry mind and saw that Syler was back to take them to the Falls. Becoming Alluran once more, Kest and Brecher took hold of Syler as one of the Kahru rushed them. They felt Syler jerk, and as they landed in the cave behind the falling water, they saw that one of the Kahru had a claw through Syler's heart and, because of the contact, had transported with them.

The Kahru ripped out the heart he pierced and ate it as Syler's body fell to the floor. Tove stepped forward to heal the fallen but was pushed back by Brecher to keep her safe. The hungry beast had smelled her and was now heading toward the Kema. Brecher told Kest to run and called Adym to help as he stepped in front of Tove to keep her safe. The beast, mad at Brecher's interference, hit him across the face with his huge paw. The treacherous claws, scraping across his face and cutting into his scalp, knocked him backward into the green waters. Tove ran to the water's edge, and placing her hand in it caused the water to roil and bubble, enhancing its healing properties.

Brecher floated unconsciously just under the green liquid, barely hanging on to life as Adym arrived to take them to safety. Kest and Adym stared in horror as the Kahru bit off Tove's head, blood flying everywhere as he shook her body loose from the morsel he held between his teeth. Tove's body fell into the hot spring of life and death, her red blood mingling with the green water in a gruesome semblance of harmony.

Kest skirted around the busy Kahru and grabbed his father out of the waters as Adym placed a hand on his shoulder and whisked them into the Myst. They were the last group to reach safety and heard the soft click of the closing of the Myst gates. The Kahru could not enter, and the Allurans, while still able to leave if needed, were kept safely inside.

Adym laid the wounded Brecher on the grass just inside the Myst and called for the Elders to come and help. They no longer had a Kema to heal their wounds. The SeiOrhii could heal themselves, but the Kema healed them quickly and in a fashion that left no marks or signs of injury. Now, the Elders and those gathered around Brecher could not be sure what to expect. He had fallen into the healing pool, and Tove had started to heal him but was eaten before she could finish the process.

Kest held his father's hand and cried. Adym felt sympathy as he had lost both of his parents a few months back. The Kahru had devoured his mother in front of him and his father. Adym had tried to whisk his father away, but his father requested that he be left to his fate in the spot his Korsyon had died. Adym, tears running down his face, had acquiesced, knowing that as a bonded pair, his father would soon follow his mother into death. He stayed connected to his father and was proud that he died after having wounded the great beast that had taken away his love.

Daija came running out of the house and sat with Kest next to their father. She looked around for Syler and saw that he wasn't among those that returned. She delved into the minds of those around her and saw what had happened to him and sobbed as if her heart was breaking. The two had not yet bonded, as Syler had said he would not accept it while they were at war. He did not want her to die just because he did. She was Chosin, and her death was for Y'ddra, not for him. Daija had argued with him over this but accepted it as there was not much else she could do. It was his choice to accept or not to accept the Korsyon, and she could not make him change his mind, try as she might.

The Elders, along with Brecher's family, sat around him for the duration of the day and into the night, watching his chest rise and fall in a labored rhythm. He was not dead. No other had survived the killing claws of the Kahru without direct help from Tove, and even then, she had not been able to save many. After all, there was only one of her.

Brecher lay in a restless coma. His mind fighting the darkness and the quiet. He could not comprehend the absolute silence. As an Alluran, he should be hearing the many voices and thoughts of his people; instead, all he heard was silence. It was painful. His head ached with the silence of the nothingness inside his mind. He knew that his face had been nearly ripped off and could feel the odd sensation of it healing closed slowly. Brecher could feel the pucker of scar tissue form across his face from chin to scalp. His eye felt as if it was being pulled closed. Healing was usually fast, and this sensation of feeling every moment of the process was strange but not nearly as strange as the quietness.

He fought the darkness and yelled into the void of his mind for other voices to answer him, but none were there to hear his screams. He searched incessantly for just one other voice, one thought that was not his own, and after hours, he gave up in despair. He was alone. His thoughts were filled with agony. Was this death? Was this what the LuZivot and the Tarikan experienced when they died? This overwhelming silence and loneliness? He knew that the death of the Chosin during sacrifice was not pleasant. Was this why?

Brecher felt he had been alone in his head for years when he heard a sound. His heart leaped in the hope that his connection with his kind was returning but was then crushed when he realized that it was only a voice. Someone had spoken aloud. He then noticed that he could hear the soft crying of those around him, and he could feel their touch. With incredible effort, he squeezed the hand of one that held his.

The silence returned as the hand tightened around his. "Talk to me." He screamed within his mind, but there was still nothing but pervasive silence. Brecher felt a small drop of moisture hit his lips and tasted the healing green of the water he was given. He wondered why the Kema just didn't heal him with her touch. Why did she give him the water to drink instead? Brecher decided not to question it and drank the liquid greedily. He would drink all the water she wanted him to if it meant getting back telepathy.

The water was taken away, and he could feel his body being moved. He soon felt the soft padding of a bed under his back. He drifted off to sleep, nightmares of the Kahru running through his dreams. He woke much later to a soft voice. He cried in happiness to hear it coming from inside his head and not from his ears. He listened to the gentle female voice and could not place who it was.

"It is me, Y'ddra." The voice answered his unspoken question. "You have been wounded beyond repair, and I cannot change that. The poison in the claws of the one that attacked you rendered you unable to hear telepathically. It should have killed you, but the Kema was able to keep you alive before she was severed in two. Interestingly, you can now hear me. Maybe due to the silence you are fighting against."

"Y'ddra?" He asked, not sure if he believed the voice.

"Yes. I cannot give you back your telepathy, but I can give you a choice. I can take you from life and give you peace, or I can waken you from your abnormal sleep. Upon waking you will still only hear the painful silence of nothing. If this is your choice, I will wake you, and I promise that you will still be able to hear me. It will be a lonely existence for one who is used to the many voices of others inside his mind. Take some time and let me know your decision." Y'ddra faded from his thoughts.

"No, don't go. Don't leave me alone in the quiet. I want to live. I want to be with my son and my daughter. I cannot leave them alone."

"Are you sure of this choice? Once given, it cannot be taken back. This terrible silence of thoughts will never dissipate. You will only be able to communicate with others through the spoken word." She told him calmly.

"And my gift? Will I still be able to feed and be an animal shifter?

"Feed, yes. Shift into the form of an animal, no, and you will not be able to communicate with anyone or anything telepathically. I am sorry."

"I will still be able to communicate with you?" He asked.

"Yes."

"Then I want to live. I can suffer this stillness of mind if I can still talk with you. This ability will be beneficial to my family. I will learn to live with this disability."

Brecher took a deep breath and opened his eyes to a darkened room, Kest sitting by his side.

Brecher came out of his revelry and cleared his throat. "I have never regretted the decision that I made. I get to see my family grow and flourish and help my people. Two things I would not have been able to do if I had chosen death."

"Thank you for telling me. Though I understand that it is a hard existence, not being able to hear others of your kind telepathically, it is something that you can live with. The Yidderians have been doing it since the dawn of time." She smiled, "But how do you communicate with the Tarikan?"

"I don't. They do not understand the emptiness of my mind but have adapted themselves to fit my needs. We have been together for so long that they know what I want before I do. Most of the people that help me are LuZivot, and they can communicate my needs to the Tarikan when necessary." Brecher stood once more and helped Diem out of her chair. Linking his arm through hers, he walked her to the door.

"Now, my dear, be careful what you think. Y'ddra knows that you love Kest and will take any opportunity you give to bond the two of you together. When I spoke with her, she laughed and told me your concerns are not necessary and whether that means that you, too, are destined to be SeiOrhii or that it doesn't matter to her whether you are, I don't know. I can only assume that you, being Yidderian, cannot live eternally, so maybe Y'ddra doesn't expect Kest to either." Brecher sobered at this thought.

"He will if I have any choice in the matter. Thank you, Brecher. For everything." She kissed his cheek and then left to find her way home to Kest.

YEAR 372

NICOLLETE SAT OUTSIDE THE chapel of Kluane and waited to see if she had heard correctly. A girl had survived birth and was being brought to the chapel as dictated by the Calling. She was now about one month old and had dark blue streaks in her hair. Apparently, her eyes also had a faint glow to them that made her parents nervous. The glow could be seen across the room at night and from a few paces away during the day. The child was due to arrive at the chapel soon, and Nicollete wanted to be among the first to know if it was true that the infant was a daughter of the Alluran moon. If so, maybe she was the one who would finally allow Nicollete to go home.

Nicollete saw a wagon escorted by a dozen acolytes enter the drive and knew the child had arrived. She hurried into the chapel and down the hall to the foyer, where she waited anxiously to take a peek at the much anticipated little one. The child would eventually go on to Alenar, where she would take up residence in the monastery, but the clerics must first verify the child's markings.

The parents passed the child to the cleric and then left after saying they had named her Kande, which they stated meant firstborn girl. They felt it was fitting as she was the first blue demon child born who survived their birth. Nicollete frowned that her parents would think Kande was a demon just because of her coloring, but then the Yidderians thought all those of her kind were demons. The cleric unwrapped the child, and sure enough, the girl had dark blue tufts of hair amongst the dark blond, and the glow of her eyes could be seen by all who stood in the foyer.

Nicollete let herself out of the room and ran across town and into the forest until she reached the Myst gates. She ran her hand across the shimmery vapor and waited impatiently for Tayin to arrive. Once he arrived, she bade him call Raighn, Adym, and Kest to join them and then waited for the three men to appear.

"I have news," Nicollete said breathlessly as soon as she saw the Myst shimmer with her brother's touch.

"We can hear you loud and clear, little sis. Are you sure the child is a blue girl?" Raighn asked her, his voice full of excitement.

"I am." She made sure the memory of the child arriving was in the forefront of her mind for all of them to see.

"I will wait to get excited once we know whether she will free us or not," Tayin stated.

"I agree." Commented Adym, "But I will keep an eye on her just in case. They are taking her to the monastery?" He questioned Nicollete.

"Yes. It was passed into law that anyone born under the moon of Allura was to be brought to the monastery. To make sure that she does not fulfill the prophecy, but also to make sure that they are safe from Yidderians who are afraid of the idea that one of them may become a demon. Of course, this would not be a fear if the Calling had not propagated a fear of the demons in order to keep you all trapped inside." Nicollete sat down in the grass and placed her hand once again on the barrier so that she might feel closer to those inside.

"Cheer up, li uhra. This means the prophecy will soon come to pass. I found the first blue girl, and now you have found the second. I wouldn't be surprised if many were born in the next few rotations. You will be home soon." Kest said.

"I will continue watching, and I will let you know as soon as I can when more girls are born. I think it may be time to move on to Alenar so that I can know the moment one is brought to the monastery." Nicollete stood up to leave. "I miss you all and cannot wait to give each of you a big hug. I must hurry if I am to catch the next boat to Alenar. If I am lucky, I can travel with the contingent sent to protect the child during her journey to the Prophetess." Nicollete hurried back to the chapel in town and succeeded in becoming part of the travel group. Within two days, she was on her way to Alenar.

Kest stepped out of Geltahn and entered the council building on Zeljani, heading toward the meeting that was called to discuss the future now that the prospect of freedom was closer at hand. He entered the room and sat down at the table next to Raighn. He waited patiently for Adym and Tayin to arrive and, when they had all been seated, waited for the council to begin the meeting.

Elder Elcrys began the proceedings. "Raighn has informed me that Nicollete met with you all two days ago to let you know that an Allurmonuhra has survived the blue moon. Now, while this is good news, we cannot be sure that she is the one that the prophecy tells of. But we can prepare for the future in case she is. First, we need to decide how we are going to contact her, and second how we are going to get the key from her. After that, we will discuss what to do with the Yidderians who are currently locked in here with us. Do we let them go? Do we keep them here? Or do we give them a choice on where they want to be?" Elder Elcrys looked around the room and then asked for ideas on how contact would be made with the girl.

Elder Brecher cleared his throat and let it be known that he had talked with the leaders of the houses on this matter already. "I spoke with Y'ddra, and she was able to tell me that the one we are waiting for will be able to speak to us telepathically. Y'ddra also said that the girl would make contact with us at some point, which would be a sign that she is who we are looking for. Y'ddra is very tired and is hoping, like us, that she arrives soon so that we can commence the sacrifices once more."

"I was told by the original prophetess that the one would hand the key to me," Adym stated. "I assume that since I am the only one of us who can cross the Myst barrier when she calls out to us, I will be able to walk through the gates and take it from her."

"How will she find the key? How will she know what to look for?" Raighn asked with curiosity in his voice.

"She will need to be taught to hear the music and understand how to follow it," Tayin replied. "The key, like all the stones of Yiddera, sings as Y'ddra does. The girl must learn how to follow the music to its source in order to find the key, which we know has been well hidden by the many Prophetesses that guard it. I suspect that it is hidden somewhere in the monastery. Of course, it could have been moved several times since it was first hidden from us."

"If Adym is indeed the one that she reaches out to, then we will let him teach her how to hear the music, and he will get her to give us the key." Elder Elcrys stated.

Elder Saniel spoke up, "And if she is not inclined to give us the key? What do we do then? The Yidderians have been warned not to do anything that might release us. Why would a blue girl choose to let us free, even if it is prophesied to happen?"

"I will handle the issue, Elder Saniel. If she does not want to give me the key, I will find a way to make her. She will not be immune to our gifts, and I can be quite persuasive." Adym replied.

Elder Elcrys and the others nodded.

"So that is decided. Unless the girl chooses to speak to another, Adym, we will let you handle her. Next on the agenda is what to do with the Yidderians who live amongst us."

"I say that we keep them here, with us. Why let them go free just because the gates are open? What happens if they close unexpectedly again? We got lucky once in that they were locked in with us, but we may not be that lucky again. I do not want to be without food should the gates become locked once more." Kest stated.

"I do not think that Y'ddra will let that happen again, son." Elder Brecher responded.

"But we do not know, now do we? I do not think she expected it to happen in the first place, or she would have done something to stop it." Countered Kest.

"I do not see why they cannot make their own choice. Many of them will choose to leave, but this is their home and has been for almost four of our years. Why would they want to leave their homes?" Raighn asked.

"For once, I agree with my cousin. They should get a choice. I believe that many will stay." Adym said.

"What is your opinion, Tayin?" Asked Elder Saniel.

"I don't care what they do. Leave or stay as long as they do not interfere with my plans once the gates are open; I couldn't care less what they choose to do."

A long discussion followed, with everyone putting in pros and cons for either decision until finally, Elder Elcrys raised her hand for silence.

"It is time to vote." She stated.

The vote was taken, and everyone voted for the Yidderians to be given the choice to stay or leave, except for Kest, who voted that they stay and not be allowed to leave the Myst. It was decided because the vote was not unanimous that they would vote again once the girl destined to free them was found.

Kest left the meeting knowing that Diem would not understand his decision and, with reluctance, headed home to tell her. He anticipated her fury at him being the one to cast the vote, which would not allow her people their freedom. Kest hoped she would understand. They had lived together for three rotations now, and while she understood the SeiOrhii's need to feed, she still did not like it when her family and friends were the chosen nourishment. Most of the Yidderians that lived in the village saw it as simply a way of life, but once Diem had heard that the arrival of girls like her signaled the eventual opening of the

Myst, she had come to believe that it no longer had to be. She decided that once the gates were open, the SeiOrhii would have a broader choice of people on which to feed, and her family would no longer have to accept the fear inflicted upon them by the SeiOrhii.

While he had told the others that his reason for voting as he did was due to the unlikely event that they should become trapped once again, his true reason was that he worried that Diem would leave him if given the freedom to join the rest of the Yidderian world. He could tell in her mind that she had no intention of this, but he was unsure what she would do once the choice was actually there and not just a possibility. Diem kept a part of her mind locked tightly against him. She had never told him she loved him, and she often stated she would not accept the Korsyon when he talked to her about it. This lack of words made him insecure in her devotion to him. If she would not tell him that she loved him, which he found curious as he could see that she cared deeply for him, then maybe she would not want to stay with him forever.

Kest did not want to contemplate what life would be like without her, so if he kept the Yidderians, who lived in the Myst currently, still locked in, then she wouldn't be able to leave him.

He stepped into their home and squared his shoulders. It was time to tell her, and he was not anticipating the coming argument.

YEAR 375

JACK BRAVELY WALKED UP the front steps and knocked on the door of his enemy and his love. The silent Tarikan that answered the door beckoned him inside and waited expectantly. Jack asked to see Diem and then was directed to a comfortable chair to wait for her arrival. He only had to wait a few minutes before he saw Diem walking sedately down the hall, smiling at him warmly. He couldn't help the flutter of excitement he always got when she smiled at him, even after all these years of her living with someone else.

"Jack, it is so good to see you." Diem gave him a big hug and a kiss on the cheek. "How are you, and how is Lela?" She sat down next to him.

"We are doing quite well. Lela is watching her brother and sister but states that she has plans with friends tonight, so I cannot take too long." He waved aside a drink and asked Diem if she would walk with him. She accepted, and the two meandered down across the expansive gardens until they came to a bench that she had long ago placed by the river so she could sit and watch the water flow by.

"What brings you here today, my friend?" Diem asked as she sat down, adjusting her skirts so that her legs were hidden and the material would not wrinkle.

"I will get straight to the point. Many more girls with blue hair and glowing eyes have been reported, and as we know, this is supposed to indicate the time is nearing for the gates to once again be opened. I was wondering what you were going to do about it."

"What do you mean what am I going to do about it?"

Jack turned to look at Diem more fully and clarified his question. "Are you going to stay in the Myst once the world is opened back up to us, or are you going to stay with him?"

"Of course, I am going to stay with Kest, but I hope that you, Lela, and the rest of your family will leave. As much as I will miss you all, I like the idea that you will not remain a regular item on the SeiOrhii menu. They will have a world full of choices, and I do not want you to be anywhere near for them to choose from." She answered.

"Why aren't you coming with us?" Jack, ever hopeful that she would leave Kest, asked.

"You know why."

"And yet I also know that you have never told him that you love him. If you love him, why not tell him so, and if you don't, why stay?"

Diem looked at Jack and decided to tell him the truth. No matter the problems that they had had in the past, he was still and always would be her closest friend, and maybe he would understand and quit asking her to leave Kest.

"I cannot say the words as they will bond me to him forever, and my forever is much shorter than his. I cannot be the one to shorten his life. I would rather die not saying the words and leave him questioning my feelings for him than live knowing that I was the reason he would not live forever." She stood up and walked over to the water's edge.

Jack stayed seated, knowing that with her words, any hope of her leaving Kest was gone forever. Her voice and her words told him how much she truly loved the animal shifter. While his heart grieved, knowing she had never felt for him as she did for Kest, he had to admit that he had known how she felt for the man the minute he saw the two of them together. Kest would have to be an idiot not to see the love in her eyes every time she looked at him. Jack stood up, walked over to Diem, and took her hand in his.

"Tell him. He deserves to hear the words. I hate the man and will never understand how you can be so comfortable around him, but hearing those words from your lips would be worth dying for."

Diem smiled at him and heard the longing in his voice. "I cannot and will not until I am ready to. Oh, let's talk of something else, please. Do you have plans as to where you might wish to go once the gates are opened?"

"We are not sure. Probably somewhere here on Geltahn, just not anywhere that we can see the Myst." Jack started walking along the river path, and still holding Diem's hand, she was forced to walk with him. "You know there is a rumor going around that Kest, again, was the only one to vote to keep us here and not allow us to leave the Myst, don't you?"

Diem gritted her teeth and let go of Jack's hand. "Yes, and the rumor is true. He and I have had words over this. When and if the time comes that the barrier is once more passable, I will help you and whoever wants to leave the Myst in any way possible to cross through. If the Allurans are free to come and go as they wish into all areas of Yiddera, then the Yidderians that live here should have the same freedoms."

"I was hoping you would say that. Once the girl who is believed to be able to open the gates is found, we will discuss this again. I have a few ideas that we can discuss at that time. Until then, just knowing that you have our backs is a relief."

"Again, if and when that time comes and if Kest still votes against the Yidderians leaving, I will help you, but I will not help before that time comes." Diem ended the conversation, and the two talked about Jack's family and how Lela was doing in school. Diem had questions about her daughter's friends and if she was interested in any particular boy. The two lifelong friends spent a pleasant hour catching up on each other's lives. Finally, Jack kissed Diem's cheek and left for home.

Diem walked back to the gardens and found Kest sitting in one of the chairs on the veranda, watching for her. She smiled and picked up her pace. She reached the veranda and was swooped up in a crushing embrace.

"How was your visit, my pet?" Kest asked, even though his voice indicated that he was not pleased with who her guest was.

"It was good, but I know that you do not want to hear about how Jack is doing." Diem untangled from his embrace and sat down in one of the rattan chairs.

"I have told you before that I will not let you leave," Kest said as he sat down.

Diem raised an eyebrow at him and gave him an aggravated look. "And as I told you, I have no intention of leaving, but I also have no intention of letting you keep the Yidderians here against their will once the gates are opened."

"And at this time, there is no reason to believe that that time will come soon, so let's not start the argument this topic always causes."

"I agree. Today is too beautiful a day to argue over something you know you are wrong about." She smiled as he laughed.

"I would ask that you stay out of my mind when I am talking to my friend. I do not like that you feel you have to listen to our every word."

"I do not know everything you talked about. I just happened to catch something about leaving the Myst, and it sparked my curiosity. Once you started talking about his life, I quit listening as that is not an interesting topic."

Diem shook her head. "Come, let's take a walk together. There is something I would like to show you." Diem said, her eyelashes fluttered seductively.

Kest jumped out of the chair and picked her up in his arms. "I will gladly see anything you wish to show me."

She laughed in delight at his words.

YEAR 825

"HAVE YOU EVER FELT as if everyone around you was moving forward but you?" Tayin asked in barely a whisper.

Neviah looked at him with sadness. "No." She said simply.

"I watched Kest falling for Diem more with every day they spent together. I watched all my friends as they eventually fell in love, and I felt left behind. My heart, my very soul, was filled with such a heavy darkness that I couldn't move forward with them. My mind was stuck in the day that Tam died." Tayin picked up a rock and tossed it across the barren wasteland.

"But you did move forward."

"Yes, and this is where I landed."

"This," Neviah waved her hand at the landscape in front of them. "was lifetimes in the making, created by

many people and much misunderstanding. You landed here because you are the only one that can fix it."

Tayin shrugged his shoulders. "How?"

"Continue your story, and let's figure that out together." She, too, picked up a rock and threw it out in front of her, smiling when it landed several feet shy of where his did. "What happened next?"

ACKNOWLEDGEMENTS

I would like to thank my mother, Carol, for encouraging me to write and publish my stories. Thank you for being there through my adventures every step of the way.

I would also like to thank LeeAnn for reading my story and for encouraging me to publish

I would like to thank my book friends for helping me pick out the blurb and book cover they thought was the best of the many choices I gave them. Sorry you had to slog through so many.

A shout out to Bookbrush/Canva for all the many options they had of pictures so that I could design my book cover.

And finally to my husband and son who let me have hours to myself to write. Thanks for the hugs and kisses that kept me going.

ABOUT THE AUTHOR

Louella Ranes writes epic romantic fantasy novels. She likes that in this genre you can create a whole new world which means anything can happen. It is not bound by Earth rules. "A Demon's Fascination" is her first book in a four book series she calls "The Demon's of Yiddera."

Ms. Ranes enjoys many hobbies including cooking, herbology, painting, and trying to learn German. She also enjoys spending time in nature with her husband and son. She has three dogs of varying sizes that keep her busy. While not working her favorite activity is being home with her family and enjoying the little things in life.

ALSO BY

Watch for the exciting next installment in the

"Demon's of Yiddera" Series

"A Demon's Desire"

www.ingramcontent.com/pod-product-compliance
Lightning Source LLC
Chambersburg PA
CBHW020519110726
47899CB00004B/1166